Now here Milly was, standing in a dark alleyway, her heart pounding, hunting demons with four boys who just so happened to be the biggest pop stars in the world.

"We're not seeing anything, Tom," Milly said, agreeing with the others. Apart from vermin, the alley was empty. Maybe the tracker had stopped working. "Unless…"

As one, JD and Milly looked up.

Milly just had time to see a cape of black hair and a swirling yellow trench coat, as the demon leaped down at them. She reached for an arrow from the quiver on her back, but wasn't fast enough. The demon landed, straddling her, knocking the arrow out of her hand. Its face, partially obscured by a surgical mask, pressed itself into Milly's.

KIM CURRAN

USBORNE

For Molly,
Devourer of books, creator of worlds.

First published in the UK in 2019 by Usborne Publishing Ltd., Usborne House,
83-85 Saffron Hill, London EC1N 8RT, England. www.usborne.com

Copyright © Kim Curran, 2019.

The right of Kim Curran to be identified as the author of this work has been asserted by
her in accordance with the Copyright, Designs and Patents Act, 1988.

The name Usborne and the devices ♀ ⊕ USBORNE are Trade Marks of
Usborne Publishing Ltd.

A CIP catalogue record for this book is available from the British Library.

JFMAMJJASO D/18   04418/1   ISBN 9781474932325

Printed in the UK

The prettiest girl in the world

"Don't let her get away!"

Neon lights flashed and pachinko machines rang as Slay raced past game arcades and dive bars, closing in on their prey. They'd left the bright lights and bustle of Shinjuku at the last turn and were now weaving their way deeper into the dark heart of Tokyo. Milly was loving every second of it. The twins, Zek and Niv, were behind her, swords sheathed but ready. She heard a thump from above and glanced up to see Connor jump across the small gap between the rooftops, his sai blades glinting in the moonlight. Up ahead, taking the lead, was JD. All of them were dressed in black combats and half-masks, disguising their identities. Milly's mask was grey, with the jagged mouth of a shark painted on one side. The whole disguise not only hid her identity, but her gender too. When she'd agreed to join Slay, the world's hottest boy band, there had been one small problem: she wasn't a boy.

However, thanks to clever styling and a tight-fitting sports bra, Milly had become Milo – Slay's shy new pianist.

As soon as she'd pulled on the heavy black boots, picked up the compound bow and slipped a quiver of arrows over her back, she'd felt a change. Not just in how she felt but in how the others treated her. They were still protective of her, but only as much as they would be of any of the other boys. They still looked out for Milly, but now they also expected her to look out for them.

"*Take the next left.*" Tom's soft voice came over the headsets. Tom had been Slay's pianist, but after a terrible incident in Mexico he'd needed to take some time out – from performing and hunting. So now, he was back at base, guiding them every step of the way. "*Left, now.*"

JD skidded mid-run and slammed into a wall on his left, bouncing off it and vanishing down the alley. "A little more notice next time, Tom," he panted.

Milly heard Tom chuckle over the line. "*Keeping you on your toes, JD.*"

She followed JD around the corner and came face-to-face with a three-metre-high brick wall. It was covered in graffiti of a panda with flames coming from its eyes.

"Bu—?" she managed to say before JD jumped, zigzagging from one corner of the wall to the next, grabbing hold of the top and vaulting over. Niv and Zek streaked past her. Niv crouched down and boosted his brother up and over, then leaped as Zek grabbed his hand and pulled him up in one fluid, practised move. Connor skipped over from the rooftops, putting in an unnecessary but undeniably cool flip as he too disappeared behind the wall.

That just left Milly.

"*Come on, Mills, you got this,*" Tom said in her earpiece, gentle and encouraging.

This was exactly the kind of thing she'd been training for over the last month. Scan the environment, find your advantage. She spotted her way over. "The wires!" she said.

"*That's my girl,*" Tom said. "*I mean, not my girl. I meant, like, the girl.*"

She heard Zek chuckle at Tom over the headsets. "Smooth, Wills. Smooth."

Milly smiled under her half-mask and rubbed her hands against the rough material of her combats. She jumped and grabbed the bundle of wires running from satellite dishes and air-conditioning units, placing her feet either side, and scooted her way up till she was level with the top of wall. She placed her weight on her left side and swung, grabbing the top of the wall and pulling herself up. Her muscles strained, and she knew she'd feel it in the morning, but for now, the adrenaline of the chase was blocking out any pain. She paused at the top of the wall to take a steadying breath, then jumped. As soon as she hit the ground, she dropped into a forward roll, protecting her ankles, and she was up again and on her feet. She glanced back at the wall and grinned. She'd made it over. And without falling too far behind. JD and the others were just up ahead. She put on a burst of speed and caught up with them.

"*Wait*," Tom said.

Milly crashed into Zek's back, and they all came to a sudden halt.

"*You should be right on top of her.*"

"There's nothing here," JD said, drawing his sword.

"Unless she's transformed into that freaking enormous rat," Zek said, pointing at a beady-eyed creature scuttling behind a bin. "In which case, I am very much out of here."

"*The tracker shows her right there in front of you.*"

Slay had come to Japan nearly a month ago, under the pretence of a publicity tour that would help them break into the country. But the real reason they'd come had nothing to do with sales figures or juicy deals, and everything to do with a nasty demon that had been terrorizing Tokyo. Gail, the band's manager – a tall, elegant woman who was just as fierce with contracts as she was demon-hunting – had got a call from a Japanese friend asking for help. And just like always, Slay went wherever they were needed.

They'd spent their first weeks in Japan researching: poring over old books, hacking police records, interviewing witnesses, finding out everything they could about the demon. How to track it, how to take it down. And while

Milly believed Gail and the others when they said this was all a part of the job, she also wondered if it hadn't also been about giving Milly time to train.

And train she had. Every day, for seven hours a day, she'd practised fighting, evading, shooting with her bow. The rest of the hours had been spent sleeping, eating and learning how to play all Slay's hit songs on the piano.

Then tonight, in the middle of Connor showing Milly how to do a one-handed chin-up, an alarm had gone off. One of Niv's rooftop traps had been triggered – the demon had been found.

Gail had winked at Milly, her one good eye flashing as brightly as her diamond-encrusted eyepatch, and said it – the phrase Milly had been desperate to hear for weeks. "Playtime is over, boys. It's slay time."

And now here she was, standing in a dark alleyway, her heart pounding, hunting demons with four boys who just so happened to be the biggest pop stars in the world.

"We're not seeing anything, Tom," Milly said, agreeing with the others. Apart from vermin, the alley was empty. Maybe the tracker had stopped working. "Unless…"

As one, JD and Milly looked up.

Milly just had time to see a cape of black hair and a swirling yellow trench coat as the demon leaped down at them. She reached for an arrow from the quiver on her back, but wasn't fast enough. The demon landed on top of Milly, knocking her to the floor and straddling her. Its face, partially obscured by a surgical mask, pressed itself into Milly's.

"*Am I pretty?*" A high, scratching voice hissed through the mask, making Milly think of nails on bones.

"I…" What Milly could see of the demon's face was pretty. Beautiful even. She opened her mouth to answer, then she saw JD standing over them. His sword flashed, slicing across the demon's back. It screeched and spun to its feet, disappearing in a swirl of yellow coat and dark hair, flying away as if carried on the wind.

JD reached out a hand and pulled Milly to her feet, before giving her a sturdy push forward. Back into the fight.

"*Milly!*" Tom gasped. "*Are you okay?*"

"Yeah, I'm fine," she said, willing her legs to keep pumping as she ran.

"*Are you sure? You don't have to—*"

"She's fine," JD said. "Stay focused."

Milly couldn't help but smile at JD defending her. She knew she'd just nearly messed up, but as JD had told her before: we all make mistakes. The important thing was not to make the same mistake twice. And there was no way Milly was going to. She pulled out an arrow and lay it across the string of her bow. That demon wasn't going to get a second chance.

"There!" Connor pointed overhead.

A shadow passed over the large Tokyo moon. Milly

levelled the bow, drew back the string, took aim and let her arrow fly. This demon was known as *Kuchisake-onna* – the slit-mouthed woman. A demon of legend who had been summoned by a man stupid enough to think he could control her. After dispatching him, the demon had begun stalking the backstreets of Tokyo – approaching people in dark alleys, her face covered by a surgical mask, to ask them a simple question: *Am I pretty?* If they said no, she would kill them. If they said yes, she would lift her mask to reveal her beautiful face, which had been sliced from the corners of her mouth to her ears, then give her victim the same, gruesome smile. The only way to survive unscathed was not to answer.

The demon woman looked back over her shoulder as she flew through the air, black eyes widening as Milly's arrow headed straight for her forehead. With a soft *thunk*, it embedded itself between two delicate eyebrows.

"*Am I pretty?*" the demon said, for the last time, before falling to the floor with a heavy, wet thud.

They all raced to the landing spot. Connor hooked up a shred of what had been the demon's bright yellow trench coat with the tip of his sai. A white surgical mask rolled out onto the floor. Both were covered in thick, black blood.

"Must have possessed that body for centuries," Connor said, "to disintegrate like that."

"Urgh," Zek said, stepping away from the growing pool of black ooze. "My boots."

"At least we won't have to bag-and-frag the body," JD said.

Milly smiled. She'd done it. She'd taken down her first black-eyed scumbag. She looked from boy to boy, drinking in their approval. Connor gave her a high five that shook her bones, Zek winked and gave her a smile and Niv held up two thumbs.

There were no smiles or high fives from JD. Just a cool look of admiration. "Good shot," he said.

"*Did you get her?*" Tom's tense voice came over the headsets. Milly could imagine him back at the base, his cup of green tea gone cold as he fretted about them all.

"Milly did!" Connor said.

"*Milly!*" Tom said. "*Have I told you just how amazing you are?*"

Zek rolled his eyes. "Oh, maybe once."

"Or twice," Connor added.

Niv slashed his thumb through the air, the sign for a thousand.

"Shut up, all of you," Milly said, but she was glad her mask hid her grin. Suddenly she was itching to get back to base. To pull her mask and goggles off and see Tom. But they had more business tonight.

"We'd better shift," JD said. "We have to be on air in thirty minutes."

Demon-slaying done. Now it was time to step back into the spotlight.

When I see you smile

Tom pulled his headset off his mop of strawberry-blond curls and spun his chair away from the desk, letting out a massive sigh of relief. Watching the others through the screens had been like playing the most exhilarating video game ever. Exhilarating and yet excruciating. He wanted to be with them, kicking demon butt, but he still wasn't feeling strong enough. Not since Mexico.

Only a matter of months ago, the boys had gone up against the biggest demon the world had ever known – a literal demon god called Tezcatlipoca. Tezcatlipoca had been summoned from the Netherworld with a single purpose – enslave all of humanity. But the demon god had needed one thing in order to cross over: a human host to possess. It had tried to possess Milly, but Tom had stepped up and offered himself. He'd been willing to sacrifice his life to save Milly's. To save them all. Had it not been for JD's quick thinking, Tom would have died right then, on top of the ancient temple, while lightning shredded the dark sky. Instead of losing his best friend, JD had made the only choice he could. Just as the demon's shadow form was about to creep into Tom's body, JD had cut Tom's hand off, denying Tezcatlipoca its host and banishing it back to the Netherworld.

Tom looked down at the prosthetic hand he'd been wearing since getting out of hospital. It looked real enough – they'd scanned his left hand and matched it as carefully as they could. And yet, it wasn't kidding anyone. Gail had promised Tom that everything would be fine – he'd learn to fight with his left hand, they'd find him a new instrument, and everything would be back to normal. Normal. He wondered if he even knew what normal looked like any more.

He glanced up at the feed from DAD – their Demonic Activity Detector – which was busy scanning all forms of digital communication for any sign of evil. Rows of data danced across the screen: numbers and charts that were a mystery to Tom but could be decoded by their tech genius Niv. All he could tell was that nothing was flashing red. He could risk taking a break.

He left the room they'd set up as the control centre and walked out into the central courtyard, which was illuminated by a string of red lights. The building they had been staying in for the last month had once been a derelict teahouse. It had a swooping, curved rooftop and paper doors. Suzume, Gail's old friend who'd contacted them about the demon, had taken over the space to save it from demolition, turning it into an art studio ten years ago. The collective who used the space blended traditional Japanese paintings with a modern graffiti style. The artworks, which covered every wall, were hugely popular with young Tokyoites and tourists alike. And one of the most popular paintings had been of a beautiful woman with a ragged, bloody smile. The *Kuchisake-onna* demon of legends. Only, as Suzume and her team learned, the demon wasn't so legendary any more. As many as ten people had died after coming face to bloody face with the demon, including one of Suzume's best artists. After failing to take the demon down herself, Suzume had called Gail for help.

Now the demon was defeated, their job was done and Tom wondered where they would be going next. Maybe DAD would throw up more demonic activity in Japan? Or maybe it was time to hit the road again? It wasn't that Tom was in a rush to leave. Tokyo was fascinating and he'd often go wandering the streets while the others were training, as much to learn about the city as to have some time to himself. The house was beautiful, if a little cramped with all seven of them living there. There were only two bedrooms. One had been turned into the control centre, the other was where Gail slept. As for the rest of them, they made do. However, compared to Agatha – their tour bus – it was positively palatial.

The rumble of Tokyo traffic was a faint hum in the background, hidden by the gentle sound of running water and the occasional satisfying *thonk* made by the bamboo water feature in the courtyard. It beat out a gentle rhythm in Tom's mind, and he began humming a melody to go with it. It started sweet and light, a gentle song that might be about cherry blossoms caught on the wind or the aching of a lonely heart. But it became harsher, darker. An all-too-familiar strain filled his mind, a high-pitched chanting – the same chanting he'd heard on the top of a pyramid, as dark clouds rumbled overhead and lightning filled the sky. The singing of an Aztec priestess calling to her demon god. Tom pressed his hands to his ears, trying to block the noise out, but it was coming from inside his head. There was no escape.

"No," he said, "no, no, no!"

"You okay?"

Tom jolted at the sound. Gail was standing in one of the doorways. The chanting had stopped and all he could hear now was the gentle running of water.

"Oh, yeah," he said, dropping his hands and forcing on his brightest smile. "Just got a song stuck in my head."

He put his prosthetic hand behind his back, trying to ignore the stabbing pain he felt in his wrist – a wrist that was no longer there. He knew the pain was only in his head.

The doctors had called it phantom pain. Demon pain would have been more accurate. The demon had tried to possess him and failed, and yet sometimes Tom still felt its dark shadow trying to find its way into his body.

"They got her. The slit-mouthed woman."

"Well, of course they did," Gail said. She'd not doubted they'd succeed for a second. Gail had formed Slay four years ago with one purpose: to rid the world of demons. She'd rescued each of the boys and trained them to become music-playing, demon-slaying machines. And she'd put Milly through the same rigorous process. Gail loved every single one of them as if they were her own children, Tom knew that. But she never seemed to feel any fear for them. Unless she was really, really good at hiding it.

She walked down the steps into the courtyard. "I'll call Suzume and tell her she can come home. Are the others on their way back?"

"They're heading to the studio. They're cutting it fine."

Gail looked at her watch. "Right, I'd almost forgotten – the interview! We'd better go."

"Maybe I should just stay here? After all, I'm supposed to be receiving treatment for 'exhaustion'." Tom smiled and waggled the fingers of his left hand, making incomplete quote marks to indicate the irony of it all.

Gail had released a press statement when Tom was still in hospital, saying he was receiving treatment for exhaustion and wouldn't be making any public appearances for a while. Most people thought it was all just PR speak for him being in rehab. Was it better the fans thought he had a drink problem rather than knowing about him losing his hand?

"And you're not exhausted?" Gail leaned against a wooden column, her wolf-headed walking stick tucked under her crossed arms.

Tom's forced smile fell. The truth was that since Mexico he was, if not exactly exhausted, then tired. Very tired. His freckled cheeks had lost their usual rosy glow and dark circles hung beneath his green eyes.

"It will be fine, Tom."

"You keep saying that, Gail," he replied, dropping any pretence. There was no point with Gail anyway. She saw more with her one eye than most people did with two. "And I keep waiting."

"Give it time."

"You keep saying that, too."

"And when have I been wrong?"

"Oh, I don't know. That green dress you wore to the Emmys wasn't exactly your best decision. And then there was that woman in Berlin…"

Tom dived for the ground as Gail swiped at him with her stick, and came up smiling, more himself now.

"That dress was designer. And that woman was… Well yes, she was a mistake. I'll give you that one."

She walked forward and wrapped her arms around Tom's shoulders. "You'll get there. I promise," she whispered, placing a kiss on the top of his head.

"I will with you to help me," he said, returning the hug.

"So, come on then. Groupie time."

Tom groaned, running his hand through his curls.

The other boys had started calling Tom their number one groupie. *"Following us around on tour, dressing like us, it's sweet, if a little creepy,"* Zek had said, teasing Tom about his decision not to join them onstage for a while. And the name had stuck.

"I have to see this for myself, anyway. JD being interviewed on Japanese national TV is going to be hilarious."

JD hated interviews. He always froze up and barely managed to say more than three sentences. Tom had been the chatty, easy-going one, who would cover for JD and keep Zek from being too sarcastic. He was happy to answer the same old questions over and over again, whereas JD had said that if he got asked about how the band was formed one more time he was going to scream. But Tom knew if he did an interview now, the only question anyone would ask would be about what happened to his hand. He couldn't face that quite yet.

No, he was happy to stay in the wings for a little while longer. Just until he got his smile back.

You're my spotlight

Milly arched up in her seat, peeling her jumpsuit off to reveal a pair of black trousers and a plain white T-shirt. To her left, Zek and Niv did the same – only they were a little more practised at the quick change and neither of them got their trouser legs caught around their boots. Milly struggled to yank her foot free, as Zek laughed.

"You have to take your boots off first, Mills." He shook his head. The patterns he had shaved into his fade were growing out a little, which Milly knew was frustrating the usually pristine bassist, but they hadn't been able to take their stylists with them to Japan.

"Do what I do," Connor called back from the passenger seat. He grinned and pulled at his jumpsuit – with a ripping sound it tore in two neat parts along the seams.

"Velcro?" Milly said. "Nice!" Despite being the youngest of the group, Connor was easily the biggest, and seemed to be getting bigger every day. If he got any more muscles, Milly thought, they might just burst out of that jumpsuit without any help.

"Yup, I got the idea from my shoes," Connor said.

"Yeah, he has to have Velcro because he can't tie his laces," Zek said, grinning as Connor stuck his tongue out at him.

It still didn't solve the problem – that Milly was stuck inside her jumpsuit. They were in a hired truck, parked opposite the entrance to the TV studio, and they had only a few minutes before they were supposed to be in make-up, and ready for the interview.

Niv tapped his forehead with his fist. *Idiot.* Milly could spot the difference between Niv and his brother easily now. Niv's cheeks were a little fuller, his skin a touch darker, and he didn't have his brother's constant sardonic smile. He rolled his eyes, then pointed to himself before reaching out with his right fist placed on his left palm, thumb up, his delicate eyebrows raised and quizzical. *Can I help?*

Milly reached out her tangle of boot and material, and he yanked. The boot went one way and Milly went the other, banging her head against the blacked-out window of the van. She was going to have to get a lot better at this. She sat up and adjusted her clothes, straightening her T-shirt and flattening down her hair.

She didn't remember seeing JD wriggling to get free of

his combats or tear them off like Connor and yet he was sitting in the driver's seat, already in his "civilian" outfit. He pulled down the visor to check his dark hair in the mirror and Milly met his intense grey eyes in the reflection.

"The hair's looking good, Milly," he said.

Milly ran her fingers through her newly cropped pixie haircut. She'd had a chin-length bob before, but they'd gone even shorter to help with her disguise as a boy. Connor had gleefully offered to shave it off for her, but she'd managed to keep him and his clippers away.

Zek considered her hair. "Yeah, it just needs…" He leaned over the back of the driver's seat and, before JD could do anything, started running his fingers through JD's hair.

"Oi!" JD said when Zek had finished, before trying to smooth his perfectly coiffed quiff back into place.

"You had too much hair gel on anyway." Zek turned to Milly, his hands now sticky, and began artfully tousling her hair. When he finished, he leaned back. "That's better."

Milly slipped on a pair of large, black-rimmed glasses, tied a flannel shirt around her waist and slipped the heavy black boots back on. Now she not only looked like a boy, but a cool one.

"Perfect," Zek said. "We shall call this look…shabby geek."

"You make a very good boy, Mills," Connor said.

Milly wasn't entirely sure how she felt about that. When

she'd first looked at herself in the mirror in her Milo outfit it had been a shock to see a young man looking back at her.

"Ready?" JD asked.

"Born ready!" they all replied, including Milly. She felt a thrill at being one of the group.

JD started the truck up again and drove towards the entrance to the studio. It was only five hundred metres and yet he slammed on the accelerator and screeched to a halt in front of the barrier. A rather unimpressed guard peered out from the security box. He was so large Milly wondered if he was wedged in there permanently. JD slid the window down and the man grunted at them. JD handed out a sheet of paper, their invitation to be on *Close-up With Nomura*, the late-night chat show.

The man grunted again, handed the sheet back, and pointed towards a stage-door sign across the parking lot.

"*Arigatou*," JD said, thanking the man. As soon as the barriers were up he hit the accelerator again as if he was in a drag race.

"JD!" Milly shouted. She went sliding across the back seat as JD threw the truck into a handbrake turn before finally screeching to a halt.

"Can you chill it with the stunt driver stuff?" Zek said.

JD unclipped his seat belt and smiled back at Zek. "Where would the fun be in that?" He threw open the driver's door and the rest followed.

"Show-off."

Milly smiled to hear Tom's voice and turned around. He was wearing a baseball cap and dark glasses to help him keep a low profile, in case there were any snooping paparazzi around. But she'd know those dimples anywhere. She hadn't been sure if he was going to join them tonight, but was glad he had. This was their first public appearance since it had been announced that Slay had a new member. The fan forums and gossip sites had run wild with rumours about what they were doing in Japan and when were they finally going to make an appearance. And so Gail had set this evening up to soothe the speculation. Milly had no idea what to expect of her first interview and could already feel her nerves building. She was grateful that Tom would be here to help her through it.

"You look great, Mil— ...Milo," Tom said, correcting himself.

"Thanks," Milly said, tugging at the shirtsleeves tied around her waist.

"Okay," Gail said, stepping up to adjust Milly's glasses. "Just remember what we practised. Keep your voice low and your answers short." She pushed the buzzer to get access to the stage door.

"And if in any doubt, just scratch your groin and burp as often as possible," Zek said. "Like Connor."

"I don't burp and scratch my groin. Not at the same time, anyway." Connor let out a small burp.

"Dear God, Connor," Zek said, waving away the smell. "What have you been eating?"

"Sushi," Connor said.

The stage door opened and a slim young woman wearing a headset and holding a clipboard stepped out. She looked stressed, and rattled off a string of Japanese.

Japanese was one of the languages Milly didn't speak, but she could get the gist of it: *You're here, at last.*

"Sorry we're late," JD said. "We had an appointment that overran."

"Yeah, by about three weeks," Connor said under his breath. The hunt for the slit-faced woman had taken a lot longer than any of them had expected.

"Welcome," the woman said, switching to English. She gave a small, polite bow. Slay returned it, matching the depth of her bow as they'd been taught. "If you could come with me."

She led them through the door and down a white-walled corridor. Pictures of a man with purple eyes, a huge grin and straggles of black hair dragged across a nearly-bald head lined the wall. In each one, he was pointing out at the camera, an exaggerated grin twisting his wrinkled face. He was easily in his late sixties, early seventies, and yet dressed like a man more than half his age. This was Nomura, the man who was going to be their host tonight. His show *Close-up* was, they'd been told, the freshest, hottest show on

Japanese TV. Nomura had been a news anchor for years, known for serious pieces exposing corrupt politicians, but had suddenly decided he needed to reinvent himself and his show format. He had dyed what was left of his hair black, thrown away his glasses and started wearing purple contacts. After being on air for only two weeks, A-list celebrities were lining up to be on the show.

"Oh God," JD said as they passed a picture of Nomura pulling his same grin while a figure stood next to him completely covered in bright pink gunk. "What have we let ourselves in for?"

Tom let out a laugh and Milly turned, surprised and happy to hear it. Tom hadn't laughed much since Mexico.

"Your face, JD." Tom pointed at JD's suddenly pale complexion. "This is going to be brilliant. I am so glad I came."

"Not too late for you to join us in the interview," Zek said. "You can have a miraculous recovery."

"Oh, I'm good," Tom said. They passed another picture. This time Nomura was standing next to a woman who had been wrapped from head to toe in neon green tape. "Oh, I'm very good."

Milly wasn't sure she quite believed Tom, but it was nice to see him smiling again. Even if it was at their expense.

"The deal was a five-minute interview," Gail said. "One game. No goop."

The woman with the clipboard smiled and nodded. "Of course."

Milly didn't buy it for a second.

"I'm up for some goop!" Connor said.

Zek shook his head. "Why does that not surprise me?"

The woman pressed a key card against a lock and opened a door that led into a small room with two grey sofas. A large bowl of fruit sat on a low table in the middle of the room and a sideboard was filled with a huge variety of drinks and snacks. Connor was straight in there, sorting through the bottles.

"You can watch the show from here," the woman said, pointing at a slim screen on the wall. "I will collect you in…" She checked her watch. "…five minutes for hair and make-up and then the interview." She bowed again and left the room.

Milly sunk onto the sofa. Her stomach was suddenly filled with squirming butterflies, and a thin film of sweat coated her skin. "Is it hot in here?" she asked. "It feels really hot in here."

Tom sat down next to her. "It's okay, Mills. You'll do great."

"What are you worried about?" Connor said, opening a can of neon green drink. "You just went up against a demon."

"This is worse."

"Worse than a demon who goes around slicing people's faces?" Connor asked.

"Much worse."

"Take a deep breath," Tom said. "It's no different to your training. Stay calm, stay focused, look for ways to use the situation to your advantage and, if that all fails, throw JD under the bus."

"Huh?" JD said, mid-sniff of a pack of mysterious snacks with the picture of a cartoon octopus on the front.

"Ooh, yes," Zek said. "Say his favourite singer is Dolly Parton and that he has a tattoo of a unicorn on his butt cheek."

"That before he was in Slay, he was a…a…"

"One of those people who paint themselves silver and pretend to be a statue!" Connor said.

"Yes!" Zek said.

"You're all aware I can kill every last one of you," JD muttered, staring into the silver packet.

"And then just sit back and enjoy as his face gets redder and redder," Tom said.

Milly laughed so hard she felt the butterflies evaporate. "Stop it!" she said. "I can't breathe."

"Har, har," JD said sarcastically, but Milly saw a smile itching at the corner of his mouth as he looked at Tom. Things had been so tense between the two of them as of late, so this felt like a breakthrough.

On screen, Nomura was running up and down the stage, throwing something out into the audience.

The door opened again and clipboard woman was back. "Please come with me."

Milly stood up, and as she did, Tom took her hand. He gave it a squeeze. "Good luck."

She returned the squeeze and held onto his hand a fraction longer than was strictly necessary. "Thanks."

Milly and the others were whizzed into a make-up room, where Milly was caked in more foundation than she'd ever worn in her life. Ironic, she thought, given here she was pretending to be a boy. Barely minutes later, the producer collected them and led them down a dark corridor. She stopped at a pair of heavy black curtains with a red light above them and held a finger to her lips.

"When the light goes green," she whispered, "that's your cue."

Zek and Niv stood at the front, Connor behind them, his hand over his mouth to make himself stay quiet, which left Milly and JD at the back.

She smiled at him and he returned it. "You'll be fine," he mouthed.

The light turned green. Zek pushed aside the curtains and stepped forward.

"Welcome, Slay!" Nomura shouted.

"So this unicorn on your butt," Milly said to JD as she

stepped out into the bright studio lights. "Does it have a name?"

She walked onto the stage, waving, leaving a gawping JD behind her.

Not goodbye

Tom rocked back and forth on the sofa, tears rolling down his cheeks. Slay had only been onstage a couple of minutes and already they were covered in fake snow, hats and scarves, and had been split into teams to make a snowman out of foam for a reason Tom couldn't work out. It wasn't even close to Christmas. Not that he cared. The look on JD's face was priceless.

Gail watched the screen, her hand covering her mouth, muttering things like "We did not agree to this" and "He is going to kill me". But Tom could see by the twinkle in her eye that she was almost as entertained as he was.

Connor was throwing himself into the glorious absurdity of the show, as expected, giving it everything he had. Rather than build a snowman, Niv and Zek had decided to turn Connor into one instead. The boy was now covered in foam, had a carrot stuck in his mouth and a top hat on his head.

Niv was trying to shove black buttons into Connor's scrunched-up eyes, but they kept falling off. JD and Milly's creation was more lump than man and whereas Milly had a large smile on her face, JD looked highly unamused. All the while, the host Nomura ran back and forth, throwing more fake snow onto the scene.

"This is amazing!" Tom said, feeling more himself than he had in a month. And all it took was the humiliation of his friends on national television.

The door opened. Clipboard woman stepped in and held it open for a young man with delicate features, thin-frame glasses and dark hair that fell in front of his eyes. He carried a silver case and was dressed in a beautiful, dark suit. Yet something about the way this young man wore it made it look more like a school uniform than the bespoke tailoring it clearly was. It was like the suit was wearing him, rather than the other way around. His nose twitched, pushing his glasses up, and Tom couldn't help but think of a bunny rabbit.

The young man bowed as he passed the clipboard woman and entered the room. He and the woman talked quietly in Japanese, then he shook his head, reassuring her of something, his nose twitched again and he nodded, before saying, "*Sayonara.*" The woman left and the three of them were alone.

There was a moment of awkwardness as Tom tried to

stop laughing at the onscreen antics and the man looked from him to Gail.

"Hello," he said in perfect English.

"Oh, I'm so sorry," Gail said. "You must think us so rude. My name is Gail Storm and this is Tom Wills."

The man nodded to Gail and Tom in turn. "My name is Hideyoshi Makoto. I am pleased to meet you both." He placed his silver case on the floor, slipped his hand into his jacket and pulled out a leather card case. With slim, nimble fingers he opened it and took out two black cards.

He handed the first to Gail. She took it with both hands and gazed down at it as if holding something of great value. When the man handed the second card to Tom, he tried to copy Gail's approach. At first, he couldn't see anything on the surface. Then, as he moved it, holographic lettering appeared, showing the man's name and a logo. *IKIR10*.

"Wow, cool card." The man smiled, accepting the compliment. Tom fished out his wallet from his back pocket and slipped the card inside. "So, are you going on the show?"

"Me?" Hideyoshi said, putting his card case away. "Oh, not really. But my band *Ikiryō* are. Tonight is their first appearance on television."

"Cool," Tom said. "We're in a band too. I mean, well, they are." He pointed at the screen. He could no longer make out who was who, as all he could see was a sea of white foam.

"Oh, no, I am not in *Ikiryō*. I merely manage them."

Tom saw Gail flinch at the mention of "merely" managing a band and was quick to change the subject. "What kind of music do *Ike-rio* play?"

"*Ah-kee-yo*," Hideyoshi said, gently correcting Tom's failed pronunciation. "Pop mostly. With an electronica edge. What we call J-Pop. The band isn't fully formed yet – which is why Nomura and I are auditioning for new girls."

"Nomura?" Gail said, pointing at the TV host on the screen. "What's he got to do with your band?" she asked.

"He owns *Ikiryō*," Hideyoshi said. "I owe everything to him."

"News anchor, TV host, music Svengali. Are there no ends to his talents?" said Gail, looking back at the screen, her amused expression somewhat muted.

"So how goes the auditioning?" Tom said.

"Very well. We are introducing the seventh member tonight. We hope to have found the remaining three girls by the end of the month."

"Ten girls?" Tom said. "That's one big group."

"It is Nomura's vision. It's why we spell *Ikiryō* IKIR10."

"Clever," Gail said, hardly looking at Hideyoshi as she was too busy watching Nomura run around onstage. "Nomura seems like an interesting man."

"Oh, he is. I am so honoured to work for him. Without him, I'd be…well, I'd probably still be washing dishes in a restaurant. I used to break more than I cleaned!"

There was something about this young man that Tom instantly liked. There was a nervous openness that he found endearing. He wondered if he would like the rest of IKIR10 as much. "Where are the rest of the band?" Tom looked back at the door, wondering if the band members would be joining them.

"They are here." Hideyoshi patted the silver case.

Tom looked from the case back to the man. "Um, sorry, what?"

Hideyoshi placed the case on the table in the middle of the room and unclipped it. He gently prised open the top and reached in to pull something out: a black box, around thirty centimetres square. It looked to be made of glass or some kind of high-tech plastic. A bead of electric blue light flowed around the edges and across the surface, marking out intricate patterns and symbols.

"It's stunning!" Tom said, which he felt was an understatement. It was one of the most beautiful objects he'd ever seen.

"Is it a Japanese puzzle box?" Gail asked, leaning over to get a closer look. "I've only ever seen photos of them."

"In a way. I built it from a design based on a puzzle box that was in my family for generations."

"I...don't understand," Tom said. "How is your band in there?"

The door opened and the clipboard woman beckoned to Hideyoshi.

Hideyoshi smiled at Tom. "I have to go and set up now, but I would very much like to continue our discussion after the show." He picked the box up and, cradling it in his hands as if carrying the most precious thing in the world, returned it to the suitcase. He bowed to Tom and Gail and left the room.

Tom looked back to the screen – the show was now on an ad break. "Well, he's interesting."

"Yes," Gail said, gazing at a framed picture of Nomura that grinned down on them. "He is."

Hai

The audience clapped, somewhat politely, as Slay finished the game and Nomura waved them over towards a bright green sofa made from an oversized beanbag. Milly wiped the foam from her hair – glad at least it hadn't been goop.

They waited till the floor manager counted them back from the ad break, her fingers counting down five, four, three, two and...

"*Okaerinasai!* Welcome back!" Nomura said, speaking first in Japanese and then in perfectly fluent, if heavily-accented, English. "And welcome again to Slay!"

He shook each of their hands in turn and gestured for them to sit down. They all took unsteady seats on the squishy sofa. It seemed intentionally designed to make you as uncomfortable as possible.

"Slay!" Nomura repeated. "This is your first visit to Japan?"

"Yes," Zek said, "and we are loving it."

"Especially the food," Connor said.

"Oh, you like our food. Do you hear that?" he said, turning to the crowd. "They like the food!"

As Nomura spoke, Milly noticed how a display board over the stage flashed a string of kanji. She assumed it was translating his words, which would explain the slight delay between him speaking in English and the audience reacting.

"Now, let me get this right. It's Connor, JD, Niv and Zek," he said, pointing at the boys.

"I'm Zek, that's Niv," Zek said, pointing at his brother.

"Ha ha ha! You should have badges! Shouldn't they have badges?" A moment later the audience laughed, agreeing with the host. "So, Zek and Niv and finally…" Nomura turned to Milly. His purple eyes bored into her and she felt a wave of hot panic, mixed with something else. A discomfort from being pinned by his stare. "We have Milo, is that right?"

Milly nodded.

"And you have only just joined Slay?"

"Yes," Milly said. *Voice low, answers short.*

"Perfect!" he said, clapping and encouraging the audience to clap along too. They were warming to the band. But Milly was not warming to Nomura and his fake, too-bright smile. Something about him just gave her the creeps. Instead, she focused on what Gail had said about winning an audience over: be humble, be grateful.

"I'm so honoured to work with these other boys, and that their amazing fans have welcomed me into their hearts."

The audience cooed, delighted with Milly's performance. The "other" boys comment might have been laying it on a little thick, but what the hell.

"So, you've officially replaced Tom Wills, then?"

"Oh no, not at all," Milly said, her voice getting a little high in her panic. Gail had made it very clear to the producers that there was to be no mention of Tom. Nomura was going off the agreed script.

JD jumped in. He looked straight into the camera. "Tom is going nowhere. We're not Slay without Tom. He's just taking some time off and he'll be back in the band soon."

Milly looked at JD in shock. He was usually too reticent to speak in interviews. In fact, it was a joke among the band that he never said more than six words at a time. She guessed his protectiveness for Tom brought out his chatty side. But she wasn't sure how that made her feel.

"I'm sure all your fans will be very happy to hear that, if any of them happen to be watching." Nomura threw his head back and laughed, delighted with his own joke.

Milly resisted the urge to roll her eyes. This man was one of the weirdest, most infuriating, most unsettling men she'd ever met. He reminded her of someone, but she couldn't put her finger on who it was.

"Now, we couldn't convince Slay to play for us today, but…"

Milly saw JD's eyes tighten in annoyance. He'd wanted to play, they all had. But the producers had insisted that they only do the game and interview instead. Nomura was lying through his unnaturally bright teeth.

"But I have a surprise for my wonderful audience – yay! Tonight, exclusive to *Close-up*, performing live. – well, as live as they get – for the very first time on television to introduce their latest member… It's *Ikiryō!*"

IKIR10 flashed up over the stage and the crowd went wild. The main lights went dark, as all the spotlights turned to pick out a point in the centre of the raised stage.

"What's going on?" Milly whispered to JD.

"Not a clue."

A young man wearing a black suit walked out, his shining shoes ringing on the hard surface of the floor. He placed what looked like a box in the middle of the stage, laid his hands on it for a moment and then stepped back out of the spotlight and into the darkness. Seconds later, a beam of pale blue light shone out of the box and the lone figure of a girl in a flowing white dress appeared, her long dark hair falling over her shoulders, her face turned to the floor. She glowed, pale blue and transparent.

"A hologram," Connor said. "Cool!"

Of course! Milly thought. When the girl first appeared, a

shiver had run up and down Milly's spine. She'd thought for a second that the girl was…but of course it was a hologram.

A single note sounded as the figure stepped forward. A second, harmonious note rang out, two more beams of light radiated out of the box and two holographic girls appeared behind the first. A third note, and a row of three more girls flickered into existence, slightly staggered behind the row in front. Six holographic girls were hovering a couple of centimetres above the floor, their feet hidden by their dresses.

"And introducing their seventh member…" Nomura said. "Nana!"

A single beam erupted and a seventh girl appeared at the end of the second row. The beat of the track kicked in and all the girls looked up in perfect synchronicity. Their faces were covered by white masks with pointed fox-like ears, long noses and bright red patterns painted on them. At first Milly thought each girl was wearing the same mask, but she slowly noticed that each one was subtly different. The girls began to sing a gentle and irresistible pop track, dancing in perfect harmony.

The crowd could barely contain their excitement. Milly spotted girls in the audience wearing long white dresses, furry fox ears and red marks painted on their faces to replicate the ones on the hologram girls' masks. She wondered how the fans had known *Ikiryō* would be playing here tonight, if it was supposed to be a surprise, and then remembered that fans always had a way of finding these things out. The *Ikiryō* fangirls sang along to the song, their hands to their faces as if they couldn't believe they were really here and this was really happening. Milly had seen that look before, whenever Slay played to their fans. Whoever IKIR10 were, they were adored. Milly couldn't understand the lyrics, but the girls' voices were beautiful.

The song ended with the high ring of a bell and a shout of "*Hai!*" from the girls. They raised their hands into the air and then the beams of light were sucked back into the black box and the girls…vanished.

A moment of silence hung in the air before the audience erupted in wild applause. Milly and the band joined in. It had been quite the performance. They were… Milly searched for the right word to describe it.

"Spellbinding, aren't they?" Nomura said, as the camera turned back to him.

Spellbinding. That was the exact word she had been searching for. "Utterly," she agreed.

"Open auditions are being held in Kyoto tomorrow night to discover the lucky eighth member! A chance for one beautiful, talented girl to be immortalized for ever. So…get on down!"

There was a scream of excitement from the audience and some of the IKIR10 fans started jumping up and down.

Nomura laughed. *"Ganbatte kudasai.* Do your best!" he shouted, before turning back to Slay. "Now, a little bird tells me…" Nomura leaned in, looked dramatically over his left and then right shoulder as if checking that they weren't being observed. The audience tittered. "You will be supporting *Ikiryō* on their tour."

Milly blinked, confused. She caught JD's eye, and he looked just as baffled.

"Um," JD said. "I…um…"

"That's why you came to Japan, yes?"

They all looked to each other, wondering what they should say. The truth was they'd come to Japan to fight demons, but Gail had been working on booking them some gigs. If they didn't play soon, people might start to wonder why they'd really come.

"Well, we're huge *Ikiryō* fans," Zek said quickly, *"obviously,* and we'd love to perform with them, but we're not sure how long we're in Japan for. It's not really up to us – you know how these things are." Zek flashed Nomura his smoothest smile.

"Oh, I do! I do!" Nomura threw his head back and laughed and laughed. "I do!"

Let's hit the road

"Tour?" Gail said, pointing at the screen and staring at Hideyoshi, who had just rejoined them in the green room. "We're not joining anyone on tour."

The young man tilted his head, as if Gail's sudden anger was a curiosity. "You had not been made aware of this offer?"

"I had not," Gail said.

"My apologies. I had been told by Nomura-san's team that you had already accepted. I do hope that you may consider it. I believe it could be a very good opportunity for you and Slay."

"Thank you," Gail said, calming down, but only slightly. "But we can make our own opportunities. We always have."

"Tell me, are you in Japan to get exposure?"

"Well yes, but—"

"*Ikiryō* only launched a month ago and are currently the bestselling, most downloaded, most adored band in Japan.

Support us on tour and you will get all the exposure you need."

Tom could see why IKIR10 were so popular. Great concept, great music. Even the idea of live auditions was a great marketing gimmick – not that Tom understood why Hideyoshi needed real girls in order to make holograms. Tom was impressed, but it seemed Gail was not.

"Slay are not a support band," Gail said, her chin held high.

"I am sorry if I have offended you, but you are not well known in my country. One week on tour with *Ikiryō* and you will have done what it takes other groups years to do: broken Japan."

Tom watched the exchange between Hideyoshi and Gail like he was watching a game of tennis. "It might not be a bad idea," he said.

Gail threw him a silencing look and he pursed his lips. But he could see that she was at least thinking about it.

Slay had never been on tour with anyone before. They couldn't afford to have another band finding out what they did. But with IKIR10, that might not be such a big issue.

"On tour with holograms, would be pretty…" He caught Gail's eye and stared meaningfully at her. "…fun."

Gail blinked, confused about what Tom was trying to communicate. Then he saw comprehension strike. The fact the girls were holograms rather than living breathing humans meant that Slay wouldn't have to worry about protecting their secret from any other band members.

Gail made a small *hmm* noise through her nose. "How big is your tour team?"

Hideyoshi held up one finger.

"Just you?" Gail said.

"Everything is preprogrammed. I control it all with the box." He patted the case.

"Don't you get lonely?" Tom asked.

"I suppose, but I am often so caught up in my work I forget other people exist." He let out a small laugh and then caught himself as if it were inappropriate to be joking about such things.

Tom didn't know why but he liked this guy. Or if not *liked* exactly then he felt a sympathy for him. There was something about Hideyoshi that reminded Tom of himself.

"In Slay, we are very much used to setting our own schedule," Gail said.

"Ah, yes, so I heard. You like to hold surprise concerts to keep your fans always guessing."

"It's just one of our things," Tom said.

"Very smart. It means your fans will always be thinking of you, always checking the websites to see if an announcement has been made. I like this idea. Perhaps *Ikiryō* should start being a little more...spontaneous. How about this? If you come on tour, you can say where and when we go. Then I can hold surprise auditions in those locations for the remaining three girls."

"We sometimes change our plans at the last minute."

"It sounds exciting," Hideyoshi said. "My sister once told me I should learn to be less controlling. Perhaps this is exactly what I have been looking for." His eyes creased at the edges and Tom thought he looked genuinely delighted at the idea of not being in control, as if the very idea was a huge novelty.

What must that be like, Tom wondered, *to be in control of every single aspect of your life?* Since the day his mother was possessed by a demon his entire life had been completely out of control. In the past, he'd loved that. He'd fed off the energy of never knowing what was coming next. But recently, he wasn't so sure. Maybe knowing what was going to happen tomorrow wouldn't be such a bad thing.

"Well, thank you for your offer," Gail said. "I will discuss it with the rest of the band."

Hideyoshi bowed low and Gail matched him. "Indeed, you must have an agreement."

"I guess that must be one of the best things about having a holographic band," Tom said. "Everyone does exactly as you say!"

A strange expression flickered over Hideyoshi's face. Tom couldn't tell if it was irritation or sadness. But it was quickly replaced by a warm smile. "Yes, I suppose."

Before Hideyoshi could say any more, the door flew open and Connor leaped in.

"Well he was a proper eejit—" Connor caught himself as he realized they weren't alone in the green room. "Delight," he finished quickly.

"Boys," Tom said quickly, "this is Hideyoshi-san. *Ikiryō*'s manager."

"Yeah, we saw you onstage," Connor said. "They are seriously cool."

"Really amazing," Milly said.

"I wouldn't mind replacing some of Slay with a hologram," Zek said. "I bet they smell better." He danced out of the way of Connor's blow and blew the drummer a kiss.

"Nomura mentioned an audition," Milly said. "Sorry if I'm being stupid, but how exactly do you audition holograms?"

"Not stupid at all. Each of my holograms is based on a living girl. Nomura-san auditions them and then the chosen girl goes through a process whereby I 'transfer' them. Their personality, the way they move, their voice – all of that data is used to build the hologirls."

Niv tapped Milly on the shoulder and signed quickly.

"He says, 'Like artificial intelligence?'" Milly translated.

"In a way, I suppose."

"And what happens to the real girls?" Zek asked. "The ones you copy?"

48

"They go back to their lives and no one ever knows they were chosen. Nomura says it offers the best of both worlds. Fame without the loss of privacy."

Niv signed, lifting the first and second fingers of his right hand in front of his eye, then moving them as if rifling through a drawer of files.

"Yeah," Zek said, translating for his brother. "Doesn't the media just hunt them all down anyway?"

"We are very, *very* careful to protect the girls' true identities. We change names, hide their faces. No one has uncovered our secret yet."

Tom knew all about keeping secrets. But he wondered what it would be like to have a normal life, while another version of him dealt with everything else.

"What's this about a tour?" JD said. He'd been watching quietly from the doorway.

"Nothing has been agreed," Gail said quickly. "But Hideyoshi-san has made us a very interesting offer."

"Perhaps I can make you another offer? Join me on my journey to Kyoto tomorrow. I can show you around my Shinkansen, we can talk more about the tour. If you decide to join, then good. If not, I can take you anywhere you want to go."

"Shinkansen? As in bullet train? You have your own bullet train?" Connor said. "That is deadly."

Hideyoshi smiled. "There is plenty of space, with more

than enough rooms to accommodate all of you, should you decide to join me. And now, it has been a pleasure meeting you, and I hope I see you again soon." He bowed and left the room.

"I don't like him," JD said, staring at the door.

"You don't like anyone," Tom said.

JD shrugged. "That's true."

"I thought he was cool," Connor said. "And cute."

Niv drew a thumb across his forehead. Tom knew that one. *Clever.*

"Yeah, and a good dresser. That was a great suit," Zek said.

"Trust you to judge someone based on what they wear," Connor said.

"Hey, what someone wears tells you everything you need to know about them. Like, your outfit tells me you know absolutely nothing about style."

"I'll give you style," Connor said, and began trying to untuck Zek's shirt from his tight trousers. Zek squealed and ducked behind his twin brother, but soon they were chasing each other around the green room.

Connor bashed into Milly, knocking her forward into Tom. He caught her by the elbow and helped steady her. "Got you."

"Yeah, you do," she almost sighed, looking up at him. They'd not been this close since the hospital. She scanned the cluster of freckles across his nose, the mole he had on his chin, his lips... Suddenly aware of how hot it was in the room, she stepped away, coughing. "I mean, thanks."

"Yeah, no problem," Tom said, running his hand through his floppy hair. "I, um, how was your first interview?" he asked.

"Well, I expected it to be less...sticky." She brushed a lump of snow goop off her jacket.

"You did really well," Gail said. "Now let's get back, we need to check in on DAD and see where we're going next."

Under my skin

It was nearly midnight when they made it back. Tired, aching and sticky, Milly opened the door to the house that had been their home for the past month. When they had first arrived, it had smelled overwhelmingly of paint. Now, it just smelled of boy.

Milly, who had been so used to being on her own much of the time, had found life with five boys took some getting used to. They never ate at regular times, or slept, or studied for that matter: the three things her old life had been built around. They would simply snatch a moment here or there, around whatever job they had to do, whether that was demon-hunting, practising or promoting. This old house was beautiful, with a stunning courtyard that she'd been training in every chance she got – some of the doorways and wooden poles were covered in arrow holes as a result.

Milly had sectioned off a corner of the living area with a

couple of privacy screens used by the artists, while the boys just slept on the beat-up couches or wherever they could lay a futon. They could have afforded to stay in any hotel in the city, and yet they chose to stay here, cramped and on top of each other, which Milly realized was just what they were used to. It was the constant noise that she'd found hardest to handle at first – the chatter, the grunts when training, the snoring. But slowly it had become the background of her life, and now she found it soothing.

Her phone bleeped in her pocket and she pulled it out to see a message from Naledi, her best friend back in London.

I miss your face! The message was over a picture of Naledi, who had put a filter on it to give herself puppy-dog ears and nose and massive tear-filled eyes.

Milly wrote a message in return. *I miss your face too! And your voice! And your hair!*

They'd left for Japan the day Tom had got out of hospital, nearly four weeks ago, but Naledi believed Milly was still in Chicago. Milly hadn't been able to think of a way to tell her best friend about what had really happened to her mother. She'd been sworn to secrecy when she'd joined Slay. And even if she hadn't, how do you go about telling someone your mother had been possessed by a demonic priestess before trying to kill you, without your friends calling in the mental-health professionals.

Instead, she'd just told Naledi that her mum had died

and she was staying with friends, without mentioning that those friends just so happened to be a famous boy band who fought demons in their spare time.

She sent the message, wondering what time it was in London and when she would be able to see her friend in real life again.

Gail clapped, snapping Milly out of her daydreams. "Great job tonight, everyone. Niv, start DAD running again in case anything new pops up in Tokyo."

Niv saluted and fired up his laptop.

"Zek and Connor, check over the weapons."

"Again?" Connor groaned.

"Again."

"Come on," Zek said, dragging Connor over to the racks of knives and staves.

"Tom and JD, how are you getting on with that song you were working on?"

JD was sitting on the back of one of the couches, cleaning his sword. "We haven't had a lot of time," he said. He looked down, his long fringe falling across his eyes. Milly had noticed that JD hardly ever made eye contact with Tom any more. In fact, they hardly spoke. No wonder they were struggling to write music together.

"Make time," Gail said. "The producers are expecting a new album from us in four months' time. And, God help me if we have to release some cheesy Christmas covers album."

"We could call it *Slay Bells!*" Connor said. "Sleigh – get it?"

Gail just shook her head.

"Okay, okay!" Tom said. "We'll work on it tomorrow."

"Can I do anything?" Milly asked, grabbing a drink from a fridge which had, for some reason, been placed slap-bang in the centre of the room.

"You can relax. You did great tonight," Gail said. "Both on the hunt and on the show."

"Thanks," Milly said. "It was a bit close when I messed up my first shot. I was lucky JD had my back."

"JD will always be there to protect you. All the boys will. Which reminds me – there's one element of your initiation into Slay that I forgot about."

"What?" Milly said, nervous that there would be some weird rite they would force her to do.

"The tattoo."

"Ooh, yes!" Connor said. "She needs one. Can I do it?"

"No, Connor, you cannot," Gail said. "Remember what happened when you tried to tattoo yourself with a picture of an angel?"

"It looked all right," Connor said.

"It looked like a demented pigeon. And it got infected and you complained for weeks," Zek said.

"Yes," Gail agreed. "You are not doing the same with Milly. I will do it."

Each of the boys had the same tattoo: a five pointed star in a circle. It was, they'd explained, a symbol of protection against possession. Connor also had a few other random tattoos which had nothing to do with protection and everything to do with his low boredom threshold and access to a tattoo gun.

"Don't you have to be eighteen to get a tattoo?" Milly asked.

"Milly, we run around with weapons and grenades, and you're worried about breaking the law with a tattoo?" Zek said.

"Yeah, good point." The boys were all standing around now, watching and waiting to see what Milly would decide. "Does it hurt?"

"Only a little," Connor said. "It's more like an irritation than a pain. Although Zek cried when he got his."

"I had hay fever!"

The others all groaned at Zek's denial.

Milly had never thought of herself as the kind of person who would actually get a tattoo. But then again, she'd never thought of herself as someone who would shoot arrows at demons or be interviewed on live television. It was time she accepted that she was a different person now. "Okay, let's do it." She smiled. "Because if I don't do it now, I'll only chicken out."

"Where do you want it?" Gail asked.

"My shoulder, I think," Milly said, reaching her left arm across her body to point to her shoulder blade. She'd been admiring the boys' tattoos ever since she saw them, but thought she'd rather have hers somewhere she could hide it.

"All right then. I'll get the stick kit."

Connor whooped.

"You'll be fine," Tom said, leading Milly over to a couch.

She hopped up and pulled off her flannel shirt, stripping down to the vest top she wore underneath. "You promise?"

"How about you hold my hand and if it hurts you can squeeze the hell out of my fingers?"

"Okay, but if I break them, it's your fault."

"Oh, I think I'll be fine," Tom said, holding up his prosthetic hand.

"Hey, that's not fair," Milly said. "I want you to feel the pain!" She hadn't meant it the way it had come out. After all, Tom had been through more than enough pain. But he only chuckled and gave her his left hand instead.

Gail returned, wearing black rubber gloves. She held a metal stick with a needle on the end in one hand and a pot of black ink in the other. She placed the items down on the arm of the sofa. "Ready?"

"Born ready," Milly said, realizing she'd never sounded more uncertain in her life.

Connor had been right. It wasn't painful so much as

annoying. The tap-tapping of the needle gnawed away at her shoulder so that after thirty minutes she was starting to think that Gail might be tattooing her bones. Just when she was thinking she needed a break, the tapping stopped.

"We're done." Gail wiped at her shoulder with a damp cloth. "Go check it out."

Milly hopped off the bed and looked around to find a mirror. She couldn't see one.

"Here," Zek said, holding up a hand mirror.

"I should've known you'd have one," Milly said, smiling.

"Hey, you don't look this good without trying."

Milly angled the mirror to look over her shoulder. The star tattoo shone on her light-brown skin like it had always been there.

"Looks great!" Zek said.

"You're one of us now, Mills," Connor said. "No going back."

Milly moved the mirror around to get a better look at the symbol. She smiled to herself. *I don't want to go back.*

"Check it out for a bit longer and then I'll wrap it up," Gail said, pulling off the gloves.

Milly hardly recognized the person in the mirror. Cropped hair, tattooed; her reflection was cooler and more confident than Milly had ever imagined herself being. Whoever that person was, Milly liked them.

"Looks awesome," Tom said. "Which reminds me, I guess I'll need to get mine redone at some point." Tom's tattoo had originally been on his right wrist – the same wrist that JD had sliced off.

"No time like the present," Gail said, holding up the stick. "You can't keep putting it off."

"I'm not putting it off. I'm—"

Whatever Tom had been about to say was cut off by a high-pitched bleeping.

Niv pulled out his phone, checking out the feed from DAD. The slit-mouth demon might have been dispatched, but Niv had set DAD running, searching for any more suspect activity. He signed, sliding his right hand up against his left palm, before grabbing a handful of air. *Found something new.*

Milly felt a fresh rush of adrenaline. The hunt was back on.

I won't bring you flowers

They'd all piled into the control centre to see what DAD had found this time. Niv was busy reading through a report and they stood around awkwardly, waiting for him to finish.

"Any second now, Niv," JD said, but Niv held up a hand, telling him to wait. Finally, Niv looked away from the screen and started signing. Tom, who had been working on learning British Sign Language, was able to catch snippets of what Niv said. In the past, they'd just relied on Zek to translate everything for his brother. It was only when Milly arrived, fluent in BSL, that he'd realized how lazy he'd been about learning to communicate with one of his best friends. JD and Connor had also been learning, although Connor mostly got Niv to teach him swear words. But when it came to a report from DAD, they couldn't risk missing a thing, and so Zek still did the translating.

"A police report came in. Two weeks ago, a young man

reported his eighteen-year-old girlfriend to the police. He said she'd gone missing for a week and when she finally reappeared she was...different. According to him, she'd gone from being the sweetest, shyest girl in the world to super confident and cruel. She dumped him and refused to reply to any of his messages."

"Sudden change in behaviour. Tickety tick," Connor said. That was one of the first signs that someone might have been possessed by a demon.

"The boyfriend is convinced she's been caught up in a cult or something," Zek said.

"Could be a demon possession," JD said.

"Could just be a bitter boyfriend," Milly said.

"The police don't take him seriously," Zek continued. "So, the boyfriend decides he won't take no for an answer. He's going to save her. He starts sending her flowers, hanging outside her apartment, playing music, begging her to take him back."

"Gah!" Milly said. "Romance films have a lot to answer for."

"Remind me never to send you flowers," Tom said, and he noticed a blush in Milly's cheeks that made his own feel hot.

"Sounds like this girl wasn't a fan either," Zek continued. "The boyfriend's body was found yesterday."

"Poor kid," Connor said.

"Police were called to the scene, but she killed three of them before escaping by jumping into the river and – get this – a witness swears that she had completely black eyes."

"Okay, boys," Gail said, then paused, looking at Milly. "Okay, kids?"

Connor pulled a face.

"Um, *guys*?"

"Y'all?" Zek said.

"Team?" Milly suggested, and they all nodded.

"Okay, team," Gail said. "Looks like we're heading to… where was it?"

Niv spelled out three letters.

"Uji?" Tom said.

Niv nodded.

"Where's that?" Connor asked.

Niv pointed at Uji on a map. It was about four hundred kilometres from Tokyo.

"That's just outside Kyoto," Tom said. A thought had just occurred to him.

"So?" asked JD.

"You know who else is going to Kyoto, who could give us a ride?"

"Hideyoshi?" Milly said.

Tom nodded excitedly.

"I've been dying to go on a Shinkansen," Connor said.

"Not just any Shinkansen," Tom said. "A private Shinkansen!"

"I don't know, Tom," Gail said, uncertain.

"Just for one night. Hideyoshi said himself that if we didn't want to stay he'd take us anywhere we wanted. This means we could be in Uji by tomorrow evening, find this demon, and be back on the road by morning."

"Just for one night?" Gail said.

"But what about Milly?" JD said. "She'll have to dress as a boy the whole time."

Tom hadn't thought of that. If he was honest, he was so desperate to get out of this cramped place he hadn't even considered that Slay now had two secrets to hide.

"He said there were lots of rooms?" Milly asked, glancing over at the corner she'd been sleeping in.

"More than enough for each of us," Tom replied.

"Then it's fine with me," Milly said.

"And what about you?" JD asked.

Tom blinked, confused by JD's question. "What about me?"

JD refused to meet his eyes. "You're not ready."

Tom felt himself bristle at JD's comment, but forced himself to stay calm. JD was only feeling guilty, he knew that, even if he was sick of it. "It's one night, JD. Besides, it's not like there are going to be any demons on the train."

JD hesitated before nodding. "Okay," he said finally. "For one night."

You were made for me

Milly stared up at the side of the white bullet train, trying to get her head around how one person could own a whole train. Not just one carriage, but eight carriages. The logistics alone were baffling.

"You sure you're okay with this?" Gail said.

Milly paused before answering. The truth was, she didn't know if she was okay with it, but there was no way she was going to say no. She'd seen Tom's face when Hideyoshi had invited them and he'd looked so excited, more like his old self than he'd been in a month. Plus, they had a demon to take down in Kyoto and this was the fastest way to get there.

"It'll be fine. It's not as though dressing like a boy is uncomfortable." She gestured to the loose jeans and black boots she was wearing. If anything, Milly thought she might like to wear these clothes all the time.

The doors of the rear carriage slid open with a hiss of

hydraulics, and a glowing blue light welcomed them on board. Tom was first to go in, followed by JD and the twins. Connor paused, his foot on the step, looking worried.

"What's wrong?" Milly asked.

"I feel like we're cheating on Agatha."

Agatha, the band's tour bus, was currently being shipped from the US back to the UK.

"Well," Gail said, "I won't tell her if you don't." She patted Connor on the shoulder and gave him a gentle push.

Milly adjusted the strap of her bag on her shoulder. Gail had told them to bring essentials only, so she'd grabbed a change of her Milo clothing and all the weapons she could carry, including a bow and a quiver of arrows. Only the essentials, after all.

If the outside of the train had been impressive, it was nothing compared to the inside. Everything was perfect, down to the last bolt. They walked past a restaurant area and a gym. There was even a small fountain trickling in a stunning white compartment which was filled with hanging plants. It was hard for Milly to get her head around the use of space – it was almost as if it was bigger on the inside. They walked through the carriage corridors until they reached one that looked more like a reception area in an exclusive hotel than a train – all white and bright with beautiful pieces of art hung on each wall.

"Is that a Rothko?" Zek asked, staring at a painting of a

yellow stripe on an orange canvas.

"Rothko. Titled *Orange and Yellow*, painted in 1956," a soft, husky voice said.

Milly looked around, trying to find the source of the voice. There, in the middle of the carriage, was a hologram of a large white fox, about a metre high. It sat with its tail curled around its front paws, and had red markings across its holographic fur.

"No way!" Connor said, running up to the projection and passing his hand through its head. "Another hologram!"

Unlike the hologram girls from IKIR10, who were so close to being real it was unnerving, this hologram was more obviously computer-generated. Created by a single source of light coming from the ceiling, it couldn't move around like the hologirls had and it looked more like a cartoon than a real-life fox.

"I am Kitsune," the holographic fox said, ignoring Connor's hand, which was currently in its long ear. "Hideyoshi's virtual assistant. It is a pleasure to meet you…" It tilted its head and gazed at Connor. "Connor McManus."

"So cool! Do him!" Connor grabbed JD and shoved him in front of the hologram.

There was the same tilt of the long head and after a moment the fox said, "Welcome, Joshua Deacon."

"Ha ha! It knows your name. You next!" Connor pointed at Milly.

She stepped forward and paused before subjecting herself to Kitsune's gaze. What if the hologram was running the face recognition against a database? Niv had assured Milly that he'd created a fake identity for Milo, including social media accounts dating back ten years and a fabricated school record. But this would be the first time it was put to the test.

"Hi there, Milo Tan."

Connor clapped delightedly. "Oh, let's see how it copes with twins." He pushed Milly out of the way and waved Zek and Niv over.

Kitsune scanned Niv first, taking a little longer than it had with the previous two boys, but finally its wide mouth curled in a smile. "It is nice to meet you, Niv Marouazi, and you too, Zekri Marouazi."

I want one, Niv signed.

"Thank you, it is nice to be appreciated," Kitsune said.

"You understand sign?" Milly said.

"Hideyoshi-san updated my protocols to include British Sign Language, to ensure that Mr Marouazi would be comfortable."

"Thank you," Gail said. "We are very impressed."

The holofox bowed its head a fraction. "Hideyoshi-san asked me to welcome you on board. He will join you when we arrive in Kyoto in two hours and seven minutes. Then we will stay in Kyoto for the night and...after that, Hideyoshi-san has asked for his schedule to be cleared.

If you are ready, we can depart."

Connor beamed. "Sure, let's go!"

Kitsune's eyes closed for a moment and then the train began to hum. Milly looked out the window and realized they were pulling out of the station. Other than the fact she could see the blur of buildings outside, there was no other indication that they were in motion. It was like they were gliding over the rails.

"You are currently situated in carriage seven. You have complete freedom to explore six of the carriages that make up the train. You will find sleeping areas, a gym, two restaurants, a meditation area and a music studio. However, carriages one and two are Hideyoshi-san's personal lab and domestic area, and he has kindly asked that they stay off limits to you. There are no staff aboard, but if you need anything during your stay, simply say, 'Hey, Kitsune', and make your request. Can I get you anything now?"

Connor opened his mouth to speak and Gail jumped in. "No thank you, Kitsune, we're fine."

"Then I will wish you a pleasant trip." The fox bowed and, with a flicker of blue-white light, vanished.

"Hey, Niv," Connor said. "Why don't you turn DAD into a hologram?"

Gail placed a finger to her lips and pointed at JD and Zek, directing them to the doors at either end of the carriage. Milly watched, wondering what they were doing.

Sensors, Niv signed.

Understood, Milly signed back. She should have realized. They were always a couple of steps ahead of her.

Gail then turned to Niv. He hefted his bag onto one of the tables and started pulling out his equipment: a laptop, cables, a couple of small black boxes and something that looked like a small airwave radio. He connected it all up, fired up the laptop, and after a rattle of keys, there was a squawk.

Clear, he signed.

"And that," Zek said, "is a signal blocker. We can talk freely now without worrying about sneaky holographic ears."

"This place is so freaking cool!" Connor said, staring at the paintings, twisting his head left and right as if trying to make the swathes of colour take shape.

"What happened to cheating on Agatha?" Milly asked.

Connor looked momentarily guilty and then shrugged. "Ah, she'll understand."

"This train is all very exciting and everything," Gail said, "but it's just a means to an end. The end being a demon in Kyoto. It's nearly four p.m. now, so we'll arrive just after six. Tom, I want you to stay close to Hideyoshi, keep him out of our way, so the rest of you can focus on tracking the demon down. It was last seen in the river, so let's start there."

Tom nodded. "No problem."

"Are you sure?" Milly asked.

Tom smiled, and it was almost his old smile. "Yeah, I like Hideyoshi. And it will be nice to be useful."

"Where are you off to?" Gail said, as Connor and Zek suddenly started running for the door.

"Bagging the best room," Connor yelled, already halfway down the carriage.

Milly and Tom glanced at each other and then ran after the others. It was only for one night, but after a month living behind a screen, Milly was going to get a room of her own, even if it meant fighting the others for it.

How can I know (if this is the real deal)?

"We are now arriving in Kyoto," Kitsune's soothing voice sounded over the train's speakers. "I hope you had a good journey."

Tom pressed his nose against the tinted windows to see the city as they pulled into the station. There were none of the looming skyscrapers he'd got used to in Tokyo, just one sweeping structure that looked like a lighthouse.

They'd spent the two-hour journey exploring the train. The race to get the best room turned out to be pointless, as all the rooms were identically lovely. And, as JD kept reminding them all, they were only sleeping on the train for one night. No reason to get comfy. Connor had run around pressing every button he could find, while Niv had followed him, undoing whatever problems he had caused. Now they'd arrived in Kyoto, it was back to business.

"Okay, everyone, tool up and—"

Niv cut Gail off with a hand gesture and pointed to the motion trackers. Someone was coming.

The doors hissed open and Hideyoshi strode through. He wore black jeans, black trainers and a black hoodie, quite a change from the stiff suit he'd worn the last time Tom had seen him.

"My apologies," he said, blinking nervously. "I wasn't able to welcome you on board earlier myself, but I hope you had everything you needed?"

"It was so fast we hardly had time to need anything," Tom said.

"Kitsune is so cool!" Connor said. "Can I have one?"

Hideyoshi smiled. "I'm afraid there is only one Kitsune. It was my first attempt at creating a hologram. My process has become more..." He paused. "Sophisticated since."

"You mean *Ikiryō*?" Milly asked.

Hideyoshi nodded. "They are my greatest achievement. Which brings me to my next apology, Gail-san. I must go to the audition now, but we can discuss the tour when I return?"

"That sounds fine," Gail said.

"And in the meantime, please look around the city all you like. Kyoto is a sleepier town than Tokyo, but I'm sure you'll still find plenty to do."

"Oh, I'm sure we'll still find some hot spots," Connor said, smiling his toothy smile.

"Would it be all right if I accompanied you to the audition?" Tom asked. "I'm fascinated to understand your process."

"Oh, yes, I'd like that. I will inform the others."

"The others?" Tom said.

The smile on Hideyoshi's face faltered slightly. "Nomura-san. He will meet us there. Are you ready to leave now?"

Tom pulled his jacket on and nodded. "Born ready." He gave Milly a quick wink as he passed.

"Have a good night, Tom," JD said and Tom sensed the warning and the worry in his voice. He looked back at the rest of the team. JD's face was etched with that guilty, angsty expression he'd worn every time he looked at Tom since Mexico. Milly was trying to hide her concern, but doing a pretty poor job of it. Connor and the twins looked worried too. Only Gail treated him exactly as she had before: expecting him to do his part.

"I will," Tom said, and stepped off the train.

The night air was cool and smelled of tree bark and something musty which Tom couldn't put his finger on at first.

"Tea," Hideyoshi said. He still carried his silver case, his knuckles tight and white around the grip. "This whole area was famous for its teahouses. And when it rains you can smell it in the wood."

A sleek black car was waiting a few metres from the train track. As they approached, Tom expected a driver to get out and rush around and open the door for Hideyoshi, but the young man climbed into the driver's seat himself, then leaned over and opened the passenger door for Tom. It wasn't till he climbed in that Tom realized there was no driver's side or passenger's side. There was no steering wheel or gear stick. Tom looked around, front and back, trying to work out how the car was operated.

Hideyoshi chuckled. "It's driverless."

Tom laughed, realizing how stupid he must have looked. "Of course it is! Wow – no team, no driver. You really are on your own, aren't you?" Tom had meant the question to be light and playful, but it came out strained.

As the car pulled away, Hideyoshi looked down at his hands. "I have Kitsune and *Ikiryō*."

Cartoon foxes and holographic girls, Tom thought. *Not the best company.* "Must be nice though," he said, trying to shift Hideyoshi's mood. "What with Gail and the others, I never get a chance to be alone."

"And is that something you want?"

Tom looked out the window as the car slipped into the flow of traffic, and thought about that. In the past, it would have been an easy no. He used to hate being alone without the distraction of the chatter and laughter of the other boys. But now, he sometimes felt like his head was so filled with angry, buzzing noise that the usual antics of the others could become almost unbearable.

He left the question hanging and instead chatted away, asking easy questions about Kyoto, Japan in general and IKIR10. Light, meaningless stuff that Tom found effortless but Hideyoshi seemed to struggle with. He was never quite present in the conversation, as if part of his mind was somewhere else. He carried some secret burden, Tom decided, some secret pain.

Don't we all, Tom thought to himself.

The roads grew narrower, the houses lower and when Tom glanced out the window, he caught a glimpse of a figure in bright green silk, carrying a red umbrella.

"Is that...?" Tom said, leaning around to try and see more of the figure as they drove past.

"A geisha, yes. We are in the Gion district, where women still come to train in the old arts."

"Wow, cool. Do you think one might audition for you?"

"I doubt that. The geisha are trained in very traditional music and dance. I'm not sure they will be that interested in J-Pop. Ah, here we are."

The car pulled up outside a building that was taller than its surroundings. It had four levels and was topped with a pointed roof that swooped down in two graceful wings. Large red lanterns hung on either side of an impressive doorway which was covered by a purple awning. In front of it, winding all the way down the street, was a row of young girls. There were easily one hundred waiting there. A girl at the front spotted the car, and the screaming started. Large men wearing bomber jackets held the girls back as Hideyoshi and then Tom got out of the car.

"This is the bit I dislike," Hideyoshi said, keeping his head down and rushing for the doors. One of the bouncers opened the door with a large hand while holding off a screaming young girl with the other. Tom paused in the doorway. If these were Slay fans, he'd stop and sign autographs, chat with them for a while. Gail always told them to be grateful for their fans, that Slay would be nothing without them. It seemed that Hideyoshi didn't have quite the same approach. Tom followed him inside.

White sheets hung from floor to ceiling, and scaffolding towers lined the walls.

"This is Minamiza," Hideyoshi said as Tom caught up with him. "One of the oldest kabuki theatres in Japan. Nomura-san bought it recently, for renovation."

"Looks like it's going to be a pretty serious project."

"I suppose. Nomura-san is not daunted by big projects. Here."

Hideyoshi opened a door and suddenly Tom saw why someone might be interested in buying this building. He was looking across a small but beautiful theatre. Rows of low-backed red seats faced a stage which was surrounded by delicate golden columns. Overhead, square panels lined the ceiling and the whole place glowed with a soft red light.

It reminded Tom of a paper theatre he'd had once as a child, where he would move cut-out people in front of beautiful scenery.

"Hideyoshi-san," a man said, jumping off the stage and coming to greet Hideyoshi.

He gave Tom the smallest of cursory glances before returning all his attention to Hideyoshi. Tom couldn't understand what the man was saying, but the body language gave everything away. He was desperate to impress Hideyoshi and clearly anxious to have his approval. Hideyoshi didn't say a word as the man showed him to the stage and introduced him to the team of people waiting. Tom felt utterly in the way as the team briefed Hideyoshi on how the audition was going to work. When he seemed satisfied with everything, Hideyoshi put his silver case down in the very centre of the stage and pulled out the black box.

Tom stepped closer, itching to see how the whole thing worked. Hideyoshi had now taken out a small handheld device: slightly larger than a mobile phone but smaller than a tablet. He pushed a button, the lights on the box flashed blue and one of the slim panels shifted out. One second she wasn't there and then she was: the glowing figure of a young woman with long dark hair wearing a white dress.

She looked up at Tom and he staggered back at how lifelike she was. She was breathtakingly beautiful – with a heart-shaped face, large, deep eyes and a small mouth.

She looked just slightly older than him.

Tom stepped closer and the girl tilted her head, following his movement. He reached out a hand and she did the same, long, graceful fingers reaching out for his face. Without knowing why, Tom felt an aching sadness well up in his chest. The girl was so beautiful, so sad.

"*Ichi! Yamero!*" Hideyoshi shouted. He pushed a button on his tablet. The hologram girl let out a gasping sigh before flickering out of existence for a fraction of a second. When she reappeared her face was covered with a fox mask once more. It had a red stripe running down the centre and a large red circle on the forehead. Her eyes peered out through the holes, intense and searing.

"Ah, she's one of *Ikiryō*?" Tom asked.

"This is Ichi. The lead singer," Hideyoshi said.

"Why the masks?" Tom said, recovering from the strangeness of it all. "You've made her so beautiful, wouldn't the fans like her even more if they could see her?"

"It made people uncomfortable," Hideyoshi said, not meeting Tom's eyes. "They said she was too…real."

"She's breath-taking!"

"Why, thank you."

Tom turned in the direction of the voice to see a young woman standing behind him wearing gold-lens glasses. She had long hair dyed blue on one side and yellow on the other, underneath a large baseball cap. She wore a long, brightly coloured coat, a green shimmering skirt and golden shoes. The style was unlike any Tom had seen before, but she made it work. She exuded cool. "Ichi does look a little like me, I suppose. I guess I should be flattered." The way the woman said it made it clear she thought it anything but flattering.

Tom looked at the woman. It took a while for him to recognize that she and Ichi shared the same heart-shaped face and delicate lips. "Wait, are you…" Tom pointed first at the young woman and then the hologram. "Her?"

"Yes. Or at least, she was created from a copy of me. He named her Ichi – his number one." She held up a delicate finger. "I'll always be your first, isn't that right, Hideyoshi-chan?"

"Kotomi-san," Hideyoshi said, standing up. He bowed to the young woman. "It is good to see you."

"Oh, Hideyoshi-chan." The woman patted Hideyoshi on the cheek, not returning his bow. "You are such a terrible liar."

"I thought you were in Tokyo."

"I invited her." An elderly man bounded up onto the stage. He wore a bright purple suit, grey-snakeskin shoes, and walked with more vigour than Tom had seen in a man of his age. It was Nomura, the TV host who had interviewed Slay just the night before. "I wanted Kotomi's assistance in choosing number eight. Especially given how behind schedule you are."

"Of course, Nomura-san," Hideyoshi said, bowing low.

"I am happy to have Kotomi-san's assistance."

Kotomi's painted lips twisted in a cruel smile. Whoever this woman was, she was enjoying Hideyoshi's embarrassment.

"And you must be the elusive Tom Wills," Nomura said. "I thought you were in rehab."

"Um, no, just taking a break for a little while," Tom said, pulling his sleeve down to cover his prosthetic arm.

"A break," Nomura said, "of course." He gave Tom an exaggerated wink and threw his head back and laughed. "Hideyoshi told me about your hand. You'll have to let your fans know about it one day."

"One day," Tom said.

"But not today," Nomura said, laughing again.

Back in the green room, Tom had laughed at JD and the others having to deal with this man, but meeting him in person wasn't quite as funny.

"Okay, let's get this started," Nomura said, clapping his hands. "Send in the girls whose lives we are about to change."

Falling

Milly headed back to her room to get changed for the hunt. She hardly noticed her Milo clothing any more, it was just so comfortable. But while dressing like a boy was easy, acting like one was hard. Gail had to keep reminding her to not cross her legs, and to be careful how she laughed. So much of being a boy seemed to be about hiding how you felt.

As Milly arrived in the narrow corridor of the sleeping carriage, JD was coming in the opposite direction. He was already kitted up in his black combats and heavy boots, with his camo half-mask around his neck. He carried his saya scabbard in his hand, its yellow tassel the only pop of colour. He spent hours sharpening and oiling the katana blade within. Milly wondered if he loved anything in life as much as he loved that sword. His guitar, maybe, which he treated with the same combination of reverence and love.

She stepped left to let him pass, just as he stepped to his right. They tried again, but as she stepped right he stepped left, until they were standing face-to-face.

"Sorry," Milly said, laughing nervously. "After you."

"No, after you," JD said, pressing his body flat to the wall to let her pass.

As she squeezed through, her arm brushed against his cool skin. He reflexively jerked his arm out of the way, as if their skin touching was troubling to him, and Milly felt a strange pang of rejection. Sometimes it felt as if JD was doing everything he could to stay away from her. To keep distance between them. It was different when they were out on the hunt or even when they were rehearsing songs as a band – then there was no awkwardness between them; they were part of one fully-functioning team. But whenever they were alone, there was a tension between them that she couldn't unravel. She often wondered if he really wanted her to be part of Slay, but Gail and all the others had reassured her more than once that JD was as glad she was here as the rest of them. She'd confided in Niv about the weirdness between them and he'd said it was because of how guilty JD felt about what he'd done to Tom.

She understood why JD must be beating himself up about that, because she did too. Tom had only lost his hand because he'd been trying to save her. *But why does that make him so weird around me?* she'd asked Niv.

The boy had smiled, his richly expressive face amused and slightly pitying at the same time. *Why don't you ask him?*

When she pressed Niv on what that was supposed to mean, he'd just shrugged and changed the subject.

"We're leaving in five," JD said, as Milly went to push the button to open her door.

"I'll be ready in two," she snapped back, feeling defensive that he was suggesting it would take her longer than the rest of them to get ready.

"I wasn't…" JD shook his head.

Milly spun to face him – she was going to do what Niv had advised her. She was going to get to the bottom of this at last; she was going ask JD what was going on.

"I…" she started.

"Yes?" JD said, moving closer, his grey eyes meeting hers.

He was actually looking at her, perhaps for the first time in a month. Milly's mouth suddenly went dry. "I… Do you think Tom will be okay?"

JD let out a small huff of a laugh and leaned back against the wall. Milly didn't know what was so amusing. "I'm sure he'll be okay. Hideyoshi is an even bigger geek than he is. They'll get on great."

"I don't just mean tonight." Milly mirrored him, resting against the closed door behind her.

JD looked away; a light from overhead caught his sharp cheekbones and cast a dark shadow in the hollows of his face. As far as Milly knew, JD hadn't spoken to anyone about Mexico, not even Tom. "He just needs time."

"Is there anything we should do in the meantime?"

"We?" JD said, closing the distance between them again. He reached over her shoulder, to pick at a speck of dirt on the clean white wall.

Why did he smell so good? Milly wondered. She never saw him put on aftershave or anything, unlike the other boys, who sometimes walked around in a fog of spice and musk so overpowering Gail would go make them shower it off. Tom smelled good too, she reminded herself, and then wondered why she was always comparing the two boys. Perhaps it was because they made such an easy comparison. Tom was warm, where JD was cold. Tom was reassuring where JD made her anxious.

"I mean, anything we can do for Tom? Together."

"I can't think of anything." JD sucked in his bottom lip. "Can you?" He looked away from the speck he had been picking at and back to Milly.

She fidgeted under the intensity of that look, and suddenly she was falling backwards. Somehow, she'd managed to push the button to open the door to her room. Now she was lying flat on the floor.

JD tilted his head and looked down at her. "You okay?"

She sat up, her ego stinging as much as her backside. "Yeah."

He checked his watch. "You'd better hurry up then. We've got to be at the bridge by seven." And with that, he was gone, leaving Milly on the floor and her dignity in shreds.

You're the one

The audition process, if it could even be called that, had been going on for an hour, and not a single girl had impressed Nomura. Most of the girls had been dismissed before they'd even opened their mouths. Some didn't even make it as far as the stage before Kotomi whispered in Nomura's ear and he shouted *"Dame!"* which Tom had learned meant "No good". The young girls who'd come in full of hope and excitement left with their dreams crushed. Many in floods of tears.

A few of the candidates made it up onto the stage and were permitted to sing with Ichi. The hologirl hovered in the centre of the stage, floating above the black box. Every time she sang, Tom felt his heart ache. It was like listening to the sound of waves crashing on beaches. It was going to be a struggle to find a voice that could match hers.

Hideyoshi seemed to find the whole process rather

uncomfortable. He smiled encouragingly at the girls and winced whenever Nomura shouted at them.

"You don't look like you're enjoying this much," Tom said.

Hideyoshi blushed as if he had been caught out doing something wrong. "I find it hard to watch them have their hopes crushed, but Nomura-san says I need to toughen up."

Gail had told Tom the same a few times, especially after he'd killed his first demon. *"They're not people any more,"* she'd said. *"What we do is a mercy."*

What Nomura was doing was anything but merciful. After a while, the old man yawned and wandered off, leaving Kotomi in charge. If possible, she was even crueller than Nomura had been, playing games with the girls who were auditioning, building up their hope, only to laugh in their faces.

"Who is she?" Tom leaned towards Hideyoshi and nodded at Kotomi, who was now seated in the second row of the theatre, her golden shoes resting up on the back of the seat in front of her.

"We went to university together. She was the…um… model for Ichi, my first hologirl."

"She's quite something."

Hideyoshi's face twitched but he stayed silent. The young woman clearly made him feel very uncomfortable. Wasn't IKIR10 meant to be his band? Tom wondered why he was letting Nomura and Kotomi make all the decisions.

"Is this process typical?" he asked.

Hideyoshi considered before answering. "I have found there is no typical audition. Sometimes we find no one good enough. Other times we may find one or two. Once, we signed four girls in one day, all from the same school in Osaka."

"Well here's hoping there's a school bus on its way." Tom was growing bored of the process and irritated by Kotomi's cruelty. Judging by how Hideyoshi kept looking at his watch, it looked like he was too.

"Can I ask you," Tom said, keeping his voice low, "why you chose to model Ichi on such a…"

"Cruel woman?" Hideyoshi finished Tom's sentence.

"Not the exact words I was going to use, but sure."

Hideyoshi looked even sadder than Tom had seen him before. "When I first knew her, she was sweet and kind. The perfect girl."

Kotomi shouted and threw a clipboard at the latest girl attempting to impress her. "What happened?" Tom asked.

"She…changed." Hideyoshi would say no more on the subject.

They must have seen over thirty girls by now. Each walked in bouncing with nerves and excitement, and each walked out bent over and broken. Tom sank lower and lower in his seat, not even wanting to look at the girls as they came in.

After another click of Kotomi's fingers, the door opened again. Instead of the heavy, happy footsteps Tom had become so uncomfortable hearing, there was a soft shuffle. He sat up in his seat to see a young girl wearing a long green dress walk slowly down the aisle. She had her face painted white, with red marks to match the markings on the fox masks that IKIR10 wore.

Hideyoshi sat up and as the girl reached the stage so did Kotomi. They all watched as she made her way slowly up the steps and stood next to the hologirl and gazed out into the theatre. Tom leaned forward, resting his chin on the back of the chair in front.

The music began, and both Ichi and this girl began to sing. It was clear to Tom's ears that the two voices were perfectly harmonious. Whereas Ichi's voice had a richness and depth to it, this girl's voice was like birdsong.

"*Yamero!*" Kotomi stood up and waved her arms around. The music stopped mid-bar.

Tom stood up too, ready to protest. This girl was amazing, easily the best they'd heard today, and she should be allowed to go on.

Kotomi pointed at one of the crew and delivered instructions in Japanese.

"What's going on?" Tom asked.

"She wants the girl to take her make-up off. She wants to see her face."

Tom looked to Hideyoshi, confused. "But *Ikiryō* all wear masks. What difference does it make what she looks like?"

Hideyoshi sighed and refused to answer.

The crew member came running onstage holding a white facecloth. The girl took it with both hands and placed it over her face. As she rubbed, trying to remove the layers of face paint, Kotomi climbed up onstage and began to walk around the girl, looking her up and down. When she lowered the cloth, not all of the make-up was off, but enough that it was easier to see the features of her face. They were round and soft and very pretty. Kotomi held the girl's chin and moved her face left and right. She then traced her hand against the girl's left cheek. The girl winced and turned away as if in pain. Tom peered closer and realized there was a soft brown birthmark on the girl's face. Tom caught his breath. Kotomi couldn't possibly turn away the girl because of something like that. If it was beauty she was looking for the girl had it, clearly. But she also had one of the most incredible voices he'd heard.

Kotomi stepped back and looked the girl up and down once more. She raised her hand and shouted out at the stage crew. A moment later, another assistant ran on, this time carrying a white envelope.

Kotomi took it and handed it over. The girl opened the envelope and pulled out a fold of paper. Her face lit up in utter delight and she squealed, before quickly covering her mouth with the paper. Kotomi reached into her long jacket and pulled out a pen. The girl quickly grabbed it and kneeled on the floor so she could sign what was obviously a contract.

Hideyoshi stood up. "It appears Kotomi-san is satisfied. We have found our eighth member. Come, let's meet her."

Tom joined Hideyoshi onstage. The girl was clearly giddy with delight as Hideyoshi shook her hand. They chatted for a while and the girl kept clutching the contract to her chest and shaking her head.

"Congratulations," Tom said. "You were incredible."

The girl covered her face with her hands, as if she couldn't believe the compliment. "Thank you," she said, bowing. "Thank you."

"What's your name?"

The girl looked up and her cheeks were wet with tears. "Ishida."

"Are you okay, Ishida?" Tom asked.

"I am so happy. My mother will be so happy too. With this money," she clutched the white envelope again, "she can go to hospital."

"Well, you deserved it. I hope your mother gets better."

"Thank you," she said again.

"You found one then?" Nomura had returned.

Kotomi pulled the young girl by her arm and made her stand in front of Nomura. The man looked her up and down, as Kotomi had done, assessing her as if she was an item of furniture rather than a young girl filled with hopes and dreams. He fired a series of questions at her in Japanese. Nomura sniffed, seemingly satisfied at her answers.

"*Owarimashita,*" he said, before spinning on his Cuban heels and bounding out of the theatre, followed by Kotomi, young Ishida and the crew. Again, Tom was struck by how agile he was for a man who looked so old.

Soon, there was only Tom, Hideyoshi and Ichi onstage. Tom watched as Hideyoshi approached the hologram and looked up at her. He then bent over, picked up the box and slid the panel back into place. Ichi flickered out of existence once more.

"So the audition is over?" Tom asked. "What happens now?"

"Nomura will make sure the girl understands the rules. No one can know she was chosen as a model for *Ikiryō*. Then we will arrange for the transfer process to take place." Hideyoshi placed the black box back into its case.

"That's where you make her into a hologram, right? How long does it take?"

"It depends. An hour, sometimes longer." For the inventor of such a remarkable process, Hideyoshi didn't sound too proud. But Tom found that humility endearing.

They made their way out of the theatre, weaving through the warren-like backstage area rather than going back out the front.

"Only two more girls to find, then? I bet you'll be glad when this is all over."

Hideyoshi smiled. "Very glad." They exited through the backstage door into a dark alleyway only illuminated by the green stage-door sign. Hideyoshi pulled out his phone. "I'll get the car to come around."

"So, back to the train then?"

"Yes, there's something in my lab..." Hideyoshi paused before continuing. "There is something I'd like to show—"

"*Omae!*"

Tom jolted at the sound, instinctively putting his hand to his pocket, only to remember he wasn't carrying any weapons and that, even if he was, he'd yet to try fighting with his left hand.

Two large men stood at the entrance to the alleyway. Everything about them, from their stance to the aggressive way they'd shouted, said trouble. Tom stepped slightly in front of Hideyoshi, stretching out his empty hands and keeping his body language open and unthreatening. Maybe he could diffuse the situation before it escalated.

"Hey, nice evening."

The two men looked at each other, confused, and then back to Tom and Hideyoshi. The bigger of the two took a few steps closer. He pointed at Hideyoshi and snapped something in Japanese.

Hideyoshi reacted by clutching the silver case to his chest and shaking his head.

So, Tom thought, *they're after the case. Well, that's not going to happen.* He might not have his bow, but he had another weapon: his voice.

He took another step in front of Hideyoshi, putting himself between the two intruders and his new friend. "Hey, now," he said softly, his voice taking on a lulling quality. "Just focus on me. Focus on my voice." But it seemed that his hypnotic powers didn't work when the person he was trying to use them on didn't understand what he was saying.

The smaller of the two men reached into his jacket and pulled out a short knife. Tom ran the scenario in his head like he'd been trained. If he was alone, he might have taken the best option, which was to run. But while he was pretty sure he could get away in time, he didn't trust that Hideyoshi wouldn't freeze. So that left the other choice. Fight.

He looked around for anything he could use and his eyes fell on a discarded manga comic on a dumpster. He casually stepped forward, talking the whole time, and picked up the magazine as if he was just curious about it. "Wow, this is so cool. I love manga, don't you?"

The two men seemed thrown by this strange English boy, chatting away as he flicked through a comic book. Tom couldn't make out the story of the comic, but there seemed to be a lot of tentacles involved. He rolled it up in his hand and took the final step forward.

"Hi," he said, smiling at the man with the knife.

The man's face scrunched up in confusion, and he waved his knife weakly. Tom struck with the rolled-up comic, slamming down on the hand holding the blade. The man dropped it with a pained yelp. Tom struck again, jabbing the comic into the man's Adam's apple. The man staggered back, clutching at his throat with both hands, coughing. Tom sensed the other man moving. He waited until the last second before ducking out of the way of the attack, sweeping downwards and scooping up the fallen knife.

He held it in his left hand, pointing it at them. They might be bigger than Tom, but he was faster, smarter and clearly better trained, even if he was using his weaker hand. They backed away. Tom smiled, expecting them to turn and run. Then, his smile fell. He stared into their eyes properly for the first time and realized this had been no simple attempt at a mugging. Both men had completely black eyes. They weren't muggers, they were demons.

One of them snarled, hissing at Tom. He needed to take them down before they had a chance to escape, but he glanced back to Hideyoshi. The young man was staring, open-mouthed, still clutching his silver case. Tom couldn't kill these demons without revealing his secret to Hideyoshi. Was it better to let them escape than be exposed?

Before Tom could make up his mind, the two demons came to a decision of their own. They both turned and ran back up the alley and away into the dark.

Tom waited a moment, letting the thrill of the fight recede. Gail had taught them it was when they thought a fight was over that they were most at risk of doing something stupid. He looked around, making absolutely certain that there was no more threat facing them, then threw the knife into a bin and turned back to Hideyoshi. "Are you okay?"

Hideyoshi lowered his case. "I think so. I... Thank you." Hideyoshi smiled a quivering smile. He looked as if he was trying very hard not to show how scared he'd been. "Where did you learn that?"

"Well, you pick up a few tricks when you have to deal with stalkers." He winked, trying to lighten the tension.

"You saved my life."

"No," Tom said, shaking his head. "They probably wouldn't have hurt us. They were probably just after money."

"They were after the box," Hideyoshi said, staring down at his precious case.

"Maybe," Tom said. He wasn't so sure. What would demons want with Hideyoshi's box? Or with Hideyoshi, for that matter? Tom would get Niv on the case as soon as they were all back together.

There was a bleep and a flash of light behind them. Hideyoshi flinched at the sound, but it was only the car finally arriving.

"Before," Tom said as they walked over, "you said you were going to show me something in your lab?"

"Oh, yes," Hideyoshi said. "I've been working on something. For you."

I'd wait all night

Milly was cold and bored. They'd been hiding under Uji bridge for over an hour and there was still no sight of the demon. Not so much as a ripple on the surface of the river.

"How much longer?" Connor said, for maybe the third time.

"As long as it takes," JD said.

"Are you sure this is the right spot?" Milly's feet had gone numb, and every time she tried to fidget to get some life into them JD would tell her to be still.

Niv nodded, pointing at a spot under the railway bridge which crossed the river. A number of witnesses had reported seeing what they thought was a woman lurking under the bridge. Little did they know they'd been looking at a demon.

"It's not all chases and rooftop fights, Mills," JD said, keeping his voice low. "A lot of the job is waiting around."

"A lot of the job is boring," Zek said, stifling a yawn.

Niv dragged his fingers over his eyelids. Milly wasn't the only one struggling to stay awake.

"Shush," JD said, pointing at the river.

Bubbles popped, disturbing the surface and then... nothing.

"Maybe she's not coming back," Connor said.

"Yeah, 'cause demons are known for their moderation when it comes to all the killing." Zek tutted.

JD hushed them all again and they descended into an irritable silence. Ten minutes later, Zek stood up and yawned. "Right, I'm calling—"

Something burst out of the river behind him. Long black hair, blended with slimy reeds, hung down past its shoulders, and black eyes stared out of a gaunt face streaked with red mud. It wore a gold necklace, almost as thick as one of its arms. The she-demon looked frail; its collarbones jutted out of its skin and its arms were like sticks. But that didn't mean it wasn't dangerous. When Milly looked down she saw the demon's hands ended in sharp, metallic nails. It hissed, revealing pointed, tusk-like teeth. Around it, the previously quiet waters now roiled and rushed like rapids.

"Finally," Connor said, leaping up, and pulling out his twin sai blades.

Milly fumbled to nock the first arrow with her numb fingers, but the demon was on them before she had a chance to release it. The creature swung, claws cutting through the air, aiming for Zek's head. He leaned back, twisting his body out of the way as the demon's metal nails passed barely centimetres from his face. Niv was swinging his weapon too, aiming for the demon's neck. The blade struck and there was a high ringing sound as metal hit metal: Niv's blade clashing with the golden necklace. The demon turned, snarling, and swiped at Niv, catching him across the chest and sending him flying into the water.

Zek used the distraction to attack – lunging out with his scimitar. It punched clean through the demon's side, plunging in all the way up to the hilt. The demon looked down at the blade embedded in its ribs and then back up at Zek. Like with most demons, it was going to take more than a blade in the side to take it down. A second swipe and the other twin went flying in the opposite direction, landing in the river with a loud splash.

Connor yelled – a high, cracking yodel – and threw himself on the demon's back. It hardly seemed to notice as Connor wrapped his legs around its slim body and began jabbing a sai into its neck. It merely reached up and pulled Connor off its back as if pulling off an annoying, itchy jumper.

Milly watched anxiously as Connor got caught in a sudden rush of water and dragged away. She hadn't fought many demons before, but this one seemed almost unstoppable. Only she and JD were left standing.

JD went first, his katana flashing left and right. The demon roared in his face before grabbing him with two clawed hands and throwing him over its head, far out into the flow of the river. Finally, Milly managed to string and release an arrow. It cut across the demon's face, slicing a thick cut in its cheek. Her second arrow embedded itself in the demon's shoulder. It paused, looked down at the feathered shaft, and brushed it away like it was nothing more than a speck of dust on its favourite dress.

The demon came for Milly, striding up the rocky embankment, a wide smile stretching its slim face. If the host's body had ever been beautiful, her beauty was gone now. All that was left was the demon spirit possessing her; twisting her body, controlling her mind. Milly reached over her shoulder and grabbed another arrow, backing away, slipping on the slimy rocks. She nocked the arrow on the second try, then drew her hand back. Her elbow hit against the thick trunk of a tree behind her. There wasn't enough room to pull the string back, and the demon was too close now anyway.

"Stupid bow," Milly muttered, throwing it to the ground. Tom had said a bow wasn't good in close quarters, but he had failed to mention how many times Milly was going to be in close quarters with a demon. If she lived through this, she was going to get a different weapon. She reached for a knife she had placed in her belt, but her hands were shaking so much she could hardly hold it. Besides, what good would a knife do when the boys' blades had had hardly any effect? She had to do something. But in her panic her mind had gone blank. Gail had warned her about brain freeze. A lot of her training had involved Gail hitting her around the head so she would be able to think through the fear.

Calm, she told herself. *Breathe.*

The demon was up to its ankles and almost out of the water, a matter of steps away from Milly. The boys were struggling to get to their feet, the heavy flow of the river buffeting them about. They'd never get to the shore in time to help her. Milly was alone.

The demon screeched, and Milly felt the hot, wet stench of death and decay on her face. Her insides felt like they were on fire and she could hardly hear for the sound of her heart pounding in her ears, but she didn't turn away. She held her knife up and roared back. "Come on then!"

The demon raised a razor-sharp set of claws, ready to strike, just as something silver wrapped around its slim arm and yanked it back. Milly looked up in wonder as a figure in black soared through the air, holding the other end of a metal whip, which had just stopped the demon from killing her.

The figure landed on the ground, knee bent, the metallic chain flowing behind it as gracefully as a gymnast's ribbon. Milly saw now the figure was female: long, dark hair pulled up into a ponytail, and a slim body covered in tight, black silk. She wore a black scarf over her mouth and had a full, heavy fringe, so only her shining eyes were visible. She glanced back over her shoulder at Milly and winked.

Milly was so startled that she almost didn't see the demon reaching for her with its other hand. She just had time to block the attack before the girl in black leaped forward to stand next to Milly and flicked her whip once more. It wrapped around the demon's chest, pinning its arms to its body. The silver was causing it pain and the demon hissed and screeched, but it was trapped. Milly picked her bow back up, ready to take aim. This was going to be an easy shot.

She felt something cold and sharp against her throat and looked down to see the girl in black holding a blade to her neck with her left hand, while her right held the whip chain. The girl shook her head. Slowly, slowly, Milly lowered the bow.

She was so confused. This girl had saved her, she'd trapped the demon. But now she was what? Protecting it? Didn't she understand that this thing was pure evil?

The boys had made it to the shore and were walking cautiously towards the two girls. Milly had only seen them look so afraid once before: the last time she'd had a knife held to her throat back in Mexico.

The blade twitched.

"*Hottoite*," the girl said.

"Woah, we don't speak Japanese," Connor said.

The girl snorted, sounding almost amused. "Step away." Her English was perfect. She took the knife away from Milly's throat, but kept it pointed at her. "Back, back."

Milly did as instructed, walking backwards until she was standing on the very edge of the bank. The girl in black yanked on the whip and the demon fell to its knees.

JD moved and the girl in black threw her knife. It cut through the air, just missing JD's ear. "One more step and I will be forced to hurt you. Believe me, I do not want that."

"What the hell do you think you're doing?" JD shouted. His face was paler than usual, his eyes wide.

"Er, yeah," Connor said. "We're the good guys."

The girl in black laughed. "This *oni* will not hurt anyone."

"How can you be so sure? You can't save them, you know," JD said. "We've tried."

"Then you should have tried harder," the girl said. She reached into a black bag with her now free hand and rifled around inside it. A moment later, there was a high-pitched screech like the sound of nails on glass. The demon in the water buckled, its body arching in agonized contortions. It opened its mouth and a black cloud rushed out into the air. It looked like a swarm of black insects battling to escape the body, but before they could flee, the cloud was sucked inside the girl's bag and all was silent.

With a flick of her wrist, the girl freed her whip. The demon's body, limp and lifeless now, slumped into the shallow water, face up.

"What the…?" Milly said, just before the girl in black turned and ran, disappearing into the night.

"Who was that?" Zek said, staring after the girl.

"Someone who just stopped us doing our jobs," JD said, scowling. His face was almost as muddy as Connor's. "Come on, let's deal with the body, then get back to the train."

The body lay still, eyes open and lifeless. She was a young woman, not much older than Milly, naked and bony, her eyes staring out at nothing. The demonic possession that had transformed her body had passed, and she was human once more. And, Milly realized, she was breathing.

"She's alive!" Milly raced forward and tried to drag her out of the water. "Help me."

JD was first to join her. "She can't be." He pushed his wet hair out of his eyes.

Milly looked at the woman's ribs again. Maybe she had been imagining it? Maybe the woman was dead after all, but then… "See!" Her ribs were moving up and down the smallest fraction.

JD pressed his fingers against the woman's neck. "There's a pulse. It's faint but…" JD pulled his hand away as if he'd been burned.

"What?" Milly said, concerned.

"Blood." JD held his hand up and Milly could see red liquid dripping between his fingers.

"Demons bleed black," Zek said.

JD looked at the young woman and then the other boys. All were staring, baffled and speechless. Milly pulled her jacket off and lay it over the woman's body to give her a small amount of privacy.

"She was definitely possessed?" Zek said.

JD nodded. "Looks like it."

"And that girl, she...what? Sucked the demon out of her?"

"Looks like it."

"And now she is most definitely not dead? And if you say 'looks like it' one more time, JD, I swear..."

"I don't know what's going on any more than you do," JD snapped. "This doesn't make any sense. Once a human is possessed, it's over. They're dead."

"Seems we were wrong," Milly said, feeling sick.

They stood there, listening to the river gurgling next to them, watching the woman breathing. She hadn't blinked or made a sound, but she was alive.

"We need to get her some help," Milly said. "Call an ambulance or..."

Before Milly could finish, the night air was cut by the sound of sirens and the darkness turned blue and then red. "Seems like someone thought of that already," Zek said.

"Milly, take your jacket. We have to get out of here." JD pulled the covering off the woman and thrust it into Milly's hand. He started to run and the others followed.

It wasn't until they were safe in the rental car heading back to the train that anyone spoke.

"Is it just me or did that girl in black look like—" Connor started.

"Don't say it!" Zek interrupted.

"A ninja?" Connor finished.

Milly didn't know about that, but she did know that the girl in black had saved her life. Maybe all of their lives. And that she knew more about demons than even Slay did.

"Ninjas," Connor said again. "This country gets cooler by the second!"

You were made for me

Hideyoshi was clearly still shaken. He twitched at every sound on the drive back and was unusually talkative, as if trying to cover up his nerves with chatter. Tom, however, hadn't felt this calm in a month. The fight had only been a small one, but he'd still won. More than that, he'd enjoyed it. Especially as it was the first fight he'd had since losing his hand. He had trained once or twice with Gail, trying to learn how to fight left-handed, but he'd never really believed that he'd be able to go back to his old life, hunting demons and playing music. But now, he felt a swell of hope that maybe Gail had been right all along. That things would work out.

Tom checked his phone as he and Hideyoshi drove back to the train. There were three unread messages.

The first from JD just read, *Hunt over. Will report on return.*

The second was from Milly. *Wild night. Demon was taken*

care of, kind of. Will explain when we see you. Important thing is everyone's okay. Hope you're good. Connor won't shut up about his belly rumbling, so we're getting food. We'll be back soon. Missed you.

The final text was from Connor. *We're off to get sushi. C. P.S. There were ninjas!!!*

Tom reread the message from Milly and smiled. It felt good to be missed.

"Are your friends having a good time in Kyoto?" Hideyoshi asked.

Tom slipped his phone away. "Seems so."

"Is it awkward there being a couple in the band?"

"A couple of what?" Tom said, looking at Hideyoshi.

"A couple. As in, together?" He glanced at Tom, who was looking at him, baffled. "Oh, I am sorry. Is that meant to be a secret? You should know that I have no problem with gay people."

"Huh?" Tom really wasn't following this.

"JD and Milo. They are together, no?"

Tom laughed, spluttering and then having to wipe his spittle off the window screen. "No, they're not a couple. What made you think that?"

"The way they are around each other. JD seems very protective of Milo, so I thought... I am very sorry. I misread."

"Oh, no, that's..." Tom couldn't explain that JD was like that because Milly was new to the group and because she was the only girl. It was kind of sexist, now he thought about it. "That's just JD. He's defensive of all of us."

"You are good friends?"

"The best," Tom said, staring out of the window at the old teahouses and temples that blurred passed. "We're like family."

"And your real family, where are they?"

"My father died in a plane crash when I was ten and my mother was…um, died of an overdose a couple of years later."

Tom had almost come right out and said that his mother had been possessed by a demon. He'd have to watch himself around Hideyoshi, he was almost too easy to talk to.

"I…" Hideyoshi clearly didn't know what to say. But then, people generally didn't. "I understand. I lost my parents when I was young too."

"Oh, I'm sorry," Tom said. Now it was his turn to not know what to say.

"It was a long time ago."

"Doesn't stop it hurting though, does it?"

"True. It took me a very long time to come to terms with their passing. I thought it was my fault, that if I could just work hard enough, be the perfect son, that they might come back. So stupid."

"It's not stupid. You want stupid?" Tom held up his phone. "I still listen to the last voicemail my mother left me. She

109

told me that she loved me and that she would see me soon. Sometimes, I listen to it at night and pretend that it's still true." Tom looked down at the phone. He'd never told anyone that, and yet here he was unburdening himself to this young man.

"To forget one's ancestors is to be a tree without roots."

"I like that. I'm sure they'd be proud of the man you have become."

Hideyoshi accepted this compliment with a nod of his head. "I hope that I can make Nomura-san equally proud."

They drove for a while longer in easy silence.

"Do you have any brothers or sisters?" Hideyoshi asked.

"Other than JD and the others, no. You?"

"I have a sister, but it has been many years since we spoke."

"I'm sorry."

"Thank you. I am sorry, too. I…haven't spoken to anyone about this in a very long time. Thank you. You are very easy to talk to, Tom-san."

"So are you," Tom said. And he meant it. Hideyoshi didn't demand anything of him, didn't walk around on eggshells around him. And he was eager to know what it was that he had been working on.

The train was dark as they pulled up, but the lights came on as soon as Hideyoshi placed his foot on the step. The living quarters that Tom and the rest of Slay had explored earlier were to the left, but Hideyoshi turned right, into carriage two – the area they had been told was off limits.

Lights flickered on, glowing from pale blue to full illumination, revealing a startlingly white room. There was nothing in there but a long white table and a single chair. But as Hideyoshi walked across the room, panels slid open revealing shelves and cubicles packed with computers, circuit boards and tangles of wires. Hideyoshi led Tom over to the far corner and laid his hand against the white wall.

"It's not ready yet, but…" He applied the slightest pressure to the wall and another panel hissed open, revealing a small pedestal on which rested a sleek, black object. The darkness looked out of place amid all the white and it took Tom a while to make out the shape. A jointed, curved cylinder ending in five slim digits.

"It's a hand?"

Hideyoshi nodded. "At the beginning, I had planned on building a robotic body for Ichi, before Nomura said that holograms would be more…effective. But after I met you I remembered I still had the parts. I made some adjustments."

"When did you have the time?"

Hideyoshi shrugged. "I don't sleep much." He undid the clips that were holding the hand in place and lifted it off the stand. He held it out to Tom. "Want to see how it fits?"

Tom looked down at the peach-coloured prosthetic he

wore, heavy and lifeless. Two rips of Velcro and it was off and on the floor.

Hideyoshi fitted the hand over Tom's stump gently, tightening the straps at the top, and placed a band lined with sensors over Tom's bicep. Finally, he placed a rubber skullcap over Tom's head, then stood back. The breath caught in Tom's chest as he looked at the robotic hand. It was so beautiful and so utterly unhuman. It was lighter than the prosthetic hand he'd been using and as he lifted it in front of his face, it felt more balanced.

"It's beautiful."

"It responds to the electronic signals your brain sends to your muscles and transmits them; you just need to train yourself to use it."

"How?"

"Close your eyes."

Tom did as Hideyoshi instructed. The light from the lab bleached through his eyelids. He felt the skullcap tight against his forehead.

"Now, imagine your hand is still there. Imagine making a fist."

Tom tried. In his mind's eye he saw the fingers of his right hand curling closed. He flinched as he heard a whirring sound and opened his eyes. The fingers of the robotic hand were bent over in a half fist. "I did that?"

"You did that."

Tom stared at the hand, and tried to imagine the fingers opening again. Slowly, the black fingers straightened. Tom let out a triumphant laugh. He was controlling it; the hand was responding to his commands.

Again, he focused, imagining making a fist, and again the hand responded, curling tighter this time, the fingers tucking against each other. Tom raised the hand up in front of his face, opening and closing it. For the first time since Mexico he felt whole. A single tear fell down his cheek and he smiled.

"How does it feel?" Hideyoshi asked.

"It feels like me."

Hideyoshi nodded. "Try this." He placed an empty drink can in Tom's open palm.

Tom concentrated and the fingers curled on his command, crushing the can.

Tom laughed louder this time. "What else?"

Hideyoshi looked around and found a wooden ruler. Tom snapped it into splinters with the merest thought.

His eyes lit up, his smile wider and brighter than it had been in weeks. "More!"

Hideyoshi laughed and placed a metal coffee cup in Tom's hand. Again, the fingers curled around, and the cup began to bend and buckle. Then there was a hissing and the fingers snapped open and lay flat.

"What happened?"

"The force must have blown a fuse. I will fix it."

Hideyoshi reached to undo the straps but Tom flinched, pulling away. He didn't want Hideyoshi to take it away from him, not when he'd only just started.

"I will fix it," Hideyoshi said gently.

Tom relaxed and let Hideyoshi take the hand.

"I also need to come up with a more elegant solution than this." Hideyoshi peeled the skullcap off Tom's head and placed it carefully on a side table. "It doesn't exactly shout pop-star cool."

Tom turned away as he placed his original prosthetic back on. Despite looking more real than the robotic arm, it felt fake. As if he was trying to hide behind it. "Thank you," he said, brushing a tear away from his cheek. "That was… amazing."

"You are welcome. As I said, I made it for you."

Tom struggled to find the words to express his gratitude. He had known this young man for only a couple of days and yet he'd done so much for him.

"There is only one small condition, and then the hand is yours."

Tom had to fight back the urge to shout, "Yes, anything." He knew enough about the danger of making deals to be cautious. "What is it?"

"Come on tour."

Come back to me

Tom was sitting on a sofa reading when they all piled back on the train. Milly was hit with a wave of relief as soon as she saw him. JD hadn't said a word over dinner, while Connor and Zek had chatted about everything *except* what they'd seen. She'd known them to do that before: using humour as a distraction from the dark things they dealt with day after day. Even Niv had kept his hands still. It seemed no one was willing to talk about what had happened tonight. But Tom would know what to say, Milly was sure. He always did.

If only he'd been there, things would have been different. He'd have been able to talk to the girl in black, rather than threaten to hurt her, for a start.

"So, ninjas?" Tom said, putting the book he'd been reading aside.

"Oh my goodness, Tom," Connor said, delighted to have someone to tell the story to. "You should have seen her."

"Con won't shut up about her," Zek said. "I think he's in love."

"Not really my type," Connor said, brushing off Zek's tease. "But that doesn't make her any less epic. She came soaring through the air and was like, *whoosh, whoosh*." Connor mimed the swinging of a whip chain. "She wasn't an actual ninja, just a super-cool girl dressed in black, but she was deadly. I hope we see her again."

"So do I," JD said fiercely. He was still fuming that the girl had stopped them from taking down the demon.

"What am I missing?" Tom said. "Why does JD look like his head is about to explode?"

Happy that finally they were going to talk about it, Milly relayed what had gone on, how this girl had appeared from nowhere, stopped the demon from killing her and then stopped Milly from killing it. And then...

"It was like she sucked the demon out of the body," Connor said. "And then...she vanished!"

"Sucked?"

"Yeah, like..." Milly made a noise like sucking something up a straw.

"And the host was left alive," JD said, clenching his teeth so hard Milly was worried he might crack them.

"Wait, *alive*?" Tom asked, looking as confused and scared as the rest of them. "That's not possible."

"Red blood and everything," Zek said.

Milly nodded. "Niv hacked the hospital. The admission report says she's in a coma."

"But…" Tom said. "That means…"

"That when we thought there was no coming back from possession, we were wrong," JD said, with his back to the group.

Tom stood up, his book falling to the floor. "No, there has to be a mistake."

"She was alive, Tom," Milly said.

Tom stared at her. "So maybe it wasn't a demonic possession to begin with?"

"You don't think I know possession when I see it, Tom?" JD spun around, and Milly saw his eyes were red with the effort of not crying.

Tom closed the gap between him and JD and rested an arm on his friend's shoulder. "It's going to be okay, JD. Gail will know what to do."

JD nodded. "She'd better. Because…"

He didn't need to finish. They all knew what he was going to say. *Because if we've been wrong all this time, Slay haven't been saving people, we've been killing them.*

"Where is Gail?" Milly asked.

"She and Hideyoshi are talking in his carriage," Tom said. "She said she wouldn't be long."

Sure enough, a moment later, the doors to the carriage hissed open and Gail walked in. As soon as the doors closed behind her, everyone started talking at once.

"Woah, slow down. JD, talk me through it."

And JD did. Gail only interrupted to get clarification about little details: what did the shadow that escaped the body look like, exactly? Where had it gone, precisely? When JD finished, Gail took a deep breath and sat down, leaning her wolf-head cane against the chair. "There's something I should have told you before." She crossed her long legs and continued. "Sometimes a demon can abandon a host and find a new one. They only have a very small window of opportunity and have to possess a new body within minutes of leaving the old one. To survive without a host, even for a moment, a demon must be very powerful."

"So, when we dispatch the demon, it's not always dead?" Tom asked.

Gail paused before speaking. "Not always." There were a few gasps and mutterings from the group. "Sometimes it gets away and finds a new host."

"So, the demon wasn't sucked out? It…jumped out?" Connor said.

Gail nodded.

"And what about the host they leave behind?" JD asked. "When the demon bails, what happens to the body?"

"They're dead. As soon as the demon enters, they're gone."

"Not this time," Milly said.

"I...I don't know what to say. In twenty-five years of doing this, I've never seen a host survive. Not a single one. It could be we're dealing with something new here. Tell me more about this ninja girl of yours. What do we know about her?" Gail asked.

Milly shook her head. "We didn't even see her face."

"Niv, get DAD on it. Search for anyone matching the description and put a shout-out on the network. Someone with her skills won't have gone unnoticed. Meanwhile, what else has DAD got for us?"

Niv opened his laptop and scanned the feeds from DAD. *Some people died when a bridge in Nara was washed away,* the last sign a swoop of his arm like a wave.

"A bridge?" JD said, managing to catch some of Niv's sign language. "Doesn't sound like our kind of gig."

Some schoolgirls went missing in Osaka.

"Missing schoolgirls sounds more like us," Zek said.

JD nodded. "Agreed, we should go check that out."

"Did DAD pick up anything else tonight?" Tom said.

Gail tilted her head and looked at Tom suspiciously. "Why?"

"Well, um, I had a run-in with a couple of demons."

"What?" Milly said. "Why didn't you say earlier, you idiot?!" She hit him on the shoulder.

"I was distracted by your whole demon-sucking thing."

"What happened?" Gail asked.

"As Hideyoshi and I were leaving the audition, we got attacked. I'm pretty sure they were after Hideyoshi."

"Demons?"

Tom nodded.

"And they were definitely after Hideyoshi?"

"I think so. Him, or his box maybe? I scared them off, but I think they'll be back."

"Hideyoshi is in danger then," Milly said. "Should we tell him? You know, about demons?"

"No," Gail said quickly. "We can't risk it."

"There's another way we can keep him safe," Tom said.

"Oh, no," JD said, holding his hands up. "I know what you're about to say."

"Come on, our job is to protect people. Hideyoshi needs protecting."

Gail drummed her fingers on the head of her cane. "I spoke to Hideyoshi earlier and his offer is very impressive. Not only will we get a fee, but he said we can have a cut of the ticket prices too. Which means we'd earn more in this one tour than ever before."

"So is that a yes?" Tom said.

"Yes, what? What are we yessing?" Connor asked.

"Tom wants to go on tour with Hideyoshi and *Ikiryō*," Milly said. She sensed that Tom was hiding something, but he also looked more excited than she'd seen in ages.

There was a jumble of sound as the boys all talked over

each other. Connor sided with Tom, while Zek wasn't so sure.

"Is it just me, or is there something off about building yourself a group of girls who obey your every command?" Zek said.

"They're holograms, not slaves," Connor said.

"Still weird."

"What do you think, Niv?"

"Oh, nerd boy here thinks it's all cool," Zek said, turning to his brother. "Don't you?"

Niv nodded and gave a double thumbs up.

"Okay, I'm in," JD said loudly, cutting through the chatter. "I trust Tom's instincts. If he says Hideyoshi is a good guy, then he's a good guy. Besides, if he's got demons on his back, what choice do we have?"

"But what about the missing girls in Osaka? Or whatever else DAD throws up? We need to be able to say where we go and when," Zek said.

"He gets that," Tom said. "I'm sure it won't be a problem."

"So that's three to one," Connor said. "Bad luck, Zek!"

"We haven't asked Milly yet."

They all turned to her.

"I...um." She looked from Zek, who was shaking his head, to Connor, who was nodding like a bobble-headed dog. JD's face was fixed, unreadable, like always. Finally, she turned to Tom. His bright-green eyes glittered. She didn't know why this meant so much to him, but it clearly did.

"I'm in."

Connor cheered while Zek groaned.

Tom sat back down, pulled out his phone, and fired off a text to Hideyoshi. Milly picked the book he'd been reading back up off the floor and sat down next to him.

"*Robotics, Mecatronics and Me* by Hideyoshi Makoto," she read off the front cover.

"Fascinating, isn't it? He only had a few copies translated into English."

She flicked through the pages, trying to make any sense of it. She'd been pretty good at maths and science at school, but this was something else. "Oh, sure. Riveting."

Tom laughed, then looked down as his phone beeped.

"All good with Hideyoshi?"

"All great," Tom said. "Check this." He read the text he'd just received out loud to the group. "He says, 'I am so very happy you reconsidered and so is Nomura-san. Osaka is an unusual place to start a tour, but we can make it work. Shall we say Friday for our first concert?'"

"That's in two days," Milly said.

"We've pulled together a gig in less time, believe me," Gail said. "Tell him yes."

"Whoop!" Connor punched the air.

"Okay," Gail said. "I'll go and update the website. Slay

will be playing Osaka on Friday night, supporting…" She swallowed after saying the word, as if it caused her pain, and tried again. "Supporting *Ikiryō*. Now, it's late. Get some rest."

Connor and the twins grumbled about not being tired, but it was JD who led them away. "You heard Gail," JD said to Milly and Tom, who hadn't left the sofa. "Get some sleep."

"Sure," Tom said. "I'll crash as soon as I've replied to Hideyoshi."

JD shrugged and left Tom and Milly alone. The carriage was suddenly very quiet, apart from the gentle patter of Tom's fingers as he messaged Hideyoshi. Milly glanced at Tom's screen and saw Hideyoshi's latest reply.

This is going to be fun. I look forward to spending time with you.

"Hideyoshi seems to like you a lot."

"Of course he does," Tom said, putting his phone away. "I am very likeable."

Milly gave him the side eye. "Likeable is not what I'd call you, Tom Wills."

"Oh, and what would you call me then?"

Milly thought about all the words she did want to use to describe Tom. Sweet, gentle, considerate, funny. Lately, sad and a bit lost too. "Cute."

"Oh no, please, not cute. Cute is the worst!"

Milly laughed at Tom's apparent angst. "What's wrong with cute?"

"Cute is like a teddy bear, or a puppy dog. Something you want to cuddle."

"I take it back. You're not cute."

"Good."

"You're adorable."

Tom slumped back on the sofa, hiding his face in a cushion. "That's even worse!"

"Okay, okay," Milly said, pushing him upright again. "You're mysterious and damaged and hot."

Tom lowered the cushion. "Hot? You mean that?"

Milly blushed a little. The Tom she had first met was none of those things, and she'd liked that about him. She'd liked how instinctively kind and thoughtful he was. But since Mexico there had been a darkness to him. A darkness she would do anything to help lift. She wanted the old Tom back; she wanted to see him smile again. And since meeting Hideyoshi, he was starting to.

"Maybe, just a little hot. In a cute way."

Tom hit her with a cushion, but he was smiling. "I'll take it."

"Good evening." Kitsune's soft voice came over the systems. "Updating schedule. The time is twenty-three forty-eight. If you are all ready, we shall depart for Osaka."

"I guess that's it then. We're on tour," Tom said.

"I guess so. I'd better get some sleep," Milly said, standing. "If I'm going to be ready for this gig I have a lot of rehearsing to do."

"You'll be amazing," Tom said. "You always are."

Milly wasn't so sure. She had handled everything being in Slay had thrown at her so far. But performing was the next test.

She said goodnight and left Tom alone, gazing out of the windows. Part of her was jealous of Hideyoshi: that he'd been able to help Tom in a way that none of the rest of them could. But mostly she was glad that Tom was slowly coming back to them.

Can you feel it?

Tom was used to the frenzy of activity before a Slay gig, but on tour with IKIR10 everything was different. It was the smoothest run-up to any show, ever; their every request was accommodated, their every need anticipated. It was almost as if Hideyoshi had planned for them joining him on tour months in advance. There had been no more demonic incidents, and while Tom tried to stay close to Hideyoshi to watch over him, the young man spent most of his time locked up in his lab.

Their first gig would be in Osaka-Jo Hall – a large arena that looked like an upside-down bowl. After that, who knew? They'd go wherever demonic activity sent them.

DAD was still tracking the missing schoolgirls. As for the girl in black, they'd drawn a blank. No sightings of girls with whip chains and no one in their network had heard of her. As for the woman who had been possessed by the demon, she was still in a coma on life support. Gail had told them to forget her. *"There's no coming back from possession."*

Tom didn't doubt it. After all, he'd almost been possessed himself, and he'd known with complete certainty that if he'd let that demon god in, he was gone. He'd felt himself slipping away as the black soul of Tezcatlipoca had crept in. No, Gail was right – there was no coming back.

He was sitting in the auditorium watching Slay rehearse, his fingers twitching at the piano parts. Milly was a brilliant player – better than him, that was for sure – but while the rest of the band had spent years playing together and worked like a smooth machine, Milly was like a cog that kept getting stuck.

"And that's when you come in," JD said, waving his hands to stop everyone playing.

"Sorry, I missed it again."

"It's okay," JD said, and Tom could see he was hiding his impatience. "You'll get it."

"By tomorrow night?" Milly said sadly.

"You're overthinking it," Tom said, clambering over the rows of seats and coming to stand at the bottom of the stage.

"Me, overthinking stuff?" Milly said sarcastically. "Never." She flexed her fingers and stretched out her neck. "I wish you could do it instead."

Tom looked back at the auditorium and imagined it filled with screaming, loving fans. It was so tempting. But no, he wasn't ready. "Sorry, Mills," he waved his prosthetic limb. "You're just going to have to suck it up."

Tom climbed up onto a speaker and then onto the stage, catching JD's eye as he passed, but JD looked away as fast as he could. When, Tom wondered, would JD be able to look at him properly again? He approached the keyboard and rested his hand on the top of the kit. He'd missed it.

"You know the notes, Mills," he said, tapping her forehead. "Now, you need to feel them." He rested his hand over his heart.

"Show me," Milly said, shifting over to give Tom room on the stool next to her.

He sat down, the two of them squeezed next to each other on the small seat, and rested his left hand on the keys, while keeping his right hand in his lap. He started to play the high part to the opening of "Bring It Home". It began with a series of dancing, upbeat notes. Tom looked up at Connor who began drumming a sharp, staccato beat. A nod to Zek and the ska bass line kicked in, followed by Niv on guitar playing the riff.

He nudged Milly. She took a deep breath and then started to play the low part: three chords on repeat.

"*Woah, woah ah!*" JD sang. "*Tell me, tell me, how does it feel to know that you're not alone now-ow.*"

"Stop trying to make it sound like me," Tom whispered in Milly's ear as JD continued. "Make it your own." He lifted his hand away and placed Milly's other hand on the keyboard. Milly took up both parts, her fingers dancing over the keys. Tom smiled as he saw her starting to improvise, adding in flourishes. JD looked back over his shoulder at Milly as he launched into the chorus, nodding in encouragement. "*No matter where I roam, it's always you, who can...bring it home!*"

Tom leaned back and let the rest of the song wash over him. It was one of the first that he and JD had written together. The lyrics could do with some work: they'd written it back before Niv joined them. The melody was good, the hooks almost irresistible. It was a great song, maybe even one of their best, but Tom couldn't help thinking it was missing something, although he didn't quite know what. Despite that, Milly was doing great. She was really getting into it and they made it through to the end of the song without a single missed note.

"Finally!" Zek said. "She gets it."

Milly stuck her tongue out at Zek.

"It was perfect," Tom said. "Better than I ever played it."

"That's true," JD muttered, but it was caught by his mic and all the boys laughed.

Milly smiled at Tom. "Why can't you be up here with me all the time?"

Tom looked into Milly's brown eyes. A lock of her hair had escaped from under her cap and was curled over her forehead. Tom went to brush it aside when there was a sound of applause from the wings. "That was wonderful," Hideyoshi said, walking onstage. Tom hadn't seen Hideyoshi since they'd arrived at the venue – he'd been hidden away in his lab while the arena staff had made all the preparations for the gig.

"Oh, thanks," Milly said, quickly adjusting her cap.

"I am looking forward to seeing you perform tonight." Hideyoshi came to stand next to the keyboards. "It's good to see a band that plays their own—"

"Watch out!" Connor shouted.

Tom looked up as something crashed towards them. He grabbed Milly and rolled off the seat onto the stage floor, wrapping his arms around her head. There was a huge smashing and splintering sound, and when Tom looked back, a large black spotlight was embedded in the keyboard. Hideyoshi lay sprawled on the floor: the light must have missed him by centimetres.

JD raced forward and helped Milly to her feet. "Are you okay?"

"Yeah," Milly said, pressing her hand to her head.

Tom clambered to his feet and watched as JD pulled Milly's hand away. There was a small cut above her left eyebrow. Blood trickled down the side of her eye. He looked to where the light had come from and squinted. He thought he saw something moving up there, a flash of blue, but he couldn't be sure.

"What happened?" Hideyoshi stood up and brushed himself off.

"You tell us," Zek said, prodding Hideyoshi in the chest. "Your shoddy stage tried to kill them. This is what happens when you try and automate everything. Robots and computers can't replace roadies, you know."

Tom pulled the bassist away. "Chill out, Zek. It wasn't his fault. It nearly killed him too."

Zek grunted and shrugged Tom's hand off.

"We'll need a new keyboard," Connor said, picking up a handful of broken keys.

Hideyoshi looked up into the rigging and Tom noticed a tightness in his jaw, a look that was more than anxiety. "I am sorry, Tom, Milo, believe me. Something like this has… never happened before. I will ensure your equipment is replaced and that whoever was responsible is dealt with."

"No," Milly said, "we don't want that. I'm sure it was just a mistake."

"Just get a pro team in here and make sure it doesn't happen again," JD said, pulling his shirt off to hold it against Milly's forehead.

Milly pushed him away. "I'm fine. And that's your favourite shirt."

Tom felt a strange twist in his stomach watching his two friends. Neither had checked to see if he was okay.

"Um, Tom." Connor pointed down at Tom's right hand.

He lifted it up to see a large shard of glass embedded in the rubber skin of his wrist. He stared at it for a moment, wondering why he felt no pain, and then remembered. With careful fingers, he plucked the glass out and dropped it to the ground.

"Tom," Milly gasped.

"It's okay, I'm fine. Lucky, hey?" He tried to laugh but it came out a little strangled.

Milly came to stand next to him. "Tom, are you sure?"

"I'm fine," he said, turning away. "You've got it now. You don't need me."

"Tom," Milly said again, pleadingly. But he pretended not to hear her.

As he walked off the stage, he looked back up at the rigging. There was nothing there now, only shadows. It had probably been his imagination earlier, the panic of it all, but he'd thought for a fleeting moment that he'd seen a pale face staring down at him. The light falling had been no accident, he was sure of it. Someone was still after Hideyoshi.

Keep me close to your heart

Milly's heart pounded in her head. She was sweating so much her glasses kept sliding down her face.

"How you doing there?" JD asked.

They were standing side by side in the wings, waiting to go on. The arena was already full of chattering IKIR10 fans and more than a few Slay fans, who must have travelled all the way to Japan to see them play. How they'd got here with barely a day's notice, Milly didn't know. But there was one thing she was learning about Slay fans: when it came to seeing their idols, they let nothing stand in their way. She risked poking her head out and wished she hadn't. There had to be easily 15,000 people waiting for them to go on.

"I think I've made a terrible mistake," she said.

"That's what I thought before my first gig," JD said.

"And you weren't wrong. That first gig was a disaster!" Zek said.

"You are not helping," Milly said, her lips so dry they stuck against her teeth.

"You'll be grand, Mills," Connor said, hugging her from behind and resting his chin on her head. "Put it this way – it's no worse than going up against demons."

Milly wasn't so sure. She'd take fighting demons over this any day.

"At least you look the part," Zek said. "That outfit is..." He kissed his fingers like a chef.

Tonight she wore white trainers, skinny black jeans ripped at the knees, a baggy T-shirt with a picture of a 1950s starlet on it and a green bomber jacket with orange lining. But even if her clothes felt good, the rest of her didn't. She wasn't ready. Not even in the slightest. She felt as if something squirming and slippery was swimming around in her stomach.

JD looked her up and down. "It's missing something."

They'd chosen not to have any outside stylists, because they didn't want to risk them finding out the truth about Milly, so the make-up and hair styling had been left to the rest of the band. She looked down at her outfit. What more could they do?

JD reached his hands behind his neck and a moment later pulled a silver necklace out from under his white V-neck T-shirt. He held it up. "Just one last touch." He reached over her shoulders to place the necklace around her neck and she felt his fingers brush against the back of her short hair as he fixed the clasp. Milly looked down at the necklace. It was a silver oval with the impression of a woman looking up to the sky, holding a sword.

"Joan of Arc," he said. "Patron saint of soldiers."

"I thought you didn't believe in saints," Connor said.

"I don't," JD replied. "But my mum did. She bought it for my dad and, well, then left it with me."

Milly thumbed the pendant. "I can't take it."

"Just borrow it," he whispered, as the lights went dark.

Milly let the necklace drop. It hung in the same place that the demon Priestess Zyanya had carved a symbol into her skin in Mexico. It had healed, but Milly would have a faint scar for the rest of her life.

A booming Japanese voice came over the tannoy. The only word Milly could make out was the last: *Slay*.

"We're on!"

Connor strode onstage, waving at the crowd. There was warm, if restrained, clapping. Zek and Niv went on next. Milly was supposed to follow, leaving JD to come on last. That's the way Slay had always done it. But now it was her turn she couldn't get her legs to move.

She felt JD's hand in hers. "Come on," he said, leading her out onto the stage.

The cheers were louder, excited. The lights turned onto the audience and Milly looked out at the sea of people, picking out faces in the crowd. Amid all the messages for IKIR10 she saw a few *We Love Slay* signs and one that read *Get Well Soon, Tom*, which made her heart ache. Tonight, they would learn if Slay's fans would accept her, or rather, if they would accept Milo. Then the lights spun back to face them and she was blinded.

JD let go of her hand and Milly took her seat in front of the brand new keyboard. Propped up on the music stand, there was a small piece of folded paper. With a shaking hand, she unfolded the note.

You got this. I'm right there beside you. T x

She felt strength flow into her. She imagined Tom sitting on the stool next to her, encouraging her when she got it wrong, congratulating her when she got it right. She could do this.

"One, two… One, two, three, four!" Connor shouted, clashing his drumsticks in time.

Well, it was too late to back out. It was now or never. Milly played the first chord, Zek strummed the strings of his guitar, and they launched straight into "Heart Attack". She made it to the end of the song, but there was no break. They flowed immediately into "Hit Me With All You Got". By the time they finished that, Milly realized that her hands were no longer shaking. She'd not messed up once and she risked glancing out at the audience. They were loving it.

"*Konnichiwa!*" JD said, after the song ended. He waited

till the delighted cheering had died down before continuing. "Thank you for welcoming us here. We are Slay and, wow, what an audience! You guys are amazing! Now, you might not know us, but I really hope you're going to like what you hear tonight." JD was a completely different person onstage. The taciturn boy who spoke only when necessary vanished to be replaced by a charismatic frontman. "So, let's get this thing started. This next song is dedicated to missing friends."

Milly took a breath and held it. This next song started with only the keyboards and JD singing. They locked eyes and she played the first chord, holding it down and letting the reverb ripple out into the arena.

"*I see you with my eyes closed*," JD sang, his voice so clear and pure it sent a shiver down Milly's spine. "*I hear you in the dark of night. Cos even when you're gone, you're here. And everything's gonna be all right.*"

On the first revisit of the verse the drums and guitars kicked in, but Milly still felt as if it was just her and JD on the stage. Everything else melted away and there was only his voice and the piano in front of her. The crowd had ceased to exist, the stage, the arena; there was just the music.

When the song came to an end she was shocked to see Niv standing next to her, grinning.

He gave her a thumbs up.

Thanks, she signed back, touching her chin with a flat palm and pushing it out.

The next song was a pounding, frantic rocky track that had JD running back and forth across the stage and Connor thrashing his drums so hard Milly didn't know how he didn't tear through the skins. She started to feel it. That transformation that she'd seen take over the others when they were onstage. The lightness. All the anxiety about whether she deserved to be here vanished, all the guilt over taking Tom's place was gone. She belonged here in this seat, on this stage. In this band.

The crowd were warming up to them, shouting, clapping, and Milly felt the love roll off them like a wave. How had she gone her whole life without this feeling? She'd watched her opera singer mother from the sidelines her whole life, and she'd never been jealous of her fame before. But now she understood why her mother would have never wanted to give this up.

She didn't even know what she was playing, only that she and the rest of Slay were in perfect harmony. In between two of the tracks, JD chatted to the crowd again, the lights turning on them so they could see their fans. Milly looked at the audience, her smile so wide it made her cheeks ache. In the first row she picked out the face of a girl a little older than her, with bright, shining eyes and a heavy dark fringe. The girl wasn't shouting and screaming like the other fans. She merely looked at Milly with a soft smile on her face, as if she was finding something amusing. And then, the girl winked.

Milly knew that wink. She'd seen it before, but where? She was so distracted by the girl that she didn't notice Zek hissing at her. She'd missed her entrance to the song. She shook her head and quickly picked it up, playing along with what she knew was going to be their last song – Slay didn't do encores. When she looked back out into the crowd, the girl was gone.

Back to me

The sound of the bass reverberated through the walls of the dressing room. Tom lay across a large chair, legs thrown over one armrest, head resting on the other, listening to Slay performing overhead. He caught fragments of the songs he knew. Heard the crowd clap and stomp. And felt the tightness in his chest again. He'd planned on watching from the wings and then couldn't bring himself to do it. He was afraid that if he stood there, so close to the music and the lights and the adoration of the fans, he'd just run out onstage to soak it all up. He heard that niggling, dark whisper that had accompanied him almost everywhere since Mexico. The voice of Tezcatlipoca. *Take it, it's yours. The power, the glory, the worship, it's all yours.*

He sat up, shaking his head to clear the voice, and tried to focus on what was in the room. Styling products covered the surfaces in front of the mirrors, the majority of which he knew belonged to Zek. The boys' boots and jeans lay in a tangled heap in the corner where Gail had shoved them after tripping over them one too many times. His prosthetic hand was somewhere under there too. He'd taken it off because the suction socket had been making his skin itch.

There was a knock on the door.

"Come in," Tom said lazily, expecting it to be the pizza delivery. It was Hideyoshi.

"Good evening, Tom-san," Hideyoshi said.

Tom swung himself into sitting position. "Hey!" He was surprised at how glad he was to see the young man. "Everything okay?"

Hideyoshi stepped inside and closed the door behind him. "Yes, everything is set up and ready to go. Your friends meanwhile are putting on quite the show. Perhaps I was unwise to ask you to tour with us – I fear you may be stealing our fans' worship."

Tom shuddered at the use of the word worship. "Oh, I don't think you have to worry about that. *Ikiryō* are pretty worshipped themselves."

Hideyoshi walked around the room, taking in the surroundings. "Is it always this…"

"Messy?" Tom said. "Sure, I guess. It's always a frantic rush to get ready."

"Why don't you give yourselves more time?"

"Um." Tom paused, wondering how best to answer that.

The real reason they were nearly always cutting it fine had a lot more to do with evil creatures than it did bad planning. "It's just one of our things."

There came the sound of clapping and cheering. Slay must be nearing the end of their set.

Hideyoshi sat on the edge of the dressing table and considered Tom. "Why aren't you with them?"

There was no messing with this young man. He just got straight to the point. "I...I'm still recovering."

"Hmm," Hideyoshi said, and Tom could tell he hadn't bought it. "That is why I'm here. It's ready."

Tom sat forward in his chair. "The hand?"

Hideyoshi nodded. "Yes."

A fizz of excitement thrummed through Tom's stomach. Ever since trying it, he'd been aching to have it back. "I...I don't know what to say."

"What do you mean?" Hideyoshi said, tilting his head to the side.

Tom stood up. "I mean, I don't know how to say thank you."

"I think you just did."

Tom laughed. This man was strange, but so uncomplicated in many ways. "I guess I did. When can I...?" He stopped himself, trying not to sound too pushy. But it didn't seem to matter to Hideyoshi.

"Now?"

"But the show!"

Tom saw that pained, sad expression flicker across Hideyoshi's face again, brief as a cloud passing. "Everything is practised, programmed. I am not needed."

"Well, if you're sure." Tom grabbed his jacket from amid the jumble and pulled it on, ignoring how it hung loose on his right side. He hadn't bothered to put his prosthetic back on, as he couldn't wait to try the hand Hideyoshi had made again.

Hideyoshi's train was waiting at Osaka station; it was only a short drive from the arena. Neither Tom nor Hideyoshi said much on the way. Tom could hardly wait to get back on board.

When they arrived, Hideyoshi let Tom go first. The lights flickered on slowly, revealing the lab. He tried to hide his impatience as Hideyoshi moved through the white space, slowly activating the lights and opening panels. Finally, there it was. The hand.

Tom felt himself being drawn towards it, almost as if it was asserting a magnetic pull. When he got closer, he noticed some adjustments to the previous version. A thin bead of blue light ran up and down the length of each finger. The joints looked smoother, the fingers longer. Instead of black nylon, the harness looked to be made of smooth black leather. It was easily the most beautiful thing he'd ever laid eyes on.

He reached out, but paused before picking it up, waiting

for Hideyoshi's permission. The man nodded. Tom didn't need any more approval. He pulled the hand off its plinth and with help from Hideyoshi, strapped it on.

"I've upgraded the brain control interface." Hideyoshi held out his fist and uncurled his fingers to reveal a silver device about the size of a battery, with a curved plastic hook coming out of it. "It tucks behind your ear." Hideyoshi placed the device over Tom's ear. It was like wearing a bluetooth headset. "Now I just need to sync them."

Tom heard the device behind his ear bleep. A blue light flashed on the hand and it instantly came to life. It was as if it had just been waiting.

"I adjusted the sensors. And I've increased the crushing force to 2.5 tonnes."

Tom opened and closed the fingers, watching as the light danced up and down them.

"I also tested it on this." Hideyoshi opened another cupboard and pulled out a large object around a metre and a half long. He placed it on the white worktable. It was covered in a black sheet, but Tom knew what was there even before Hideyoshi pulled it off to reveal a brand-new Yamaha keyboard.

"I bought two when replacing the model that was, ah, broken. It's an upgrade to the one you had." Hideyoshi switched the keyboard on and stepped back.

Tom rested his left hand on the keys, feeling the smooth

coldness against his skin. He then placed his right hand next to it and flinched when he felt a sting of coldness in his fingers. It was like touching ice. "It's cold."

"I added temperature sensors. They're not calibrated, so perhaps it's a little oversensitive." He typed a string of letters and numbers into his laptop. The lights on the arm blinked red for a moment and then returned to blue. "Try now."

Tom lay his hands once more on the keyboard. This time, the sensation from both hands felt more balanced. He applied a little pressure and felt a wave of delight wash over him as the keys sang in response.

He started playing, the same piece he'd worked on with Milly: "Bring It Home". At first, it was a little awkward and the fingers of his right hand missed the odd key. But slowly, the action became smoother and faster. And faster. Until the fingers of his right hand were a blur. Tom laughed, high and loud.

"You are happy?" Hideyoshi asked.

"I am…" Tom threw his arms around Hideyoshi and hugged him. "Thank you!"

Hideyoshi waved the gratitude away. "It's nothing. Maybe one day we can write a song together?"

"I would like that," Tom said.

He held the robotic hand in front of his face, curling it up into a tight fist.

It was perfect. He was finally ready to get back to work.

You saved me right back

Back in the dressing room, Milly was still buzzing from the high of the performance. It had been the most incredible feeling in her life. She'd never felt so connected – to the boys, the fans, everything. There was only one thing niggling at the back of her mind: the girl she'd seen in the front row. There was something familiar about her that Milly couldn't place.

"Where's Tom?" JD asked, cutting off Milly's train of thought.

They'd left him in the dressing room, and he'd said he'd be watching from the wings.

"Off bromancing with Hideyoshi, no doubt," Zek said.

Milly noticed a pained expression flash across JD's face and then remembered: this wasn't just her first gig, it was also their first without Tom.

JD pulled out his phone and selected an app. It was slow

to open, and he shook the phone, frustrated, as if that could make it work faster.

"What are you doing?" Milly asked.

"Tracking Tom's phone."

Milly stared at JD's screen and started to feel some of his frustration at how long it was taking to locate. Eventually the map came into focus and Tom's position was marked clearly next to the station.

"He's on the train. He probably just needed some space," Milly said, laying a hand on JD's arm. "He'll be fine."

JD laid his hand over hers and gave it a squeeze. They caught each other's eyes and then quickly stepped away. Onstage, everything had been so easy between her and JD. Offstage, the awkwardness was back.

Niv banged on the wall to get everyone's attention. *I've got something*, he signed, holding up his phone.

"Is it ninja girl?" Connor asked hopefully.

Niv shook his head, tucked the phone under his arm and signed. *The missing girls.*

"You found them?" Milly asked, taking the phone off Niv.

Niv nodded. *And they're causing trouble.*

Zek translated for the others while Milly read the latest feed from DAD. It was from a nearby area called Kamagasaki, where there had been reports of a disturbance in a bar. On social media, people had been posting about thugs with black eyes beating up a bouncer. But the weirdest thing was the men weren't alone. With them were four schoolgirls matching the description of the missing girls.

Connor grabbed the phone off her and read the report. "How did they get into the bar? They don't look old enough."

"They're demons, Con," Zek said. "I don't think they worry so much about being carded, you know?"

Connor groaned. "I hate demon kids. Makes it so much harder when you have to, you know." He threw the phone back to Niv before drawing his finger across his neck.

"So you've gone up against this before?"

"Once," JD said. "It wasn't pretty."

Milly felt that shift again; that the world was not as she'd once known it. "Who knew there were so many demons everywhere?"

"We did," said JD, pulling his stage T-shirt off and pulling on a fresh one.

"What did we tell ya?" Connor said, shoving a slice of pizza into his mouth. "Demon whack-a-mole!"

Gail walked in, smiling. "Brilliant performance. Milly, you were on fire! I don't know where that came from, but keep it up."

Milly held a cool can of drink against her blushing cheek. "Thanks."

"I take it you've seen the message from DAD?"

They all nodded.

"More she-demons," Zek said. "Seems to be a lot of them here."

Zek was right. So far, they'd gone up against the slit-faced woman, the Uji bridge demon and now these schoolgirls. She'd not seen a single demon in male form since they'd been in Japan. "That's weird." Milly paused and looked up at the others. "Is that weird?"

"Well, most of the Japanese demon lore I've been reading does seem to lean heavy on the wronged women and broken-hearted mothers," Connor said. "So not really."

"What difference does it make?" JD said. "Whatever they look like on the outside, it's still a demon inside."

"Yeah, we're all for gender equality when it comes to slaying!" Zek said.

"Okay, then. I'll deal with the press here, you get moving and try and keep it low-key. We don't want to draw any attention to this. We play and then…" Gail paused, waiting for the others to finish.

"We slay!"

"Well, there goes keeping things low-key," Zek said as they pulled up at the bar where the reports had been coming from.

It was nearly ten p.m. They sat in a hire car, watching young men and women running out of the bar doors, screaming and disappearing into the streets. Some held cameras up, filming over their shoulders even as they ran.

Milly watched as Niv pulled out a small black box and pushed a button. He slipped the box away and smiled. *Phone blocker*, he signed.

She noticed that some of the people running away stopped their fleeing to gawp at their now-dead phones.

"Okay, let's do this," JD said, placing his hand on the door handle.

"Wait!" Milly said, laying her hand on his shoulder to stop him.

"What's up?"

"Are we sure – I mean one hundred per cent sure – that they can't be saved?"

JD turned to look at her. "Gail said…"

"I know what she said. But she wasn't there, under the bridge. I know I'm new to all of this, but I think something different is going on in Japan."

"I'm with Milly," Connor said. "I've been doing some reading and something isn't adding up."

"Not adding up how?" JD asked, but Milly could tell he was curious more than confrontational.

"I don't know yet. I'll keep reading."

JD looked to Niv and Zek.

Zek shook his head. "I don't know."

"Okay, till we know what's going on, we take them down but we don't kill them, got it?" He reached into the glove compartment and pulled out a large handful of electric ties, and handed them around.

"Phaser set to stun," Zek said, sliding a few of the ties into his top pocket as if adjusting a handkerchief. "Got it."

They piled out of the car and pulled their masks on. The flow of escapees had stopped. The doors hung still. As Milly and the others approached, the sounds of crashing and laughing could be heard.

Milly was last into the bar, her bow already drawn. The bar was a mess of smashed glass and broken tables, and it reeked of spilled alcohol. Five large men wearing dark sunglasses strode around, knocking over tables and smashing pictures. And at the centre of it all were four girls in blue-and-white school uniforms. The first girl's hair was in two tight buns on either side of her head and looked like the ears of a teddy bear. The second girl wore her hair in long pigtails that bounced as she skipped around the room. The third girl had a short bob and blunt fringe that almost totally covered her eyes. The final girl, the one Milly instinctively knew was the leader, wore her hair long and loose over her shoulders. They looked like any of the schoolgirls Milly had seen in her short time in Japan. But despite their angelic appearance, they were trouble: laughing as they threw bottles against the walls. The girl with pigtails grabbed a man who was trying to hide behind the bar by his throat. Tears ran down the man's face and it looked as if he was close to passing out. The whole scene strangely reminded Milly of one of the boarding schools she'd gone to.

The pigtail girl-demon holding the barman twisted her head and smiled at Milly, revealing small sharp teeth and totally black eyes. Milly notched an arrow and aimed for the head, before remembering the plan from the car. She shifted her target and let it fly. The arrow thudded into the demon's shoulder, causing her to drop the man. She pulled the arrow out and licked blood off the tip, as if licking a lollipop. The blood was bright red. Black eyes but red blood. This wasn't making any sense. Demons normally bled black.

The demon with the long loose hair shouted something in Japanese. The large men in sunglasses lined up, while the demon and her three schoolgirl-demon friends made a run for it out the back.

One of the men cracked his muscle-bound neck and smiled. Another pulled out a butterfly knife and began to flick it over and over in his hand. The other three were also armed, with broken bottles and chair legs. Milly hesitated. She couldn't see their eyes behind their glasses. Were these men the same as the girls? There was one way she could find out. She notched another arrow and fired. It caught one of the men on the side of his face, knocking his glasses off and cutting his cheek. Milly smiled as she saw both the man's eyes and blood were a deep black.

"Yes!" Connor said, jumping into the fight.

Blades met with bottles, and knives with bats. Milly finished off her demon with an arrow to the throat. It fell to the floor, clutching the shaft, black blood pouring through its fingers. It took Slay less than a minute to take down all five of the demons. The demons had had no idea what they were up against.

"After the girls!" JD led the chase – through the bar and out the back door and onto a construction site. Downed tools and equipment littered the rubble-strewn floor; a bright yellow crane arched overhead and from it hung a large steel girder attached by two chains.

The girl demons were waiting. They held knives, and Milly realized one of them was spinning a spiked metal ball on a chain as if spinning a skipping rope. Taking these girls down without killing them was one thing. Doing it without getting killed themselves was another.

"Flashdance!" Connor yelled and let a light grenade loose. The area exploded in white light and the demon girls hissed, covering their eyes. JD pulled a grenade off his belt and threw it after Connor's. It went off with a bang, filling the air with yellow smoke. Blinded and stumbling, the demons backed away, trying to escape the aerosolled salt that was burning their skin.

Before Milly had a chance to strike, a spiked ball smashed into the wall behind her, just centimetres from her head.

The demon tugged at the chain and the ball tore free, nicking Milly's cheek as it passed.

The urge to kill these things was getting stronger, but she had to stick to their plan. Wound not kill, so they could find out what was going on. She loosed an arrow and it drilled through the air, heading for the leg of the demon with the spiked ball. The demon dodged and the arrow only grazed its knee.

The others weren't having much luck subduing the demons either. Sparks flew as JD's sword was blocked by the knives of one of the demons. Zek and Niv were being backed into the corner by a demon with a baseball bat covered in spikes. Only Connor was gaining some ground, against the one with long pigtails: he'd disarmed her and had her pinned to the floor, one of his sai to her throat. Connor spun his sai around, ready to use the butt to knock the demon out, when he was hit in the side by the demon with the spiked ball. He went rolling across the floor towards Milly, and knocked her off her feet too. Milly got a mouthful of dirt as her face hit the ground.

"Right, that's it!" She rolled over and windmill-kicked herself up onto her feet. "Playtime is over." She loaded up a grenade arrow and let it fly. It slammed into the brick wall behind the demons. The arrow flashed once, twice, and then exploded in a blast of white light, throwing both boys and demons to the ground. As the boys lay groaning, one of the demons managed to get to its knees and flung a knife high over Milly's head.

"Ha, missed!" she said.

But the demon hadn't been aiming for Milly. There was a sound of metal on metal and then a crunching, creaking sound.

Milly saw JD's eyes widen in horror as he looked at something behind her. "Watch out!"

She turned just in time to see the girder swinging. The demon had broken one of the chains attaching it to the crane and now it was heading straight for her. She just had time to duck and close her eyes; waiting for the strike, waiting for the pain. But there was nothing. When she opened her eyes, she couldn't take in what she was seeing at first. It was Tom, standing over her, his arm raised, holding the end of the girder in a sleek black hand, as casually as if he was holding a door open for her.

He pulled the girder back like he was pulling back a swing in a child's playground and sent it flying towards the demons. It tore free of the final chain and caught all four of them in one neat row, pinning them to the floor. They screeched and wiggled under the weight, but they weren't going anywhere.

Milly looked back to Tom, as he held his hand out for her. She felt the cool, slick smoothness of it as he helped her to her feet.

"Are you okay?" he asked.

She just shook her head, struggling to process what she was seeing. How was he here? How had he done what he'd just done?

"Okay, let's wrap this up," JD said, taking the electric ties out of his pocket.

All six of Slay stood over the trapped demons. Milly looked down on a youthful, pretty face and into the black eyes filled with nothing but hate. The demon hissed and spat. Milly wrapped an electric tie around her ankles and took a small amount of pleasure when she screeched as she tightened the tie. She didn't know what they were going to do with these girls once they had them tied up: they didn't look like they'd be willing to answer any questions. She couldn't see any vestige of humanity in them, only the snarling demons that had taken possession. Gail had to be right, once a demon gets in, the human soul is gone. That's it. Milly had to believe that, because if not, it meant that she'd killed her own mother rather than freeing her.

Before Milly could pin her hands together, the demon threw back her head and screeched. A black cloud burst out of her mouth, nose and eyes, swirling like tiny tornadoes. Milly glanced down the line of demon girls and saw the same thing was happening to each of them. Four black clouds were being sucked from their bodies. Milly followed the trail up and up. There, crouched on the crane, was the girl in black.

The demonic clouds were being drawn to her, wrapping themselves around her and then vanishing inside her bag.

"Oh, no," JD shouted, pointing at the girl with his sword. "Not again."

But before he or any of them could do anything, it had stopped. The last tendril of smoke vanished inside the girl's bag. She stood up, flicked her whip chain towards a scaffolding pole, then swung off the crane and vanished inside the half-finished building.

"No!" JD shouted, kicking at a brick and sending it flying across the construction site.

Milly looked back to the four figures still pinned by the girder. Each now had their eyes closed and looked as if they were sleeping.

"Help me get this off them," she said, heaving at the steel beam.

Connor crouched down and slid his fingers under the end of the girder, managing to lift it a fraction off the floor.

"Let me," Tom said. He took the other end and lifted the girder in his slick black hand and gently pivoted it off the girls before letting it crash to the floor.

Milly lay her hand on the neck of the girl she'd been fighting a moment before. There was a faint, hardly-there pulse. She saw Connor do the same to one of the other girls.

"Still alive."

"Are they in comas?" Milly asked, not sure she really wanted the answer.

"This doesn't make any sense," JD said, coming to stand next to them. "They should be dead."

"One demon host in a coma could be an anomaly. This is starting to look like a pattern," Zek said. "Gail is going to freak."

"No," JD said, holding his hand up. "We don't tell Gail, not till we know what's going on. Connor, call an ambulance, then, Niv, you can hack the hospital and find out what we're dealing with. Till then, it's business as usual, okay?"

Milly wasn't sure she agreed with keeping this from Gail, but she understood why JD was doing it. She was beginning to feel guilty and she'd only been slaying demons for a month, starting with the one who had possessed her mother. Gail had been doing it for half her life. If she found out that she could have been saving people all along, what would that do to her?

"The important thing is that we stopped them," Tom said.

JD seemed to only then register that Tom was with them. "What are you doing here?"

"Um, saving your butts, by the looks of things."

Milly looked down at Tom's new hand. "What is that?"

Tom held it up in front of his face. "Cool, isn't it?"

"Cool doesn't come close," said Connor, grabbing it and holding it higher so he could get a better look in the low light. The sleek black material reflected the flickering bar sign. The smooth curve of the wrist swooped down to jointed skeletal fingers, which Tom waved.

"How? When?" JD asked. He reached out to touch it and then pulled his hand back.

"Hideyoshi made it for me."

Milly saw the expression on JD's face change from curiosity to suspicion. Tom must have read the shift too. He stepped back, shaking his head. "No, JD, I know what you're going to say, but don't even start."

"What?"

"You're going to ask how I know I can trust him and what does he want in return... Just don't."

"But come on, you have to—" Zek said.

"I have to nothing. This is the first time I've felt whole since..."

Tom didn't need to finish. JD dropped his head and swallowed hard.

Milly looked between the two boys, their pain making her chest tighten. "I don't know about Hideyoshi," she said. "But I know that you and your new hand just saved my life."

Tom gave her a small, grateful smile.

JD looked back to the comatose girls. "I guess we'd better—" Once more, he was cut off by the screeching of sirens. "Come on," he said, almost wearily. "Let's get out of here."

"So that was your ninja," Tom said, as they all started running back to the car.

"Yup," Connor said. "Isn't she the best?"

Bring it home (remix)

"What's it made of?"

"How does it work?"

"Can I have a go?"

"Whoa, one at a time." Tom lay back against the soft leather of the sofa, trying to get away from the barrage of questions about his robotic hand. They were back on the train in the living quarters, and Gail and the others had been demanding answers ever since they arrived ten minutes ago. In the bright lights of the carriage, with all six of them standing over him, it felt like he was in an interrogation room. Most of the band seemed delighted with his hand and what it could do. But JD was as suspicious as ever.

"Why did Hideyoshi make it for you?" he asked.

"Why?" Tom said. "I don't know. Because he could? Or maybe he's just a good guy and he wanted to help. What does his motive matter? The hand works."

"And then some." Connor held up his hand and Tom high-fived it.

"How does it feel?" Gail asked.

"Amazing. I can hardly describe it. It just feels like… my hand. Only better."

She nodded. "Good. But just to be sure, Niv, can you run diagnostics on it?"

Tom went to complain but Niv signed, ending in a thumbs up.

"You already scanned it?" Tom said, feeling slightly betrayed.

Niv held up his phone and shrugged before signing again.

"He says it automatically scans all tech within a five-metre radius."

Tom put aside his irritation that Niv had somehow gone behind his back. He looked back to Gail.

Her mouth twisted as she seemed to think about what to say. Then she relaxed. "If Niv says it's okay, then it's okay with me."

Tom saw JD open his mouth and prepared himself for whatever protest was to come. What happened to trusting his instincts and "*If Tom says he's a good guy, he's a good guy*"? But before JD could say anything, Gail threw him a look and he sat back down.

"Do you think you can play keyboards again?" Connor asked.

"I…" He caught Milly's eye. She stood away from the rest of them, watching. She smiled a strange, happy-sad smile, and Tom understood. Milly had said she was only going to join Slay till Tom was better. And now, he was. It would be so easy for him to step back into his old role, to pretend nothing had happened…but he'd seen Milly play. Not only was it clear how much she'd loved it, but she was better than him. Tom couldn't deny that he hungered to be back up there, centre stage, but it was that very hunger that scared him. He closed his eyes and saw a flash of black lightning and smelled the tang of ozone. He flinched as the wrist that no longer existed ached underneath the socket of his new hand. He couldn't go back to how it was, in the spotlight, all eyes on him. But there was a way he could still be a part of it, while staying in the background.

"Follow me." He stood up and headed out of the carriage. The others hesitated for a moment and then followed him further down the train. They passed through the smaller of the two restaurants, which was designed to look like a fifties diner, through the meditation area with its bonsai trees and trickling water, and arrived in the carriage that had been set up as a recording studio. A large mixing desk stood to the side, the multi-channel sliders lying in a neat straight row. Tom lay his left hand on the desk and switched it on. The sliders came to life, moving in an undulating wave.

"So, I've been thinking," he said, coming to stand behind

the desk and adjusting a few of the settings. "Maybe Slay need a new sound."

"They do?" Gail said, eyes tightening.

"I was listening to *Ikiryō*, and they have something so fresh. A five-piece band, it works, sure, but maybe we're missing something. Hideyoshi got me thinking." At the mention of Hideyoshi's name, Tom caught the twitch of annoyance on JD's face, but he ignored it. "Niv, remember back in Manchester, when you recorded the banshee? Do you still have the recording?"

Niv nodded and pulled out his phone. A moment later, a high-pitched, blood-curdling screech blasted over the speaker system and they all covered their ears, shouting at Niv to turn it down.

When they'd recovered, Tom said, "Again, but not so loud as to kill us all. Okay?"

Niv played the sound again, at a more reasonable volume, and Tom hit record. He plugged his own phone into the desk and flicked through all the songs, selected "Bring It Home", and hit *import*.

It was a great song, catchy and upbeat. But it could be better. As the song began playing over the studio speakers, he started to move the sliders. He introduced a stronger, syncopated beat, a pounding wobbling bass, and dropped in some rewinds. Then, with a hit of a button, he played the sound of the demon's screech, adding enough reverb so it sounded like a synth violin: haunting rather than terrifying. He loaded up another sound from his phone, the recording they'd made of JD saying "For the music" at the radio interview back in Chicago. He looped it, dropping it in at just the right point in the song. The samples layered over the existing track, adding to it, and all the time Tom's fingers flew across the buttons, the sleek black material of his hand blending in with the sliders. Then he muted each channel one after the other and ended with an echoing, reverberating beat, before stepping away from the desk.

"That was next level," Zek said, finally.

"Seriously incredible," Milly said, and Niv nodded.

"That was so cool, Tom." Connor bounced around, making *wom wom wom* bass noises.

Tom looked over at JD, waiting. There might be six people in this band, but when it came down to it, JD would have the last word. Even Gail would wait for his approval. Even though Tom was the oldest and he'd been part of their weird family the longest, JD was the leader. Tom had never really given it much thought before now; he'd just settled into this way of doing things because it made the most sense. But now, waiting to see if JD would accept his new vision for the band, if JD would accept him back at all, Tom felt a bubbling bitterness.

"I love it."

Tom sighed, the acid heat in his stomach flowing away.

"You can do that live?" Gail said.

"With some more practice, sure."

"Then I think we've just found the sound for our next album."

"Yes! It's going to be epic," Connor said, slapping Tom so hard on the back he nearly fell over. He then hugged him so tight Tom could hardly breathe. "You're back!" Connor shouted in his ear.

"I'm back," he said, returning Connor's hug with both arms.

Connor let him go. "He's back, everyone!"

The others joined Connor in his congratulations, each taking a turn to come over and hug Tom. Milly was last. They misjudged the hug, both trying to go in the same direction and ended up banging heads. On the second go it worked. He felt the slight roughness of her flannel shirt through the sensors of his right hand, felt the pulse of blood running through the skin in her back. As he let go, he ran his hand gently down her arm, feeling the skin turn to goosebumps under his touch. They both stepped away, avoiding each other's eye.

"We killed it at the gig, sent some more demons back where they came from, and Tom is now officially a cyborg!" Connor said. "This has been the best night ever, and we need to go out and celebrate."

Tom smiled. He wasn't sure about "cyborg" but he wasn't

about to fault Connor's enthusiasm. It had been a pretty awesome night. "What do you suggest, Con?"

"Oh, there's only one place we can go…"

It was near midnight but Tom wasn't close to being tired. They all waited for Connor to finish: "Karaoke!"

Breaking free

"You have to be kidding," Gail said as they entered the karaoke booth. The room was barely three metres square, and apart from the screen that covered one wall, every other surface was covered in paintings of demons. Red-faced, razor-tusked *oni* snarled down at them. Ink-paintings of floating women with black eyes ran from ceiling to floor. There was even a huge pile of soft toys of creatures with big cute eyes and fluffy claws.

"It's demon themed! Can you believe it?" Connor said, launching himself into the pile of plushies. "All the rooms are themed. There was a unicorn room, a mermaid room, and this one!"

The others squeezed in, marvelling at the cramped surroundings. Tom was the last in. He stopped by the door and stared at one of the paintings. It was of a large man who looked to be made of smoke. Milly stopped too. Whether intentional or not, the picture bore an uncanny similarity to Tezcatlipoca, the demon god they had fought in Mexico. She looked from the picture to Tom, trying to judge his reaction.

He held his chin with his new robotic hand. "They've not caught his eyes." Before he could say any more, he got a plushie toy to the face, as Connor started throwing the toys in all directions. Milly was smacked around the head with a fluffy red devil. She caught it on the rebound and stroked the fluffy tuft of its forked tail against her cheek.

"Are we here to sing or not?" JD said, randomly pressing buttons on the karaoke machine. It burst into life, blasting a Japanese pop song out at a volume that would fill a stadium.

JD and Zek slapped around, trying to find the volume. It was Niv, leaning against the wall, who finally found the switch and turned it to less ear-splitting levels.

"How does this work?" Zek said, shaking a microphone.

"Have you never done karaoke before?" Milly asked.

All the boys and Gail looked dumbly at her.

For Naledi's fifteenth birthday they'd had a karaoke party for two, and it had been so much fun. Just the two of them in a booth, screeching songs at each other. Milly hadn't known any of the songs, as her mother had banned her from listening to "modern" music, but what she lacked in knowledge she'd more than made up for with enthusiasm.

"Well, you select a song." She squeezed her way between

JD and Zek to get to the machine, and started by switching the language setting to English. She then pressed the button marked *Select* to pull up the list. "You can search by title or artist."

"Have they got any Slay songs?" Connor said, leaning across the machine and prodding at the letters with his thick fingers.

"No way!" JD said, slapping Connor's hand away. "Don't you dare."

"But we never get to sing!" Connor said.

JD raised his hands, and stepped back. Zek and Connor scrolled through, trying to find a Slay track. There were none.

"Good," Gail said. "Or I would have had to have a word with the management. You know, artists don't get royalties from these things."

The boys groaned and a salvo of toys flew in Gail's direction. She batted them out of the way with her stick, using it like a baseball bat.

"Yes!" Connor said. "I've got one. And this is for you, Gail."

They all waited to see which song Connor had selected. When the title and artist flashed up, they all cheered. "Take Off" by The Cyclones.

Gail took less convincing than Milly had initially imagined and after only a little jostling she grabbed a mic and started to sing. Her voice had the most incredible deep rasp and Milly could see why she'd been so successful as a lead singer. It was hard to take your eyes off her as she sang. The song came to an end and Gail bowed. "Thank you, thank you. Now, how do you order drinks in this place?" Gail passed the mic back to Connor and left the booth in search of alcohol.

Connor chose the next song. "This one goes out to Zek," he said, before launching into "You're So Vain".

Milly didn't know the song, but it seemed the others did. Zek took it well and grabbed a mic of his own, joining in at the chorus and adding in some sweet harmonies – although Milly noticed he was changing the words from "You're so vain" to "You've no brain". But Connor seemed to be having too much fun to notice.

"Come on, Milly!" Zek said, when the song ended. "Your turn."

"Nope," Milly said, heading for the door. Singing with Naledi was one thing. In front of a world-famous pop band was quite another.

"Nice try," JD said, wrapping his arm around her waist and picking her up. He put her down in front of the monitor.

"Yeah, come on, Milly," Tom said. "Show us what you've got."

"Milly! Milly! Milly!" The others chanted.

"Okay, okay. But only if JD sings with me," she said.

This suggestion was met with much whooping. JD didn't need any more encouragement. He grabbed a bright pink microphone and spun it around. "Bring it."

Milly reluctantly accepted the mic that was shoved into her hand by Connor, and took her place in front of the screen. "What are we going to sing?"

"I've got just the track." Zek scrolled through the songs and a moment later the screen was filled with images of a sunlit pasture scattered with wild flowers.

"Oh no," Milly said, when she realized what track he had chosen for them. "Breaking Free". It was a duet from a teen musical that even she had seen. She'd hated it and yet she'd seen it at least five times, because Naledi loved it and knew every word and every dance move.

JD raised an eyebrow and grinned cheesily, before starting to croon the boy's part. It was in a much higher register than his usual voice, which made him sound ridiculous, meaning that Milly didn't have any choice. If JD was going to make an idiot out of himself, then she had to too. When her part came, she started to sing, to much applause and encouragement from the rest of the band.

"Holy cow, she can sing!" Connor said.

"Watch out, JD," Zek said. "You might be relegated to playing the triangle."

When it got to the chorus, Milly and JD stood, forehead to forehead, just like the characters in the film had done.

JD stroked her cheek with the back of his hand and she turned away, in pretend bashfulness. When she turned back, JD's playful expression had gone. He was staring across the room. Milly was suddenly acutely aware that it was only her voice echoing through the speakers and she faltered. The track continued, the high-pitched backing singers oohing alone. Milly followed JD's gaze to see what had caught his attention. He was staring over at Tom, whose eyes were fixed on Milly's neck as if he'd seen something terrible. She touched her chest, trying to work out if there was something on her, and her hand brushed against the silver necklace JD had given her. Was there something wrong with it? Something that was causing this reaction in Tom?

"Tom, are you okay?" Milly stepped off the small stage and reached out to touch him. Her hand fell on the cool material of his new hand. He flinched and blinked, as if he'd just woken up. He glanced from Milly to JD and then looked down.

"I, um, I'm not feeling well." He pushed his way through the group, heading for the door.

"Tom!" Milly said, staring after him. "Wait!" But he wouldn't listen.

As the door closed behind him, Milly looked back to JD, hoping he would know what to do. But JD just shrugged and looked away.

Standing in the way

A single thought beat inside Tom's brain like a fly trapped behind a window. *JD likes Milly. JD likes Milly.* How had he not realized it before? It had been staring him in the face all this time, and he'd just not seen it. As he pushed his way through the now-packed bar, he replayed all the moments between JD and Milly since they'd met. It was so clear that his best friend liked the same girl he did. Maybe even more than liked. The necklace she was wearing was one of JD's most precious possessions. He'd have only given it to her if he really, really cared about her.

JD was like a brother to him, and he couldn't let a girl get between them. Even if that girl was the most amazing girl he had ever met. If JD liked Milly, then there was only one thing he could do, and that was step aside.

And then another thought struck him. Why should he? Why should JD get to have this, along with everything else?

Tom was so used to deferring to JD in everything; his immediate instinct was not to get in JD's way. But Milly wasn't a strategy. She wasn't a demon to take down.

Tom finally made it to the front doors and practically fell out onto the street. He looked left and right, not knowing which way to go. One of the others would follow him soon, he knew. JD or Milly probably, and he didn't want to see either of them. It looked darker to the left, so he chose that way. He kept going – just walking, not knowing where he was going – until he found himself in an open park. It was cold and quiet, with a light mist cooling his hot cheeks. He felt like he could finally breathe. He closed his eyes and turned his face to the night sky, trying to take deep, slow breaths. His calm was disturbed by the sound of laughter.

He opened his eyes to see two people walking towards him, huddling under a see-through umbrella. It was a man with long, floppy hair and a black suit, and a teenage girl in very high heels. They both looked as if they'd been drinking. A lot. The man stumbled and fell to the floor, while the girl just stood and giggled. Tom went to help the man, when suddenly he recognized the girl. The side of her round face was marked by a dark birthmark. She was the one from the audition, the sweet girl with the voice of a bird. Ishida. What was she doing here? It had only been a few days since he'd seen her in Kyoto, and hadn't she said she'd be looking after her sick mother?

"Ishida?" he asked.

The girl glanced over at him, an annoyed, weary look on her face. She looked Tom up and down as if she was examining a particularly unpleasant pile of dog's droppings. She sniffed. "*Nani?*"

He walked towards her. "Hi – it's me, Tom. We met at your audition."

The girl slipped her arm away from her companion who was struggling to get to his feet. She walked closer to Tom, twirling the umbrella over her head.

"What are you doing in Osaka?"

"Partying," Ishida answered. "Kyoto is boring."

"What about your mother?"

Ishida reached her hand out from under the umbrella and ran her fingers through the falling rain. "She died."

"I…I'm sorry."

The girl shrugged. "She was old."

Tom had seen money change people. Seen how they'd used it to transform themselves: their clothes, their faces, their lifestyles. How they often left their old friends behind, now that new doors were open to them. But the change in this girl was deeper. More fundamental. Physically she was still the same; the same pretty face with the dark birthmark. But other than that, she was completely unrecognizable. It was almost as if…

"Tom-san." Tom turned to see a woman walking across

the park wearing a red fur coat that glistened in the rain. It took a moment for Tom to place her. Kotomi – Hideyoshi's university friend and model for his first hologirl. She smiled, and peered at him through her tinted sunglasses. "Well, well. What are you doing here?"

"I might ask you the same thing."

"Checking in on Ishida." She gestured towards the girl, who was now blowing a bright-pink gum bubble. "Like I do with all the girls who have been chosen for *Ikiryō*. Once they've been copied, I make sure they go back to their lives and that they don't break their contracts by opening their mouths." She lay a long golden nail against her nose. "Can't have anyone revealing our secrets now, can we?"

"I guess not," Tom said.

"We were going for karaoke, would you care to join us?"

"It's late."

"One a.m. The night is only beginning."

"I'm fine," Tom said. "I've had quite enough of karaoke for one night."

Kotomi leaned in conspiratorially. "One thing you will have to learn in Japan – there is no such thing as 'enough karaoke'." She arched back, laughing at her joke. "Come, Ishida."

Without so much as a goodbye, she wrapped her arm around the younger girl's shoulder and walked away. The drunk man, now finally on his feet, stumbled after them.

Tom watched the three leave. An idea itched at the back of his head, but he couldn't quite grab at it yet. The rain grew heavier, starting to weigh down his hair and light jacket. Cold drops trickled down his neck and made him shiver. Instinctively, he reached his right hand out to sense the heaviness of the downpour and flinched when he remembered it wasn't skin and blood picking up the sensation of the raindrops – it was electrodes and sensors. He smiled. Whatever it was, it worked.

He pulled out his phone and dialled a number. It was late, but Hideyoshi had said he didn't sleep much.

"*Moshi moshi?*" Hideyoshi answered.

"Hey, it's me, Tom. You doing anything?"

Not alone

"Tom?" Milly called out, her voice drifting down the train carriage. "Tom, are you here?" There was no answer.

She'd chased after him when he'd left the karaoke booth, but there had been no sign of him when she'd got down to the ground floor. So she had returned to the train, hoping to find him here. Gail and the others must still be back at the karaoke bar, having fun.

She walked from the lounge into the sleeper carriage, listening out for any sounds. It felt strangely unwelcoming, like going into a school at night, almost as if it resented her being here. The low lights in the corridors threw her shadow out in front of her. But other than that, she was alone. She checked each of the bedrooms in turn. Connor's was surprisingly neat. He'd jammed a chin-up bar in the cupboard, and all his clothes were folded in neat, square piles on the floor. Zek's was a mess of clothes and hair products. Niv had unpacked his computer equipment and she could see a constant stream of data running across one of the monitors as it ran checks and cross-checks throughout Japan. JD's room had hardly anything in it, just a few folded T-shirts and a book lying open on the bedside table. She turned it over to read the title: *The Wind Among The Trees*. Flicking through the pages, she was surprised to realize it was a book of poetry. Feeling as if she'd violated his privacy, she put the book back and left his room. Tom's room was last. It smelled of him; of his deodorant and aftershave. She picked a shirt up off his bed and breathed it in. Where was he? And why was he ignoring her? Then an idea hit her.

"Hey, Kitsune," she said, calling out to the train's personal assistant.

"Hello, Milo," the voice replied.

"Can you tell me who is on board?"

"Milo Tan is in carriage eight and…" Kitsune paused for a moment. "A second individual is in Hideyoshi-san's lab."

Hope fluttered. "Tom Wills?"

"I'm sorry. Something is interfering with my scan. Can I do anything more to help?"

"No, it's okay. Thanks, Kitsune."

"You're welcome, Milo."

It was probably just Hideyoshi, Milly thought. So where was Tom and why was he ignoring her? She kept seeing the look on Tom's face as he'd stormed out of the karaoke booth.

How could he be such an idiot? If only she could explain to him that it had just been a stupid song and nothing more. Okay, so the way JD had stared into her eyes as they sang had made it feel as if butterflies were dancing in her stomach. But that was just the way JD was when he was performing. It was so obvious that day-to-day he saw her as nothing more than one of the band. A little sister, maybe. Whereas her and Tom...

She had to find him. And even though it pained her, she knew Hideyoshi would know where Tom was. She made her way back through the carriages. There was a sound coming from somewhere, a gentle murmuring that she had to strain her hearing to catch. She reached the doors to carriage two and raised her hand to knock, wondering if Hideyoshi would answer.

The doors hissed open.

Milly paused. They'd been told that the area was off limits. She knew Tom had been in here before, but as far as she knew it was only when he was invited by Hideyoshi. The carriage was in darkness, but Milly could make out a glimmering light in the far corner and heard that sound again, louder this time. She could make it out now, a girl humming.

"Um, hello?" she said, stepping inside. "Hideyoshi-san, is that you?"

Soft, blue lights flickered on, responding to her presence.

But instead of staying on, they continued to blink on and off, on and off. In the strobing flashes of light she caught glimpses of the room. A table to her left, a computer console to the right, and tangles of wires all around. It was warmer than the other carriages and there was a strong smell in here, like a hint of incense. *Solder,* she thought. She remembered the pine-like smell the rosin core sometimes gave off from her Design Technology classes.

She moved in further, heading for a door she could see at the far end of the lab. The lights flickered off and she was thrown into darkness. When they came on again, the temperature suddenly dropped, and her breath clouded in the low light. The hairs on the back of her neck prickled and she knew, with complete certainty, there was someone, something, right behind her. She turned to see a figure about a metre away. A glowing girl in a white dress, with ragged, dark hair falling in front of her face. She looked like one of IKIR10, but she wasn't wearing her fox mask. The light pulsed off and when it came on again, the figure was standing face-to-face with Milly. She had closed the distance between them in the blink of an eye. The hologirl looked up, her head moving in jagged twitches, and spoke.

"*Tasukete.*" It came out as a whisper, like the sound of a breeze in a willow tree. She reached out a long, delicate hand and laid a finger on Milly's shoulder.

Electric pain shot through Milly. She grabbed her

shoulder and staggered back, hitting a table. The touch had been ice-cold and yet her shoulder now burned as if she'd leaned against a hot iron. Holograms were pure light; there was no way that one could touch her, let alone hurt her. So what the hell was going on?

The hologirl took another jerking step towards Milly, but Milly dodged out of the way, and ran for the glowing lights of the doors. She had almost made it to the exit when there was the figure again, blocking her way. It was impossible – she'd been behind her a moment ago.

Milly ducked and rolled through the doors, up and onto her feet again, and ran like she'd never run before. She'd left her bow with the swords and knives in her room at the back of the train. She had to get to it.

She made it through the next carriage and there, standing in the middle of the living room, was the glowing girl.

The hologirl looked up and opened her mouth, blue-tinged lips curling in a snarl. "*Tasukete!*"

"I don't understand. I don't know what you want!" Milly shouted, frantically looking around for something she could defend herself with. But all the weaponry was locked up.

"*Tasukete!*" the girl said again, louder.

A sleek, silver lamp stood on one of the tables. Milly wrapped her hand around it and yanked, tearing the cable out of the socket. She threw it at the figure with all of her strength. The lamp flew straight through the girl's body.

Milly swore under her breath. So the thing could hurt her, but she couldn't hurt it.

"*Tasukete!*" the girl in white screamed, zooming forward as if on rails, till she was screeching in Milly's face. "*Tasukete!*"

Milly felt a blast of freezing cold air on her skin, smelled the stench of rotting flesh. She stared into dark and empty eyes, and knew she was looking into the face of death.

"*Yameru!*"

The lights in the train slammed on and the girl stood still, her head bowed peacefully.

Hideyoshi walked into the room. Milly slumped against the wall. She was safe, at last.

Second first kiss

Tom had heard the screaming and come running, only a few paces behind Hideyoshi. After Tom had called, Hideyoshi had picked him up from the park and driven him back to the train. They'd planned on playing around with some music, but now it seemed as if that would have to wait for another night.

Tom looked over Hideyoshi's shoulder to see Milly, panting and shaking, staring at something in front of her. He could only make out a glow of blue light. He pushed Hideyoshi out of the way and recognized the hologirl, Ichi, without her mask again. She was hovering in the centre of the room, her head held low and her hair in front of her face. Milly, meanwhile, looked terrified.

"*Yameru,*" Hideyoshi said once more, and Ichi blinked out of existence.

Tom raced over to Milly, checking her up and down. She didn't appear to be hurt, but clearly something terrible had happened. "Are you okay?"

She slid onto the floor, as if whatever strength had been holding her up was gone. Tom kneeled down next to her and took her hand. It was freezing.

"Are you okay?" he asked again.

"I…I think so," Milly said, her voice high and quavering. She gingerly slipped her hand under the collar of her T-shirt, as if checking for a wound.

Tom stopped her hand and pulled her top back up to cover the strap of her sports bra. "Are you sure, *Milo*?" He stressed the name, glancing over at Hideyoshi. Whatever had happened to her was enough to make her forget about her disguise.

Milly adjusted her top and nodded. "Yeah, I'm fine," she said, her voice lower now.

"What happened?" Tom helped Milly to her feet.

"I don't know. I was looking for you, and then there was this girl…"

"Ichi," Hideyoshi said. "There must have been an error in her programming."

"Programming? Are you trying to tell me that was one of your hologirls? One of *Ikiryō*?" Milly said. "No way. I saw her eyes. I felt her breath on my face. She…touched me." Milly laid her hand against her shoulder again. "There is no way that was a hologram."

"I've seen Ichi without her mask on before," Tom said.

"It's a bit unsettling how lifelike she is, isn't it?"

Milly shook Tom's hand away. "It wasn't unsettling," she said. "It was terrifying."

"Please, there is no need for you to be afraid. Ichi cannot harm you," Hideyoshi said, sounding as concerned as he had when the spotlight had fallen and nearly killed them both.

"Exactly," Tom said. "She's just light. It must have been your imagination."

Milly glared at Tom and he was taken aback by how fierce she looked. "I think I know the difference between my imagination and something that was trying to kill me." There was a tense silence as Milly continued to glare at him.

Hideyoshi coughed. "I will go to the lab and check on what happened. I am very sorry that you have been so disturbed." He bowed slightly and left the carriage.

Tom waited till Hideyoshi was out of hearing distance. "Milly…"

"Don't 'Milly' me. I know what I saw."

"But Hideyoshi—"

Milly cut Tom off with an exasperated sigh. She took her cap off and threw it onto the sofa. He could see her hands were still shaking. He reached out, wanting to reassure her that everything was going to be okay, but he stopped himself.

"Don't you believe me?" she asked.

"I believe that you think you saw something."

"I think if there's anyone who's seeing things that aren't there, Tom, it's you."

"What's that supposed to mean?"

Milly spun around to look at him. "Why did you storm off earlier tonight?"

"I'm surprised you even noticed, you were having so much fun up there with JD," Tom said, instantly regretting it. He knew he was being an idiot, but he couldn't help it. The image of the two of them singing, staring into each other's eyes, had been burning away at him.

"I knew it! You're jealous."

"Can you blame me?" he said, surprised at how angry he suddenly felt. "You and JD are just so…perfect together."

Milly looked taken aback. "Oh my God. You don't get it?"

"Get what?"

Milly charged towards him, and for a moment he thought she was going to hit him. Instead, she grabbed his face in her hands and pulled him towards her. Their lips crushed against each other in a frantic kiss. Tom resisted, confused, but as he felt the kiss linger he softened, responding in kind. He wrapped his hands around her waist and pulled her closer to him. All the heat of his anger and stupid jealousy melted away into the passion of the kiss. Time stopped having any meaning. The kiss might have lasted seconds or an hour, Tom couldn't tell. When it did end, they stared into each other's eyes.

"I have been wanting to do that for such a long time," Milly said at last.

He brushed a lock of hair off her forehead, and kissed the spot where it had been. "What stopped you?"

"Everything."

Tom held her a little tighter, not wanting to let the moment go. But she was right. Everything stood between them. They couldn't let this, whatever *this* was, happen. Tom might have been wrong about Milly's feelings for his best friend, but he was almost certain JD had feelings for her. He'd never known JD to look at a girl the way he'd looked at Milly tonight.

He let her go, running his hand up and down her arm. "So?"

"So…"

"That was quite a first kiss."

Milly laughed. "Not our first. Remember Mexico?"

"I don't want to ever think about Mexico."

"Okay then, let's say this was our first kiss."

"And this is our second." He leaned in to kiss her again when they heard the sound of an engine followed by laughter. He and Milly quickly stepped away from each other.

"Hey," Connor said, leaping through the door. "Where did you two go?"

"We, um…" Milly said, stuttering.

"We just went for a walk," Tom said.

"And then Hideyoshi's hologram tried to kill me," Milly said.

"What?"

Milly filled them all in and Tom tried his hardest not to interrupt or correct her. When he'd arrived on the train, all he'd seen was Ichi in the middle of the room. It hadn't been anywhere near Milly. Besides, it was made of light – it couldn't hurt anyone.

"That's it," Gail said. "We are leaving the train now. I don't care what the contract says, I will not have members of my band put in danger like this."

"No, it's okay," Milly said, looking at Tom. "Maybe Tom was right and I was imagining things. Freaking myself out."

"Milly, you've gone up against demons and you didn't freak out. A damn demon god tried to possess you and you didn't freak out. You do not freak out easily," JD said.

Tom was annoyed by how protective JD was being. He felt a sudden urge to run forward and kiss Milly again, to stake his claim on her; to make it clear to JD that Milly was his, and his alone. He pushed the dark compulsion aside, troubled that it had even flicked across his mind.

"It's fine, JD. I'm safe now."

"Are you sure?" JD asked.

"She's fine," Tom snapped. "I'll speak to Hideyoshi tomorrow and find out what went on."

JD laid his hand on Tom's shoulder. "I know you trust

him, Tom, but there's something up. What do we really know about Hideyoshi?"

Tom shook JD off. "Not this again! Well, okay, we know he's still in danger. Twice something has tried to kill him."

"Twice?" Zek said.

"First the demons at the theatre." Tom held up one finger, then another. "Second, the light falling. That was meant for him, I'm sure of it. So I don't care if you don't like him. It's our job to protect him."

"And what about protecting Milly?" JD said.

Tom clenched his jaw. "I would never let something happen to Milly. I would die first."

The group looked between Tom and JD, and Tom could tell they didn't know which side to take.

Gail finally broke the deadlock. "Milly, you've had a shock. You should go get some rest."

Milly said her goodnights and went to leave. She paused at the door. "One thing. Does anyone know what *tasukete* means?"

Tom racked his brain for the basic Japanese he'd been studying, and came up blank.

Niv signed, hitting the open palm of his left hand with the fist of his right, thumb extended, and then moving it slowly towards his body. Tom noticed how Milly's jaw tightened and her face paled.

"What?" he asked. "What does it mean?"

"Nothing," Milly said, refusing to meet his eyes. "Night."

191

Break my heart

Milly went back to her room, locking the door before collapsing onto her bed. It was past one in the morning but her mind was working furiously. The karaoke, Ichi, the kiss; it all rushed around in one confused mess and she wasn't sure what any of it meant. She brushed her fingers over her lips; they still felt tender and she could taste the trace of Tom.

In one night, everything had become so confused. Just as Tom had come back to them – back to himself – and there was hope that they could all return to some kind of normality, she'd kissed him, throwing things out of kilter again. She liked Tom – a lot – but could they really be together? What would the rest of the group think? And did she even care? She'd wanted to kiss Tom since the night they'd met and he'd loaned her his T-shirt to sleep in. But why had she kissed him tonight – just when she'd been so annoyed with him? It was so stupid, the kind of thing she and Naledi would roll their eyes at when they'd seen women in films doing it. How was it possible to want to hit someone and kiss them all at once?

If only Naledi was here. If only she had someone she could talk to. She pulled her phone out and went to contact her best friend. There was a mass of unanswered messages, getting increasingly worried, from Naledi. How could she even begin to explain what was going on? *Oh, hey, Nal. Google "Slay Japan Tour" and you might recognize someone. Oh, and yeah, you know that J-Pop band, IKIR10? One of them tried to kill me. How are you?*

It was all too much. Too wild. She put the phone down.

There was a knock at the door. If it was Tom, she really didn't want to talk to him. She really didn't want to talk to any of the boys.

"Milly, can I come in?" It was Gail.

Milly slid across the lock and sat back on the bed. Gail opened the door, stepped inside and closed it behind her.

"DAD has something."

"The girl in black?" Milly wanted to tell Gail about what had happened tonight with the girl in black appearing again, but she didn't want to go against JD.

"No, nothing on her, I'm afraid. But DAD flagged a report of another missing girl in Tokyo. Now, we can stay on board, stay on tour, support *Ikiryō* in Tokyo in a couple of nights, giving us the cover to check the activity out. Or…we can get off the train now, cancel the whole tour. Just say the word."

Milly closed her eyes and got a flash of the figure who had chased her through the train. But it was quickly replaced by an image of Tom. She didn't believe he would ever put her in danger and he was so sure there was nothing to worry about. And now that the fear had passed, she was starting to question what had really happened. "No, no I want to stay. I promise. Besides, I think we'd have a tough time convincing Tom to leave Hideyoshi unprotected."

"Ah, I see. So this is about Tom." Gail raised a querying eyebrow.

Milly felt her cheeks go pink. She couldn't hide anything from Gail. "We kissed."

"Ah," Gail said again, folding one of Milly's T-shirts and setting it aside. "I'm surprised it took you so long, really. So, do you like him?"

Milly thought about this for a moment. "Yes, I think I do."

"And what about JD?"

The heat in Milly's cheeks turned up a notch. "I… What?"

"Milly, we spend our lives lying to the world. The most important thing is that you don't lie to yourself. Or to me, for that matter." Gail fixed Milly with her one dark eye.

"I…I'm not sure. Is it possible to like two people at once?"

Gail laughed. "Sweetheart, it's possible to like fifty people at once. This whole idea of there being one soulmate for everyone was cooked up by writers to sell songs. Believe me, I wrote some of the best of them. But who you like is almost academic, because you and Tom, you and JD, hell, you and any of the band is a bad idea."

Milly looked down at her hands. "But…why?"

Gail sighed softly. "Dating within a band can cause complications. I know, I dated my bassist for a year and it was a roller coaster. We'd break up, get back together and then break up again. And every time we broke up, it was hell for all the other members of the band. Plus, imagine having to share a stage with someone who you could hardly stand to look at."

Milly couldn't imagine a time when she wouldn't want to look at Tom.

"It's not that I don't think you and Tom could have a future – or you and JD for that matter. It's just, what if you don't? What if you end up hating each other? What happens then?"

"I could never hate Tom!" Milly said.

"You'd be surprised at what heartbreak can make people do, Milly. But I'm not telling you 'no', because I know teenagers better than to do something so stupid. God knows if I forbid it you'll only end up sneaking around anyway, and get yourself into even more trouble. I'm just asking you to press pause for a little while, and think about the consequences. Because what we do, this war we are fighting against darkness – it's bigger than any of us. Do you understand that?"

Milly nodded. "Of course."

"Good," Gail said, standing up. "Because I've already lost too many people I care about, and I don't want to have to lose you."

Milly understood that, as sympathetic as Gail was being, it was a warning too. Put their mission in jeopardy, and she was out.

"We stay on the train? Final answer?" Gail said.

"Final answer," Milly said.

Gail nodded one last time and left the room.

Milly laid back on her bed and stared at the smooth white ceiling above. Why did things have to be so complicated? Why couldn't she and Tom just be a normal couple of teenagers who could go to the cinema and hang out in parks rather than chasing demons? She liked him so much. Maybe too much.

"Help me," Milly whispered to herself. That was the translation Niv had signed. It's what the hologram Ichi had been saying: *Tasukete*. Help me.

Maybe Milly wasn't the only one who was in trouble.

Back where you belong

"One, two… One, two, three, four!" Connor clashed his sticks and the set began.

They were about to play to a crowd of 55,000 people in the Tokyo Dome – one of their biggest gigs yet. Tom waited in the wings, his legs jittery with nerves. He checked his watch. Seven thirty-three. They were running bang on schedule, which never normally happened, but the Tokyo crowd had been in and ready for the show to start at exactly seven thirty. Slay had launched straight into their opener – "The Road Keeps On Callin'" – and after it there'd be one more song and then he would be joining them back onstage. He clenched and opened his right hand over and over, making sure it was working. It had been less than two months since he had played with the others, but he felt like he'd been out of action for years. Plus, he wouldn't be slipping back into his old place at the keyboards tonight.

He would be trying something completely new and it might go horribly, horribly wrong. What if the fans hated the new sound? What if they didn't want him back? What if…

"No," he said out loud. *Don't go there,* he told himself. *Don't even think it. Don't think about shadows and darkness and the real reason you're itching to get out on that stage.* But of course, as soon as he'd had the thought, it was all he could think about. He closed his eyes and saw the flash of black lightning, heard singing, smelled sulphur. He couldn't do this. He couldn't go out there, precisely because it was all he wanted to do. He wanted to hear all those voices worshipping him, adoring him. Calling him by his name, Tez—

A hand on his shoulder made him flinch. "Tom?"

It was Gail standing behind him, but it took him a moment to recognize her. He blinked, confused at her presence, confused by where he was. And then the sound of Slay launching into their second song brought him back.

"You okay?" Gail said. "If it's too soon, you don't have to do this."

"What? No," Tom snapped. "I want to do this." He turned back to the stage and saw the spot at the back, waiting for him. "I need to do this."

Gail pulled on his shoulder and turned him to face her. "Tom, remember, this is all just a game. This is the fun bit, remember that. You and your best friends in the world making music you love to make people happy. Remember that feeling. Remember the joy. The rest – the fame, the money, the sales – it's all just sprinkles."

Tom laughed. It wasn't the first time Gail had given him the "sprinkles" talk.

"So I want you to go out there and have fun, okay?"

"Okay." Tom turned back to the rest of the band. They were more than halfway through "Just Go", which meant he was about to join them onstage to play the remix of "Bring It Home" any minute now. "Sprinkles," he said, swallowing hard. "Sure."

With a triple smash of cymbals and a strum of guitar, the song came to an end.

"Thank you," JD said, pushing his damp fringe out of his eyes and laying his hand on his chest. "You're all amazing. Thank you. But now," he continued, "I am… Well, I don't really have the words to say just how happy and excited I am…" JD looked offstage and caught Tom's eye. He smiled and Tom felt the fear melt away. Whatever happened, tonight on this stage, or tomorrow, or ever – he knew JD had his back. How could he have ever doubted that? Tom flicked his eyes across the other members of the band. Connor, Zek, Niv – they would all die before they let anything happen to him. Finally, he looked at Milly. He only had to be around her to feel that everything was okay.

"… How delighted I am to welcome back onstage – back where he belongs… Tom Wills!" JD stretched his hand out, and waved Tom forward. "Get out here, buddy."

Tom walked out into the lights, and it didn't feel as if his feet were touching the floor. The crowd went wild when they realized what was happening, and Tom felt their love for him as if he'd been wrapped in a warm blanket. He took his new position, behind a brand-new deck desk, just to the side of Connor's kit. Spotlights turned and focused solely on him.

He leaned in to the mic. "Hey! It's so good to be back. As you can see, I've had a bit of an upgrade." He waved his black hand. A confused hush settled over the crowd. "I know you've heard a lot of rumours about why I've been away, but the truth is, there was an accident and I lost my hand." Those that understood English in the crowd gasped. There was a slight delay as they then explained it to the others. Tom heard cries of distress move like a wave across the audience. "But I'm all good now," he said quickly. This was supposed to be a celebration, and he could already hear some fans wailing.

"He's better than good," Connor said, leaning forward so he could reach the mic positioned over his cymbals. "He's the best!"

The crowd cheered and Tom saw tears on the faces of Slay fans. He looked over to see Milly, her face turned away from the crowd as she wiped her own tears away on the sleeve of her bomber jacket. He had to fight to keep his own tears from falling. *Welcome home,* she mouthed to him, and he felt his heart swell.

"Okay then, let's do this."

Connor counted them in once more and they launched into the remix of "Bring It Home". Tom's hands flew across the decks as he played the samples, weaving them in and out of the live performance. It sounded even better than he'd hoped it would. The remix gave the song a new life, a new energy, and he sensed the crowd responding to it.

They went straight into "Last Goodbye", which was to be their final song.

"Thank you, Tokyo," JD said afterwards. "You have been amazing, and we have been Slay!"

JD waved and, along with the rest of the band, left the stage. The crowd were clapping and stamping for more. But Slay didn't give encores. *Why not?* Tom thought. Why not give the fans what they wanted? What *he* wanted.

Before anyone could stop him, he ran back out onstage. "Thank you!" he said. "We love you all. One more song."

JD and the others were shaking their heads frantically as Tom stood behind the decks. He ignored them all. If they didn't want to come back out, that was fine, he didn't need them. He had everything he needed right here. He pressed a button on the decks and a haunting sound, like wind in the trees, began. Another button and a sample of JD's voice played, distorted and echoing. *"I'm all alone."* Tom looped it,

slowing it down and then speeding it up. "*I'm...I'm...I'm...
all alone.*" He selected a glitching beat and laid that down.
He started clapping his hands and the crowd joined in. They
were loving it, and so was he.

Milly was the first to come back out and join him. She
began playing the keyboards, riffing off the track he was
creating on the fly. Tom glanced over at JD and felt that
pang of petty victory that Milly had once again chosen
him over JD. The others came out and picked up their
instruments, picking up their place in the song. JD finally
started singing.

When they came to the end, Tom came out from behind
the decks and raced towards the front of the stage, grabbing
JD's hand and lifting it into the air. The crowd boomed in
response.

"Tell me you didn't love that?" Tom said, leaning in so JD
could hear him over the cheers.

JD pulled his hand away. "We have rules for a reason,
Tom."

"Come on, JD, you're the one who taught me how fun it
can be to break the rules." Tom wrapped his arm around his
friend's neck and pulled him so he could kiss the top of his
head. He couldn't remember the last time he'd hugged JD
like that, and he realized he'd missed that maybe even more
than being onstage. It was like Gail had said: him and his
best friends in the world, creating music together.

"Sprinkles," he said, and JD looked at him as if he was crazy.

Tom turned around to see if Milly had enjoyed it too. She was staring out at the crowd, a look of shock and surprise on her face. Before he had a chance to ask her what was wrong, she pushed him aside and threw herself off the stage.

Take a leap of faith

Milly had run to the front of the stage, ignoring the confused looks from JD and Tom, who were still drinking in the wild applause. There was that girl again, a few rows from the front – the same one she'd seen at their last gig. The same one she'd seen in Osaka, dressed in black and sucking souls out of demons. She was certain of it. The girl smiled, gave that infuriating wink, and started to push her way to the back. Milly knew if she didn't get to her soon, she'd be gone again. She looked around, trying to think through her options. If she went through the backstage area she'd lose sight of her. And there was no way she'd make it *through* the screaming crowd before the girl escaped. There was only one thing for it: go over them.

She took a step back and ran, launching herself and spinning backwards off the stage and into the air. As she flew, arms outstretched, a thousand thoughts raced through her head: she was going to break every limb, the crowd were going to crush her, this was probably the dumbest decision of her entire life. But she landed on the sea of people and the waves of hands picked her up and carried her.

Gentle hands pushed her over their heads, cradling her. It was the strangest form of intimacy she'd experienced. She had literally put her life in the hands of thousands of strangers – thousands of strange girls – and they had accepted her. Ever since she'd joined Slay, she'd been scared of the fans, who she'd only seen at a distance, screaming behind barriers. But here, she felt embraced and welcomed by them.

She gestured wildly towards the back, like someone directing a plane in for landing, and the crowd followed her directions. At last she was placed back on her feet. Right beside the girl in black.

The two girls paused for a moment, sizing each other up. The girl's hand twitched for her belt and Milly reacted, grabbing her wrist before she could make a further move. They stood like that, frozen. The fans all around Milly reached out to touch her, squeeze her free hand or thrust pens at her, wanting a signature from a member of Slay. Even if this girl wanted to hurt Milly, she'd have to go through all the fans to do it.

Milly relaxed and let go of the girl, holding her hand up to show she meant no harm. The girl tilted her face, looking

Milly up and down. With a small jerk of her head towards the back door, she leaned in and shouted in Milly's ear. "Let's go somewhere we can talk."

Milly looked back at the stage. The boys were at last making their exit, waving at her to join them. She should absolutely tell them she had found the girl in black, and she positively shouldn't follow this deadly stranger by herself. Slay's number one rule was never go it alone. And yet she knew if she told JD and the others, they'd only scare the girl off. Fight her, even. Milly didn't know why, but she trusted the girl in black. She looked back at the girl and made her decision. She followed her.

They pushed their way through the crowd – past the bouncers, who, with a word from Milly, stopped any of the fans from following – and exited the arena. The girl led Milly across the road and down a tight alleyway lined with tiny restaurants. Steam billowed out of the open windows and Milly's stomach rumbled from the amazing smells. She kept checking to see if anyone had followed them, but they were alone. Ducking through shops and down side roads, they finally came to a restaurant that was mostly empty, apart from a few old men slurping at noodles. The girl nodded to a tired-looking waiter behind the bar and took a seat in a booth at the back.

Milly slid into the seat opposite her. She opened her mouth and couldn't even think where to begin. What did this girl want? Whose side was she on? Milly started simple. "Who are you?"

The girl looked at her through a heavy fringe. "I could ask you the same. Demon-fighting boy band. You play music by daylight, fight evil by moonlight. You're straight out of a manga."

Milly laughed – it was a relief to be able to share this secret with someone, especially another girl. "Speak for yourself, ninja girl."

The girl seemed to find this funny. "Call me Aneki."

"I'm Mil...Milo." Milly caught herself just in time. One secret at a time, she thought. "What are you doing here?"

The girl leaned back. "Why, can't a girl like pop music?"

Milly shook her head. "Are you following us?"

Aneki didn't answer. She gestured at the waiter, and a moment later a pot of steaming green tea and two cups were slammed on the table. The girl then slid the paper covering off a pair of chopsticks, folded it quickly into a zigzag pattern and then laid the chopstick on top of it.

"Nice," Milly said, looking at the chopstick holder the girl had made. "I'll remember that. But you didn't answer my question."

"Answer me something first."

Milly matched the girl's pose, leaning back in her seat. "Go on then."

"Why do you fight demons?"

"Because they hurt people."

The girl snorted through her nose. "It's lucky you're cute, because you're stupid."

"What's that meant to mean?"

"I'm not following *you*," Aneki said, switching tracks again.

"But you are following someone?"

"Why do you play at being a boy band?"

Milly was starting to see how this was going to go. A question for a question. "Because the money is good and it gives us a reason to travel anywhere in the world. Who are you following? Is it someone else in the band?" Milly wondered if maybe this girl was after Tom or JD.

"No. How long have you been fighting demons?"

"Me? Only a few months. But the others, I don't know. They've been doing this for a long time. Do you fight demons too?"

"I fight evil wherever I see it."

Milly leaned forward again. "So why did you stop us killing those demon schoolgirls, and that demon in Uji?"

"I didn't stop you killing the demons. I was stopping you killing their hosts."

"But...I was told that once a human had been possessed, the host was dead."

The girl shook her head. "Normally, yes. Normally, when an *oni*, a demon spirit, enters a human, the two energies become one. Inseparable from the moment the possession takes place." Aneki reached for a bottle of chilli oil on the table, and poured it into her cup, where it created a red, swirling film over the green tea beneath. "The dark spirit of the *oni* traps the human soul. Crushing it, destroying it. The *oni* spirits are stronger than ours. Once an *oni* spirit has merged with a human soul, there is no way back for the human. The *oni* always win."

Milly had seen that, when the demon priestess Zyanya had possessed her own mother. Her mother had tried to fight back, had tried to hold on, but in the end, the demon was too strong for her.

"You did something that sucked the soul out of the body. We saw it."

"Yes."

"So, if you can take the demon out, then…" She paused. This was the question she hadn't wanted to ask. Because if it was possible to save humans after they'd been possessed, then what had she been a part of for the past month? What had Slay been doing for years? Gail had promised them all that there was no way back. But what if she was wrong? "Then can't you save the human?"

Aneki poured the mix of tea and oil into a new cup, the two liquids swirling together. "Once an *oni* and human soul have merged, there is no way to separate them. Even if it leaves a host, it will take whatever remains of the human soul with it."

Milly let out the breath she'd been holding. "So there is no way back." The guilt she'd been carrying for the last few days lifted. She leaned back in the seat, watching as Aneki continued to pour the now frothing liquid from cup to cup. And then something Aneki had said replayed in her mind. "You said 'normally'. What's so abnormal about what's going on here?"

Aneki stopped, and then, with a flick of her wrist, she tipped the tea and oil mix out onto the floor. The waiter complained but Aneki snapped back in Japanese and he went back to grumpily filling up soy bottles. She then continued with her demonstration, picked up the bottle of chilli oil and poured it – this time into an empty cup. "If an *oni* were to possess a human body without a soul, there is no crushing. No battle. The soul remains intact, only trapped."

Milly looked at the mess of oil and tea on the floor and back to the cup with the red oil in it. "A body without a soul, that's why they're in comas?"

"Yes, and they will stay that way until their souls return."

"So... Where are the souls?"

Aneki smiled and put the cup down. "Now you are asking the right questions. Why don't you ask your friend Hideyoshi about that?"

"Hideyoshi? But...what's he got to do with this?"

"Everything." The girl's eyes blazed with intense hatred. "That's why I'm here. To stop him."

"Stop him doing what?"

Aneki reached into her jacket pocket and pulled out a photograph. She handed it to Milly. It showed Hideyoshi standing next to a girl. Her hair fell in front of her face and she had her arm thrown over Hideyoshi's shoulder as she pulled him into a hug he didn't look happy about.

"Who is she?"

"That was my best friend."

"What happened to her?"

"Hideyoshi."

"What do you mean?"

Before the girl could answer, Milly's phone buzzed. She looked down to see a call from Tom. "I... Sorry, I have to get this."

She clambered out of the booth and walked slightly away from the table, so that she wouldn't be heard.

"Where are you?" Tom said when she answered. She could hear Connor whooping in the background and the bustle of backstage. "Are you okay?"

"I..." Milly tried to think of a way to explain. "I'm fine. I just needed some air. I'm on my way back."

Milly looked back to the booth. There was only the one exit in the restaurant, the same way they had come in. Milly hadn't seen anyone go past her and yet the booth was empty. The only thing left behind was the photo and a black business card.

You can tell me

"That was…epic!" Connor roared, as they piled inside the dressing room.

"I know," Zek said, brushing a speck of dust off his suit. "I *was* incredible."

"You were all incredible – especially you, Tom!" Gail said.

"Thanks." Tom was trying to smile and joke with the others, but struggling. The high of being onstage had crashed, dragging him down and down, and now he felt empty, as if something vital had been sucked out of him. He looked down at the phone in his hand. Milly had sounded distant. Was she upset about him joining the band again? Or was she freaking out about the kiss?

"Was that Milly?" JD asked, jerking Tom out of his thoughts.

"Yeah, she's on her way back."

"You should definitely do that remix at our next concert," Connor said. "Speaking of which, where are we going next?"

"Don't know," Zek said. "The girl reported missing turned up safe and sound and DAD hasn't kicked up anything else. But you have to check out this freaky thing Niv found."

Connor followed Zek and soon the three boys were laughing at something on Niv's phone. Tom couldn't tell what it was, only that it had nothing to do with demons.

Gail was on her phone, as per usual, shouting at someone about something. She left the room so she wouldn't be overheard, which always meant that someone was really getting a grilling.

"Everything okay?" JD said softly, coming to stand next to Tom.

"Sure."

"And why am I not believing that 'sure'?" JD knew him too well.

"It's just…weird, I guess."

"Being on the decks?"

"No, actually that's great. I loved that. No, I mean, just being up there. It's like sometimes…I…" He wanted to tell JD about the darkness he saw sometimes, about the flashbacks – if that was even what they were – to Mexico. He knew that if he could just tell his best friend, then everything would be okay. They would be able to work it out together.

"That's good, because with Milly playing keyboards now and all…"

"Milly?" Tom said. The confession he had been about to make died on his lips. "Oh yeah. I mean, she's amazing."

"You know…if you want to tell me anything, like, if there's something going on between you two…" JD looked pained and uncomfortable and Tom saw again just how much his friend liked Milly. "Then that's cool, you know?"

A pang of pettiness struck Tom. What if he told JD about the kiss? What if he told him to back the hell off and that Milly was his? How cool would he be then? Tom wondered. The feeling passed. "Ah, man, you know it would be too complicated."

"Yeah, I guess. Shame," JD said. And Tom wondered who exactly he was sad for.

"The gig went down well on social. Especially your return, Tom," Zek said, handing Tom his phone. He flicked through post after post all tagged with #SLAY followed by a dagger emoji. There were videos of the show, photos, and post after post about how incredible it had been. *Tom's back and better than ever*, one read. Tom smiled, feeling a little of the buzz of being onstage again. He kept flicking, looking for more posts about himself. He stopped on one and was only able to catch a glimpse of a cartoon drawing before Zek grabbed the phone back.

"What was that?" Tom asked, wondering why Zek had been so keen to hide it from him.

"Oh, you don't want to see that."

"Um, yes I do," Tom said.

"Trust me, you don't."

"Trust me, I do."

"Okay then." Zek held up the phone.

Tom looked at the picture and it took him a moment to work out what he was seeing. It was a drawing of JD caught in a passionate embrace with... "That's me!" Tom said, snatching the phone out of Zek's hand.

"I told you," Zek said, reaching for the phone. But Tom refused to give it back, spinning around so that Zek couldn't get to him.

"What? I...I don't get it. Me and JD?"

"What's this?" JD said, and he grabbed the phone off Tom before he had a chance to stop him. JD stared down at the image.

"The fans who ship you call you 'Jom'," Zek said.

"The fans who *what* us?" Tom asked.

"Ship, as in relationship. They like to think you're together."

"Me and Tom," JD asked, pointing first to himself and then to Tom.

"Yup."

JD looked back at the picture, and a smile itched at the

corner of his mouth. "It's a good drawing." He threw the phone back to Zek.

"Don't you think it's weird?" Tom asked.

"Not really."

"There's Jom, Jonnor."

"Sweet!" said Connor.

"I am not even going to go into Ziv. And of course there's Jilo," Zek said, with a devilish grin.

Tom ran this through his head, trying to work out what Jilo meant. "JD and Milo?"

Zek nodded. "Ever since 'Milo' joined us," he said, putting air quotes around Milly's fake name, "there has been a lot of fiction about it. Photos of Milly and JD looking at each other, touching each other's arms – you know, stuff like that."

"I...I don't touch her, I don't look at her," JD said, a red tinge appearing in his pale cheeks. "I mean, I look at her the same way I look at any of you."

"Hey," Zek said, holding his hands up. "I'm not saying anything."

"And keep it that way," JD muttered under his breath, going to pick at a piece of pizza.

Tom knew he was lying. Ever since he'd seen JD and Milly singing, he knew there was more to their relationship than just friendship. But Milly had chosen Tom, and he was just going to have to trust in that.

The dressing-room door opened and in came Milly, looking a little dishevelled. Her cap was skewed to the side and her flannel shirt was untucked, but her boy disguise was still intact.

"Hey, Mills! How were the tubes?" Connor said, putting on a terrible American accent.

"Huh?" Milly said.

"Tubes, like waves? When you're surfing?" Connor explained, dropping back into his Irish lilt. "You were crowd-surfing and... Ah, why do I bother?" He turned back to the pizza.

"That's the question we've all been asking ourselves, Con," Zek said, spinning around in an armchair. "Why *does* he bother?"

"Hey, that was the last slice!" JD shouted, pointing at Connor.

"Oui downt noo wha ou ween!" Connor said, his mouth clearly filled with pizza.

"Milly, did you even get a... Hey, what's wrong?" JD switched from annoyed to serious.

JD was too good at reading her expressions sometimes. But she ignored his concern and looked directly at Tom. "Tom, can I talk to you?" she said.

"I, um, sure," Tom replied, looking at JD. Milly took his hand and led him outside the dressing room and into a busy corridor. Music floated from the stage above and Tom could hear the roaring of the crowd. IKIR10 were in full flow, playing a song that was sad but sweet at the same time. Milly led him further away and into a quiet stairwell. Her hand felt warm in his. Nerves started to flutter in Tom's stomach. Was this about the kiss? Were they about to kiss again? Is that why she had brought him here? He wished he had mints, he'd just been eating pizza.

Milly looked left and right, checking they were alone. "I need to ask you something."

Tom's lips were suddenly dry. Milly's shirt had slipped down and her shoulder was showing. He stared at a freckle there, wanting more than anything else to kiss it. "Okay?"

"It's about Hideyoshi."

Tom paused. This was not heading where he had expected. "Huh?"

"Do you trust him?"

"Of course I do. Why?"

"I met someone tonight and they said…"

"Said what? Milly, you're scaring me. What's wrong?" He gripped her shoulder and she reached up to run her fingers over the back of his hand. He felt the tingles run all the way up to his neck.

"Ahem."

Tom looked up the stairs to see Hideyoshi walking down towards them. He looked at the space between him and Milly, how her fingers were trailing over his and realized what it must look like. Tom quickly stepped away. "Oh, hey. Yeah, Milo and I were just going over the set."

Milly looked up at Hideyoshi and back to Tom. She didn't even bother trying to back him up, she just dropped her head and walked away. Tom watched her go, feeling a mix of anger and confusion.

"Is your bandmate okay?" Hideyoshi asked, walking down the few remaining steps.

"Yeah...no. I don't know." He ran his fingers through his hair. He didn't know anything any more. "How is the show going?"

"Oh, good, I think." He looked up and they listened to the muffled music for a while. "The fans seem to enjoy it. I held another audition today and we have found our ninth member."

"That's awesome. And you'll have number ten in no time, I'm sure."

"I think I already know who I want for ten."

"Well – congratulations, I guess," Tom said. "And is Nomura happy with the selection?"

"Yes, very. In fact, I was hoping to find you. Nomura-san has invited me for a meal in the finest restaurant in Japan to celebrate the end of our search, and I wanted to know if you would care to join us?"

Tom looked back down the corridor. After a show, he and the others would either go hunting or hang together, eating pizza and going over what happened. And yet, for some reason he wasn't up for it tonight. Maybe it was all this Jilo stuff or the way Milly was acting, but he needed a break. "Sure," he said. "Let's go."

Lost souls

Milly curled her hand around the photo Aneki had left on the table. Had the girl been right, that they shouldn't trust Hideyoshi? He seemed like such a sweet guy, and he'd done nothing but help them. Especially Tom. Looking at her phone again, she reread Tom's text saying he was going for food with Hideyoshi and he'd meet them back on the train. She'd not heard anything else since. She was sitting on a low sofa in the lounge carriage of the train, half-watching the boys as they played a game that involved not being able to touch the floor. They tried to get her to join in, but she was too distracted worrying about Tom. Should she text him, just to check? But then he might think she was being clingy. Gail was right, relationships in bands were complicated. She put her phone away and tried to put Tom out of her mind.

"Right, you lot." Gail came in, sat down and hardly raised

an eyebrow as Connor clambered over her head. "Where's Tom?"

"Having dinner with Hideyoshi," Milly said.

"Okay. Well, I have to go out. Nomura is sending a helicopter to pick me up at nine p.m. Apparently he wants to take me to his mountain retreat to talk about a possible European tour. Don't worry!" she said as they started groaning. "I'm only meeting to tell him no, face-to-face."

"A helicopter!" Connor said. "Can I come?"

"No you cannot! Try not to break a leg while I'm out."

"Hope you get covered in goop!" Connor called after Gail. She waved over her shoulder as she exited.

JD jumped down from a sideboard and landed next to Milly. His large smile faded the moment he caught her eye. "What's wrong?"

She looked at his face, ruddy from the game. His eyes darted left and right as he looked at her. "It's nothing," Milly said.

"Tell that to your lip."

"Huh?"

"You're chewing it." JD pointed towards her mouth. "You only do that when you're worried about something."

"I... Do I?" Milly hadn't realized she did that.

"Is this about Tom?" JD said, his voice sounding strained, and Milly noticed he had stopped looking at her.

"No. I mean, yes, but...I'm just worried about him."

222

Milly's stomach twisted. If Aneki had been right, being around Hideyoshi could be dangerous.

"Seriously, Milly," JD said. "What's going on? Your expression is scaring me."

"You look like you need a cuppa," Connor said. He was swinging by one arm from a hat rack. "Do you need a cuppa?" He landed on the floor in front of her.

"No, I'm fine."

"You've been all mysterious ever since you and Tom went off together," Zek said. "Come on, spill, Mil. Spill, Mil. Get it?"

"Start by telling us where you went after the gig," JD said.

"Okay. Well, you know that girl who keeps turning up, the one in black?"

JD nodded. "Hot ninja girl?"

Milly blinked. She'd never heard JD talk about a girl like that before, and she wasn't sure she liked it. "'Hot ninja girl'?"

JD pointed over his shoulder. "It's what Zek calls her."

Zek shrugged. "She is hot."

They were getting off topic. "Right, anyway. She was here tonight. At the back of the crowd."

"Is that why you risked breaking your limbs, throwing yourself offstage?"

Milly thought this was a little ironic coming from Connor, who was always throwing himself off things.

"I spoke to her."

"Alone?" JD leaned back, looking both angry and worried. "She's dangerous, Milly."

"No, no she's not. She does what we do, only...differently. I know you guys are always telling me not to trust anyone. But I thought I could trust her, and then she told me not to trust Hideyoshi."

"Milly, you're babbling," JD said. "Why shouldn't we trust Hideyoshi?"

"I don't know for sure, but my gut says something isn't right."

"Okay then," JD said, as if no further explanation was needed. "Then we'll get to the bottom of it. Niv, did you already run the checks?"

Niv nodded.

"What checks?" Milly asked.

"Hospital records, cross-referencing Hideyoshi's name against any of our contacts, seeing if there was any sudden change in his character reported by friends," Zek said. "We wouldn't go on tour with someone without knowing everything about them."

I can look deeper, Niv signed. *But we risk him finding out.*

Milly paused. Maybe she was being paranoid. But who cared? "Do it," she said.

Niv opened his laptop, cracked his fingers and typed two words into DAD. Hideyoshi Makoto.

A processing bar ran, and Milly watched as the different databases that DAD had access to flickered across the screen. Police databases, government records, newspapers, university, health systems. There wasn't a firewall that DAD couldn't get its way around. A moment later, the screen was filled with pop-ups on all the information it had gathered. There was a lot of it. Niv began flicking. Son of a businessman, younger sister, both tragically orphaned. Youngest person to graduate from the University of Tokyo. First Class degrees in Artificial Intelligence and Robotics. A photo of him shaking hands with Nomura flicked past to be replaced with one of him at a science fair winning an award. He looked younger, maybe just out of university, fresh-faced and excited, but even more shy than he was now.

"Keep going," Milly said.

More photos appeared. One was from Hideyoshi's social media account and showed him with a girl. They were both smiling at the camera. The translated caption read: *UTokyo Graduation Day with Kotomi*. Milly held the photo Aneki had left up and compared them. It was the same girl; Milly was sure of it. So now Aneki's best friend had a name. Kotomi.

Milly stared at the girl. There was something so familiar about her, and yet she couldn't quite place it. She wracked her brains and then it hit her. "It's her!"

"Her who?" Zek asked.

"The girl who chased me through the train."

"Ichi the hologirl?" Connor said. "How can you tell? She wears a fox mask."

"Not always, she doesn't." Milly took Niv's computer off him and flipped back through the files until she had found the picture of Hideyoshi in the newspaper receiving his award. She dragged her fingers across the screen, zooming in on a spot behind Hideyoshi's head. There, behind him, hovered a hologram girl. She held up the photo next to the hologram. She was certain. Kotomi and Ichi had the same face.

"So, Hideyoshi modelled Ichi on a girl he went to university with. A bit creepy, sure, but nothing necessarily evil," Zek said.

Milly paced up and down. They were so close, she knew it. Her gut that something was very wrong. "Can you do a search for Kotomi?"

No problem, Niv signed, before doing a search. There were a few Kotomis who had been to the University of Tokyo, but only one who had been in the same year as Hideyoshi. More information, more photos. Milly's head was already spinning with the effort of trying to focus. And then an article popped up. "Stop!"

Brilliant young woman recovers from mysterious coma.

The photo that accompanied the article showed a girl lying in a hospital bed, smiling a cold, satisfied smile. But even with the wires and a cannula it was clear that it was the same girl.

"A coma?" Milly said.

JD rubbed the back of his head. "Who else have we seen in comas recently?"

Milly was confused for a moment and then it clicked. "The demon in Uji! The schoolgirls! That's what Aneki meant with the cup… Of course, why didn't I realize it? They were empty vessels."

"Milly, this whole private revelation thing is loads of fun to watch, seriously, but do you think you could bring the rest of us up to speed?" Zek said.

"The demons have been possessing humans whose souls were already gone. It's why when Aneki sucked the demon spirit out of the girls, they were still alive but in comas."

"Is that possible?" JD asked. "To live without your soul?"

"Sure," Connor said, and they all looked to him. "There are load of Japanese myths that mention souls leaving the body of a living person to go haunt other people or places. I guess what we might call an out-of-body type affair. In the Endo period, there was even a disease they called *Kage No Yamai* – the shadow illness – when people's souls were sucked out of their bodies and went off to cause trouble. And while they did, the person was left in a coma."

Milly stared at Connor, amazed and impressed.

"Okay, putting aside the fact that Connor has turned into some sort of super-nerd, let me get this straight," Zek said.

"Demons are possessing girls whose souls have already been taken?"

"Yes," Milly said.

"And hot ninja girl—"

"Her name is Aneki."

"Okay, this Aneki... She can suck the demons out, leaving the bodies behind. Only they're in a coma?"

"Pretty much."

So that leaves one question, Niv said.

"I know," Milly said. "Where did their souls go? I asked Aneki that and she said..." Milly glanced at the image of Hideyoshi and his first hologirl. "No."

JD followed her line of sight. "You're not thinking? He couldn't. Unless... Could he?"

"Are you really suggesting Hideyoshi is stealing souls and passing them off as holograms?" Zek said. "That's not possible, is it?"

"I don't know," Connor said. "It kind of makes sense."

"It does?"

"I mean, *Ikiryō* means 'living ghost' after all."

"What?" Milly and JD said together.

"*Ikiryō,*" Connor said again, as if he'd said the most obvious thing in the world. "Am I the only one who read the book on Japanese myths Gail gave us?"

Milly hadn't done the reading and, looking at the guilty expressions of the others, she wasn't the only one.

"Well, Japanese mythology makes a distinction between a *shiryō* – the ghost of a dead person – and *ikiryō* – which is more like a wandering spirit, like when the person is still living."

"*Ikiryō*," JD said. "How did I miss it? It was right there all the time."

"Don't beat yourself up, Jay," Connor said. "I knew what the word meant and I didn't think they were *actually* ghosts."

"The auditions," Milly said. "That's what he's been doing. Finding girls and then 'copying' them." She made quotation marks around the word.

"But wouldn't people realize what was going on?" Zek said. "Girls going for auditions and then suddenly going into comas? It's hardly subtle."

Milly stopped. "Not if they were still walking around."

"With a demon inside them," JD said.

They all looked from one to the other. Could it be true? Was Hideyoshi really stealing girls' souls and then putting demons in their bodies to help cover it up?

We need to be sure, Niv signed, hitting his left palm with the edge of his right one.

"Yeah, we can't confront Hideyoshi until we are one hundred per cent certain," Zek said.

JD picked up one of their weapon bags and threw it to Zek. "Then it's about time we found out just how much our girl in black knows."

Don't say no

Tom and Hideyoshi were welcomed into the restaurant by a woman wearing a stunning blue kimono. She bowed and directed them in. Hideyoshi let Tom go first and as he walked in he couldn't believe what he was seeing. Overhead was a large glass arch filled with brilliant blue water the same colour as the woman's dress. In the water swam three women with neon-blue fish tails. They waved at Tom as he walked underneath them and if it wasn't for the tiny breathing devices he spotted, he might have believed them to be actual mermaids.

He caught the glinting of metal out of the corner of his eye and saw two chefs throwing large knives around and bringing them down in quick movements onto the fish they were preparing. Like the maître d' and the mermaids, they too were wearing electric blue. Their hands blurred as they worked, but there was something unusual about them. Tom squinted, trying to work it out, and he noticed their eyes were pure white.

"They're blind?" he said, marvelling at how they were throwing the razor-sharp blades around at high speed.

Hideyoshi nodded. "They use their other senses to create the dishes."

Tom had been so distracted by the mermaids and the blind chefs, he hadn't noticed that there wasn't a single guest in the restaurant.

"I thought you said this was the best restaurant in Japan," Tom said.

"It is."

"So how come no one is here?"

"Because I booked out the whole restaurant."

Tom couldn't begin to imagine how much that must have cost.

"Nomura doesn't like to be disturbed when talking business."

Tom saw a man sitting at the only occupied table in the whole restaurant. His strands of black hair were dragged across his wrinkled head like a barcode, and he wore a suit the same purple as his eyes. He smiled, revealing bleached teeth. There was something familiar about that smile.

"Mr Wills!" Nomura stood and threw his arms wide, as if welcoming Tom onto his chat show. Next to him, still seated, was Kotomi, Hideyoshi's university "friend". She was talking on the phone and seemed deeply unimpressed by his presence.

"Please." Nomura gestured to an empty seat. "Join us."

Tom sat down at the table and Hideyoshi joined him.

For a while, there was nothing but the sounds of the chef's knives and the bubbling of the water overhead.

"So, Mr Wills, it is a pleasure to meet you again."

"You too," Tom said, before adding "I guess" under his breath. Nomura's smile belonged in the tank overhead, with the fishes.

"And how is being on tour with *Ikiryō*?"

"It's a lot of fun. They're incredible," Tom replied genuinely.

"Yes. I made them, you know? When I met with Hideyoshi and saw the potential in his...project, I knew that he was on to something quite extraordinary."

"Well, they are that," Tom said, fiddling with the chopsticks in front of him. They were carved from a bright blue stone.

"But I think they can be even bigger still – isn't that right, Hideyoshi?"

Tom was wondering where this was going.

"With Tom's help they could be," Hideyoshi said.

"My help?" Tom said. He was starting to feel uncomfortable under the staring eyes of the women above him and the intense gaze of the man in front of him. Kotomi still hadn't stopped talking on the phone. "I don't know what you mean."

Before either man could answer, the woman in the blue kimono arrived at the table and began placing small dishes of unidentifiable food in front of them.

"*Ikiryō* are spectacular, but their music is…"

"Weak," Nomura said, popping a piece of sliced fish into his mouth. "Empty-headed pop nonsense."

Tom poked at a tentacle on one of the plates. It wiggled. He shuddered and instead turned his attention to a safe looking square of white fish. He tried twice to pick it up with his chopsticks but it kept slipping through. Before he could try a third time, the kimono woman appeared with a traditional knife and fork and placed them next to him without saying a word.

"We heard your new sound tonight. We would like something like that for *Ikiryō*."

"Are you suggesting a collaboration with Slay?" He stabbed the fish with his fork and placed it in his mouth.

"No, we're suggesting that you leave Slay and join *Ikiryō*. As our producer," Hideyoshi said.

Tom coughed on the mouthful of fish.

"But…I mean, I can't leave Slay."

"Why not?" Nomura said. "It doesn't seem to me as if they have a place for you any more, now that Milo Tan has joined the band."

"I… It's not like that."

"Isn't it?"

"With us, you will have total creative control," Hideyoshi said.

"You won't have to share the spotlight with anyone. Apart from a bunch of hologirls!" Nomura laughed – a forced, pained laugh.

Tom put down his fork and dabbed at his mouth with the corner of a bright-blue napkin. What troubled him even more than this whole weird set-up was the fact that he was seriously considering their offer. Ever since Mexico, ever since he'd stood alone on the top of a temple and tasted pure, unadulterated power, he'd been fighting back the dark impulse that haunted his dreams. That had made him withdraw from the others. The desire for fame that was his alone.

It's what he'd tried to tell Milly back in the hospital, and why he'd asked her to take his place. He wanted it so badly he could feel it eating away at him. And here these two men were, offering him everything he wanted. He'd never been ambitious in the past. But since Mexico he'd had an alien-longing to be in the spotlight. To have all the fame for himself. And he didn't like it.

"I can't," he said at last.

"If it's an issue of money," Nomura said, "I can assure you that won't be a problem."

"It's not money. Slay is more than just a band. It's my family."

"I think we both know that families don't always have your best interests at heart, Tom-san," Hideyoshi said.

"Slay does," Tom said.

"Are you trying to convince us," Nomura asked, "or yourself?"

Tom didn't have an answer for that. He stared down at his cutlery, watching the reflection of the restaurant bend in the blade of his knife as he moved it back and forth. He couldn't possibly be considering this, could he?

Something flashed in the knife's mirrored surface and he moved the blade back a fraction to catch it again. He saw Hideyoshi, the mermaids swimming overhead, and Nomura. There was something very wrong with the old man's reflection. It kept twitching and spasming as if Nomura was fighting to keep control of something. And yet, when Tom looked up at the man's face for real, it was perfectly calm.

Tom dropped his knife and it clattered to the floor.

"Is everything okay? Has the food disagreed with you?" Nomura asked, his purple eyes fixed on Tom.

What was behind those purple contacts? What was Nomura hiding? Tom couldn't believe he hadn't seen it before. Too late for guilt, he had to do something.

Rule number one, Gail's voice came back to him. *Never go up against a demon alone.*

Trying to take on a demon alone was the quickest way to get yourself killed. He had no idea how powerful this demon might be. All Tom knew was that he had to get out of there and find the rest of Slay. And fast.

He stood up. "I…um, I have to leave."

Hideyoshi stood up, and Tom suddenly realized how much taller the young man was than him. "Nomura-san is not a man you insult." An angry snarl twisted the man's usually smooth and handsome features.

Hideyoshi might be an innocent victim under this demon's thrall, or he might be a willing minion. Hadn't Hideyoshi said that he owed everything to Nomura? Maybe that even included his soul?

Tom backed away, knocking his chair over.

"Oh, good," Kotomi said, putting her phone down at last. She slipped off her heart-shaped sunglasses, revealing completely black eyes. "We can all stop pretending. It was so boring."

Tom looked from Nomura to Kotomi. Two demons. And maybe more waiting. He was unarmed and outnumbered.

"I had hoped we could all stay friends." Nomura leaned his head back and plucked at his eyeballs, tugging out a set of purple contact lenses. When he looked back at Tom, his black eyes shone like oil. "But it seems we're going to have to be a little more persuasive."

You called

"Any word from Tom?" JD asked.

Milly checked her phone for the fifth time since leaving the train. "Nothing." His phone wasn't showing up on the tracker either and Milly was starting to seriously freak out. It was nearly midnight and it had been three hours since she'd heard from him.

"We'll find him," JD said, but Milly could tell that he was just as worried as she was. Only he was better at hiding it.

We don't know he is dangerous, signed Niv, tapping the edge of his right palm against his forehead as if saluting, brow furrowed, before raising his palms in question.

"If Hideyoshi had wanted to hurt Tom, he'd have done it by now," Zek said, wrapping an arm around Milly and giving her a reassuring squeeze.

"Sure, like, he's had loads of opportunity. He could have just turned Tom's cyber-hand against him at any time, with the push of a button," Connor said, miming choking himself with his own hand.

"Not helping, Con," Milly said.

"Tom will be okay," JD said. "We have to focus on the job. We need more information."

Milly put her phone away and looked at the run-down building they were waiting outside. In the flickering street lights she could see the windows that weren't smashed were boarded up, and there were piles of rubbish and scraps of wood blocking the door.

"You're sure this is the place?" Zek asked.

Milly had texted the number on Aneki's business card, asking to meet. A reply had come a moment later, giving them this address. "This is where she said."

"And it couldn't have waited till the morning?" Connor asked. "I'm knackered."

"No, Con, saving our friend couldn't wait," Milly snapped.

"I was only joking," Connor said, his face flushing and Milly felt a pang of guilt. Snapping at Connor was like shouting at a puppy.

Where was the girl? Milly wanted to know. Would she even turn up? The tightness in Milly's chest clenched.

"I didn't expect all of you." Aneki stepped out of the shadows. *How long had she been there?* Milly wondered. How much had she heard?

238

"We try not to meet with armed girls in dark places alone," Zek said. "Kind of a rule of ours."

The girl seemed to find this amusing. "Come." She gestured with her head towards the building, and they all followed. She pushed a plank of wood aside to reveal a door. The door itself was covered in graffiti and some stains Milly didn't want to think about. Aneki opened it with a key and stepped aside, letting them go in first.

The room was dark and large enough that the far walls were swallowed in shadows. Weak light cut through the holes in the windows, creating spotlights on the concrete floor. It smelled of rubber and damp. "What is this place?" Milly asked.

"It was my old gym," Aneki said, flicking a switch on the wall. Lights slammed on, row after row. The room must have been at least ten metres by ten metres. At the back, there was a set of asymmetric bars over a faded blue crash mat, a row of climbing ropes and a pommel horse. "I was training to compete as a gymnast in the Olympics when my parents died. Now I use it for a different kind of training."

Milly spotted a large hunk of wood covered in cuts and holes from blades.

"It's...lovely," Zek said, stepping over a rolled futon mattress lying in the centre of the open room.

To the side, there was a table with a box serving as a chair, and three computer monitors. Abandoned noodle cups lay scattered across the table. Niv wandered over to the set-up and hit the space bar on the keyboard. The screens came to life and Milly glimpsed various photos of Hideyoshi before Aneki pushed Niv out of the way and hit a sleep button. "Do not touch my stuff."

Sorry, Niv signed.

"So, you've discovered *Ikiryō*'s secret?"

"They're not holograms," Milly said.

Aneki clapped her hands together in an ironic round of applause. "Took you long enough. And are you going to help me stop him?"

"First, we have some questions for you," JD said.

Aneki leaned back on her desk and considered JD. She nodded.

"The demons. How did you banish them?"

"It's not banishing."

"Then what is it?"

Aneki walked over to the makeshift nest that she'd made and threw a blanket to the side, revealing a black bag. She pulled out a cream-coloured box covered in the most intricate carvings inlaid with gold. The thought of the craftsmanship involved in making something so delicate, so precise, made Milly's head hurt. "What is it?"

"We call it the *Yurei Bako*. The spirit box. It's been in my family for generations upon generations. Legend says it was created by a dark magician who would use it to summon *oni*."

"*Oni* are demons, right?" Connor said.

"Yes. He would summon the *oni* and then trap them so that he could harness their power for himself."

"Like a genie in a bottle," Zek said. And Milly caught a cold look pass between Zek and his brother.

"Exactly. The box was given to my family to stop it getting into the wrong hands."

"How does it work?"

Aneki ran a finger around the patterns. "It's a puzzle box with ten different compartments. It took me years to find all the compartments. If you open it within a few metres of an untethered demon, it will suck their spirit inside. Then you have to close it before they can escape."

"Untethered?" JD asked.

"When it has not attached itself to a human soul."

"So, that box has demons inside it?" Connor moved away nervously.

"Five."

"The Uji bridge demon and the four who were in the schoolgirls," Milly said.

"And while the demons are in there," JD said, pointing to the box, "Hideyoshi still has the human souls."

"Eight of them. Kotomi was the first to go through his 'copying process'. I don't think he really knew what he was doing at first. She was in a coma for months. When she came back, I thought everything would be okay. But then,

I realized: it wasn't Kotomi any more."

"Her body had been possessed by a demon?" Milly asked.

The girl nodded. "While her soul was trapped by Hideyoshi and made to perform in his stupid band. He called it Ichi. Number one. Then he started collecting more. Ni, San, Shi, Go, Roku, Nana and Hachi."

"Two, three, four, five, six, seven and eight," Connor translated. "He didn't even bother giving them names. Only numbers."

"Do you think they might try to escape?" Milly asked.

"What do you mean?"

"Ichi, I saw her on the train. At first I thought she was trying to attack me, but I think she was asking for help. And the light that nearly fell on Hideyoshi, I think it might have been her then too."

"That sounds like Kotomi. She would try and do everything she could to break free from Hideyoshi."

Niv pointed to his eyes and then the box.

Aneki looked him up and down, suspiciously. "As long as you are extremely careful. If the *oni* escape we can't trap them again."

Niv picked it up and delicately moved it around, looking at the inlay work. With one hand holding the box, he used his other hand to sign, moving his upright fingers as if waving at someone behind him. *Hideyoshi's is similar.*

"It is?" Milly said.

"What did he say?" Aneki said.

"That Hideyoshi has a similar box." Milly remembered the sleek black box she'd seen Hideyoshi place in the middle of the stage the night IKIR10 had performed on Nomura's chat show. It did look similar, now she thought about it. Like a black glass, high-tech version of Aneki's ivory box. But instead of gold patterns, Hideyoshi's box had glowing blue lights.

The girl laughed, a snort of air through her nose. "Hideyoshi has a *replica*." The word "replica" was dripping with scorn, the way someone might describe a fake copy of a beautiful work of art. "He was obsessed with that box growing up. He'd spend hours and hours trying to find all the secret compartments. After our parents died—"

"Wait," Milly said. "*Your* parents? Hideyoshi is…your brother?"

"Was that not clear?"

"Um, no," said Milly.

"Well, he is. My big brother." She made that same snorting laugh again.

Milly tried to process this. "And yet you're trying to stop him?"

"It's my duty. My family are supposed to protect the world from evil. And yet, Hideyoshi…" She looked down, unable to go on.

"What happened to him?" Connor asked.

"The death of our parents broke him. But it wasn't until the will was read that I started to see just how much. The box should have gone to him as the eldest, and yet it was left to me. I don't know why my parents didn't trust him. Maybe they saw the darkness in him that I had never seen. But the day I was given the box, I'd never seen Hideyoshi so angry. He demanded I give the box to him. I refused. One day, he threatened to smash it to pieces if I wouldn't give it to him – that if he couldn't have it, no one could. I told him to smash it. There was this terrible moment where I thought he would actually do it. But instead, he put the box back in its case and left home. We haven't spoken since."

"So he made a copy from memory?" Zek said.

Aneki nodded, and laid her hand on the box, her delicate fingers tracing the golden patterns.

"This box is a thousand years old, made by craftsmen whose skill was unparalleled even then and no longer exists. It is the only one of its kind in existence. Hideyoshi's copy is a marvel of modern technology and an abomination. Instead of trapping *oni*, his box traps human souls and makes him their master."

"So that's how he's turning the girls into holograms," JD said.

"And while he has their souls, their bodies are being possessed by demons," Milly said. "So they're still walking around and no one realizes that the girls have been taken."

"Until Aneki sucks the demons out and they go into a coma," Zek said.

"A body left without a soul," Milly said.

"It's the darkest, deepest perversion of everything the Makato family stand for. We fought demons, protected people from them. Hideyoshi is…making deals with them." She spat on the floor.

"The one bit I'm not getting here," Zek said, "and I realize this is going to sound peculiar coming from *us*, but why the girl band? If you're able to trap souls, why bother showing them off to the world? It's pretty high risk that someone might notice."

"I just put it down to Hideyoshi's arrogance," Aneki said.

Milly wasn't sure. "What if it works like a normal summoning?" she said. "That the person has to make the agreement to lose their soul?"

"Why would anyone agree to that?" Aneki said.

"You'd be surprised," Zek said. "Money. Power."

"Fame," Milly said, as the final piece slotted into place.

"The auditions," JD said. "Tom said hundreds of girls came forward, wanting to be part of *Ikiryō*."

"Willing volunteers," Milly said. "Happily signing their souls away. Literally."

"And they probably have no idea what they're really signing up to," Connor said.

"Does anyone who makes a deal with a demon?" JD said.

Niv tilted his head and signed three letters.

"NPA?" Connor said, doing his best to follow Niv's signing.

"NDA," Milly corrected. "That's a good point. The girls don't get fame – they sign contracts saying they have to keep their involvement secret."

"Money and power then. I've known people to do more for less," JD said.

"So, what's the plan?" Connor said.

"Destroy the box. Free the souls. Stop my brother."

"Simple," Zek said. "I like it."

"I'll call Gail," JD said. He dialled and held out his phone, putting it on speaker. It took a while for the phone to connect. When it did, all they could hear was the rushing of wind and screaming.

"Tom!" They could just about hear Gail's voice shouting over the line. "You've got to save Tom!"

There was another screech, which turned Milly's blood cold, and the line went dead.

We meet again

Tom was back on top of the pyramid, staring up at a purple sky, his arms outstretched, calling to the lightning. It was his to control. The whole world was his to control. He only had to say the word, and all the power would be his. Below, at the base of the temple, humans were bent and cowering, kneeling before their living god. He smelled the copper tang of blood and looked to his left to see a body on an altar. A sacrifice offered up to him. The strength of this young warrior was his to take.

Lightning struck again, and this time he felt pain in his face. Once more, a sharp hot pain ringing across his cheek. And suddenly the pyramid was gone and he was staring up at a curved white roof.

"Hit him again," a man's voice said, and Tom recognized the drawl.

"No need. He is awake." This was Hideyoshi.

Tom went to sit up and realized he was bound. Straps across his chest, arms and ankles pinned him to a large reclined chair that looked like something you might get in a dentist, if that dentist happened to be on a spaceship. He strained against the straps, but they cut into his skin.

He managed to raise his head, and saw three people in the lab. Hideyoshi, who stood to his right, Kotomi to his left, currently examining her fingernails, and sitting on a stool in front of him was Nomura. The man smiled. "Didn't I tell you that I always get what I want?"

"I have to say," Tom said, looking at the bindings, "you do drive a hard bargain. But I think I'm going to have to talk to my manager about some of the conditions."

Nomura laughed, clapping his liver-spotted hands together. He'd changed out of his purple suit into a sharp silver one, and the strands of black hair he'd dragged across his nearly bald head were now cut short and smart. "Funny! Isn't he funny? I like that. The human spirit, fighting back. It makes a refreshing change." His accent had changed too: now it had an American twang. "Don't get me wrong, I like the screaming and the sobbing and the begging to live. But after five hundred centuries, it can become a weensy bit tiresome."

Five hundred centuries, Tom thought, closing his eyes. It was bad enough he hadn't spotted what Hideyoshi was up to, but to have had dinner with this man and not realize he was a demon was beyond stupid. Just wait till the others found out – he wouldn't hear the end of it. Assuming, that was, he lived to tell them.

"I have to give you credit," Tom said. "You hide the fact you are a black-souled dirtbag pretty well."

"Well," Nomura said, brushing his hand across his newly shorn head. "I have had a fair amount of practice. And it's easier to hide in plain sight. The eyes won't see what they don't want to see, and you, my little pop princeling, were so easy to fool."

Tom glanced at Hideyoshi – who turned away, pretending to stare at his computer tablet, but Tom knew it was just because the man didn't have the guts to meet his eye.

"It was almost too easy," Nomura continued. "When I heard that you'd run into Kotomi and our newest recruit in Osaka, I was sure you'd work it out. But I hadn't counted on quite how stupid you are. Lucky for me that Hideyoshi's sister has been running around causing problems, or this whole project could have been quite dull."

"His sister?" Tom said.

"I think you met her. Dresses in black. Likes knives. Keeps sucking my demons out of their bodies and trapping them in her dumb ivory box. When I get my hands on her, I swear—" He mimed wrapping his hands around something and squeezing and shaking. The fit of rage passed and he ran his hand over his hair to smooth it back in place. "Where was I?"

"You were going to let me go," Tom said.

"Funny. No, I couldn't do that. Not when I still have a need for you." Nomura grabbed the chair Tom was strapped to and spun it around, so it faced a screen. "We thought you might want to have a look at what's to come."

The screen flickered to life. It showed Hideyoshi's lab from the angle of a camera positioned above the door. Tom saw the same chair he was strapped to, and sitting in it was a young girl who couldn't be much older than fifteen or sixteen. She jiggled in the chair, nervous with excitement.

"Meet Kyu," Nomura said. "Number nine."

Tom realized what he was watching: this must be the transfer process that Hideyoshi had spoken of. His top-secret means of creating his holograms. Kyu was the ninth member of IKIR10.

He sensed he was about to witness something terrible, and yet he couldn't take his eyes off the screen. He watched as Hideyoshi gently placed straps around the girl's wrists, ankles and chest and then placed a rubber skullcap over her dark hair. This was the same cap Hideyoshi had originally used to help Tom control the hand, before he'd upgraded the brain control to the small silver device now tucked behind Tom's ear.

Sitting next to the chair was the black box. On screen it looked even darker, even as the blue lights pulsed on and off. Wires trailed out of it and snaked across the floor and back up again, connecting to the skullcap.

There was no sound on the video, but Tom saw Hideyoshi speaking to the girl. She nodded enthusiastically in return. Another gentle question from Hideyoshi, and the girl nodded even more eagerly. Hideyoshi raised his hand and laid it on the black box. With his other hand, he pressed a button on the computer.

And that's when she started screaming. The fact Tom couldn't hear her made it somehow worse. The girl's body started to thrash in the chair, her slim limbs slapping against the soft leather covering.

"Stop it!" he shouted, even though he knew he was watching something that had already taken place. He closed his eyes, unable to watch any more, tears falling down his cheeks.

"Oh, no," Nomura said, pulling Tom's eyelids open. "You're missing the best bit."

Forced to look at the screen, Tom saw the girl was still now, her eyes open and staring ahead. Next to her was a glowing blue figure, who was like her in every respect. The figure looked around, panicked, and opened her mouth ready to scream again. Hideyoshi pressed a button on his computer and the glowing girl's mouth slammed shut. Another press of a key and the glowing figure stiffened her arms tight against her sides, her head jolting to the centre. But her eyes were still moving, darting wildly left and right.

Hideyoshi walked out from behind the console holding a small computer tablet, and started walking around the figure, completely ignoring the body lying limp on the chair. He looked her up and down, consulted his tablet, and pushed a button. Her clothes changed from jeans and jumper to a long white dress. One more push and a white fox mask appeared over her pretty, soft face. It had a single red line running from forehead to chin and three stripes on each cheek. Hideyoshi seemed pleased with his selection. The transformation was complete. IKIR10 had its latest member.

The screen went black.

"Impressive, isn't it?"

"You're sick!" Tom spat. "All of you. How could you do that to an innocent girl?"

"He's so annoying," Kotomi said with a sigh. "Can't we just kill him?"

"But I need him alive so I can add him to my collection." Nomura turned to face the others. "The tenth soul. The final piece. And gathering it from a demon-slayer slash pop star? Well, that's just the cherry on the top! So, will you do the honours and get a demon lined up, to pop in when he's popped out?"

Kotomi rolled her eyes, as if she'd been asked to take the rubbish out. She walked over to Tom and started to stroke his skin, dragging a long fingernail across his arms, and around his neck. She took hold of his T-shirt and tore it in two, and continued her examination of his chest.

"No marks," she said finally.

The tattoo, Tom realized. He didn't have any mark protecting him from possession. He'd been so stupid avoiding having it redone. And now it was too late. Kotomi pulled a small blade out of her pocket. She lay the blade against his neck.

"I said alive, thank you very much."

Kotomi sighed again and moved the blade to Tom's bare left arm. She pressed down, smiling as the knife cut deeply into his skin. He clenched his jaw, not wanting to give her the satisfaction of hearing him cry out in pain. Blood poured freely from Tom's arm and Kotomi looked around for something to catch it in. She settled on a crumpled coffee cup, holding it under his arm until it was a quarter filled with his blood. She dipped a finger in the cup, then sucked her finger clean. "Yummy."

She spun on her gold trainers and went to a corner of the carriage. Tom twisted around to watch her as she began drawing symbols on the white walls using his blood. A summoning ritual. They were going to bring across a demon to take over his body.

Nomura and Hideyoshi were also watching as Kotomi slowly drew the complex symbols needed for a summoning. While their backs were turned to him, Tom looked around for something, anything he could use to get out of here. The carriage was bare except for the chair he was strapped into, a small tray table to his right and Hideyoshi's worktable to his left. Sharp metal tools were lined up in a neat row on the table, any one of which could cause some serious damage if Tom could get his hands on them. But the worktable was too far away. He turned to the tray table and saw a clipboard and a pen with the contract that the girl had signed before Hideyoshi had stolen her soul. The pen had a shining silver clip. If Tom could just get to that, he might be able to use it to pick the clasp holding him in place. With Nomura and Kotomi concentrating on the summoning ritual and Hideyoshi refusing to look at him, this could be his chance. He focused on making his robotic fingers move just a fraction. If he could just get to the pen, if he could just—

"Uh-uh," Nomura said, yanking the tray away and then wagging his finger. "Naughty, naughty. In fact, why don't we just take that away?" He undid the harness attaching Tom's robotic hand and tossed it down on the worktable next to the tangles of wires and the black box. "After all, the last time I let you anywhere near me with a sharp object it was most inconvenient."

"The last time?" Tom said, wondering what the demon was on about.

"Oh, you really are so very stupid. It's rather adorable."

254

And then everything made sense. Tom had met this demon before – only that time, he had been in a different body. The body of a middle-aged white man with a terrible taste in suits. Hadn't Gail said he might be more powerful than they gave him credit for?

"Mourdant?"

"Ta-dah!" the demon said. He threw his arms wide as if he'd just walked out onstage. "It is me!"

"I thought you were…"

"Dead? Banished? Sorry to disappoint you, but all you did was kill my host. Luckily, Nomura here," he indicated his body, "was in the museum in Chicago to do some tedious interview or other, and his hunger – for fame and fortune, and anything but another dreary interview with dreary academics – called out to me. A small whisper in his ear, a gentle nudge towards a certain ancient book which happened to be on display in the medieval section, and hey presto, I had myself a new body. I had business interests in Japan already, so it was convenient. It's a little old and decrepit, but I did what I could with it."

"The next time I kill you," Tom said, "I'll make sure you stay dead."

"The next time? Ho ho!" Mourdant wagged his finger at Tom. "You are a cheeky one. And if I'm not very much mistaken, your friends have just arrived."

Hideyoshi turned on a screen. It was showing a feed

255

from outside the train. JD, Milly and the others were there. Tom felt a rush of excitement at seeing his friends. "You are in for it now, Mourdant!"

"Oh ho," Mourdant said. "You think so, do you? Well, I'm afraid I will have something waiting for them. Hideyoshi, whenever you're ready."

Hideyoshi picked up the black box and held it in both hands, twisting and sliding panel after panel until nine transparent girls stood in a line, facing the door.

"If your friends make it this far," Mourdant said with a wave of his liver-spotted hand, "they will die. Oh, won't this be fun? If only I had popcorn."

I can't lose you

The train was still waiting in the station when they finally made it there. The lights were off in every carriage apart from Hideyoshi's quarters at the nose end. Milly raced out of the car and started towards the front.

JD grabbed her by the shoulder, spinning her around. "We can't just charge in there."

"Why not?" Milly said. Anxiety for Tom twisted in her chest and she found she could hardly breathe.

"Yeah," Connor said, "why not?"

Aneki looked like she was itching for a fight too. Her whip chain twitched in her hand.

"This is Hideyoshi's home," JD said, pointing at the train. "If we go charging in there, weapons waving, he'll lock it down. He doesn't know that we know yet. We've got a better chance of getting Tom out safe if we play along. It's what Gail would do."

At the mention of Gail, Milly felt the weight of fear turn in her stomach. They'd no idea where Gail was or what had happened to her. They were utterly helpless to do anything for her. But Tom was a different matter. It wasn't too late to help him.

"Okay," Milly said. "But as soon as I lay eyes on Hideyoshi, he's getting an arrow in the neck."

"Not if I get to him first," Aneki said.

Weapons away, they approached the train. The doors hissed as they approached and the blue lights flickered on.

"Welcome back, Slay," Kitsune's voice said. "We will be departing in three minutes."

"Where is Tom?" Milly said.

"He is with Hideyoshi-san and two more guests in his quarters."

Milly and JD shared a look and they started walking towards the front of the train. When they arrived at the doors to Hideyoshi's lab, they were locked.

"Open them," JD demanded.

"I'm sorry, these are Hideyoshi-san's private quarters. They are not to be opened by anyone apart from Hideyoshi-san. We will be departing in one minute."

"They opened for me two nights ago," Milly said.

"That's not possible. The only situation when I would allow anyone else to open these doors is in an emergency."

"This is an emergency," JD said.

"Please state the nature of the situation."

"Um… The train is on fire?" Connor tried.

"My systems tell me that there are no fires on board. I am sorry. Have a pleasant journey."

The train juddered a fraction as they started to move. Milly glanced out of the window to see the station outside become a blur as the train quickly reached its top speed.

"Where are we going?" Connor asked.

"It doesn't matter," Milly said. "The only thing that matters is getting Tom."

Milly started tugging on the door, but it wasn't budging.

"Hey, Kitsune," Zek said.

"Hey, Zek."

"You and me, we have an understanding."

"I do understand you, Zek, yes."

"So will you open the doors, just for me?"

"I can't do that, Zek."

"If you don't open these doors right now," Milly said, "I am going to find your motherboard and…and…" Milly didn't know if Kitsune even had a motherboard or what damage she could do to it. "And, well, I'll break it," she finished lamely.

Niv pulled out his screwdriver and tried to lever off one of the panels. As soon as he touched the wall, there was a fizzing sound and Niv went stiff, shaking, a golden bolt of electricity twisting up his arm.

Connor went to pull Niv away.

"No!" Zek shouted. "Don't touch him!" Zek looked around.

"What?" Milly said desperately. "What do you need?"

Zek closed his eyes, as if listening to something. "Wood. Something wooden." His eyes snapped open. "There." He yanked a large framed picture off the wall and smashed it over his knee, then used the broken wood to knock the screwdriver out of Niv's hand. The connection broken, Niv collapsed to the floor, pale and shivering. It had only been a matter of seconds, but to Milly it had felt like it had been hours watching Niv convulsing in pain.

"How did you know that?" Connor asked. "About the wood?"

"I didn't," Zek said. "He did." He rested his hand on his brother's forehead.

"Is he…?" Connor asked, his face pale and screwed up in fear.

"He's just unconscious," Zek said, letting out a long sigh.

Milly took a deep breath, relieved that her friend was all right. She looked back to the door. "Forget this." She picked the broken frame from the floor and ran at the door, smashing against it as hard as she could.

"Ah, I see the whole gang are here."

A voice echoed through hidden speakers. Milly stepped away from the door, looking up and down to try and find the source of the voice. She recognized something about that smug tone. But it wasn't possible…

"Where are you?" JD shouted.

A panel in the door slid open, providing a window into Hideyoshi's lab. Milly pressed her face against it to see Hideyoshi standing next to a young woman she recognized from the photo. Kotomi – the girl he had modelled his first hologirl on. Here she was, looking almost bored by everything that was going on.

"Hideyoshi!" Aneki shouted, banging on the door. "It's not too late to stop all this."

Hideyoshi looked up and stared straight at his sister. All his usual nervous energy was gone. He looked like a broken man. "Yes, it is, sister." He glanced over at the third figure in the room.

It was Nomura, the TV host. His aching smile was gone, as were his purple contacts. In their place were shining black eyes. Milly had a fleeting moment of self-congratulation that she'd been right about him.

"Where is Tom?" JD shouted.

Nomura stepped aside with a sweeping gesture, revealing a large white chair. Tom was strapped to it, his T-shirt torn open.

"Get ou—" Tom began to shout, before Kotomi slapped him around the face.

"Let him go or…or…" Milly struggled to put words to

what she was going to do to Nomura. Tom was just on the other side of the door, but it felt like he was a thousand miles away.

"Or what?" Nomura said, his voice crackling over the speakers.

"We'll kill you," JD said simply.

"Didn't work last time, did it?"

Last time? But they'd never so much as raised a finger against Nomura. And then the man smiled, and it was like looking at a shark. Now she understood. The whole time, it had been a trap. Revenge for what had started in Chicago. And they'd walked straight into it. "Mourdant."

"The one and only. Now if you wouldn't mind, Hideyoshi and I have work to do. I'm afraid you're going to have to leave."

"Not without our friend."

"Oh no, he is staying with us. Isn't that right, Thomas?" Mourdant laid a hand on Tom's head and pushed it up and down, making him nod, as if operating a toy. Tom snarled and tried to shake Nomura's hand away. "We think it's time that a boy joined *Ikiryō*. Anyway, it's been just great catching up. Must dash. Bye-ee!" He waved a hand and the window in the door was covered again.

Milly charged at the door again, smashing it again and again.

"Oh, Mills…" Connor tapped her on the shoulder.

She turned to see what had made his usually rosy cheeks go so pale.

Nine ghostly girls stood at the back of the carriage, long black hair covering their faces. In perfect unison, the girls looked up, their faces free of masks, their eyes empty. Each of them was beautiful in their own way, and each of them was terrifying.

"Kotomi!" Aneki said, taking a step towards the first hologirl. "Fight him!" Ichi raised a hand and shoved Aneki back, sending her flying off her feet and crashing into the wall.

Milly stepped back. If one of them had that kind of strength, what chance did they stand against nine?

"Line up," JD said, coming to stand on Milly's right. Connor dropped in on her left and Aneki dragged herself to her feet and stood next to him. Zek stood over the unconscious body of his brother, his sword ready. "Do you have any grenades, Connor?"

"I *always* have grenades." Connor slipped his hands into his pockets and pulled out two black canisters. One had a red top, the other was yellow. He flicked the safety off each.

IKIR10 took a step forward, staying in perfect formation.

"Now!" JD said.

Connor threw the first grenade, and their world exploded. Milly could hardly breathe. Yellow smoke filled the air and her eyes were streaming. The atomized salt was holding the trapped souls back: they hissed every time they came into contact with it. But it wasn't stopping them. As fast as Connor could throw the grenades, the train's filtration system was working to clear the air.

"Down to my last one," he said, throwing another canister, which exploded. When that cloud was gone, they'd have only their weapons to defend themselves. And yet, their silver weapons didn't seem to be having any lasting effect on the holograms. Milly let loose arrow after arrow, but they only managed to stop the hologirls for a moment. The figures would vanish as soon as the silver made contact and then reform a few seconds later.

Out of the corner of her eye, Milly saw Aneki's whip chain flying. It was proving a little more effective than her arrows in pushing IKIR10 back, but nothing seemed to be actually hurting them. How, Milly wondered, could you hurt something that didn't have a body? How could you fight something that wasn't even there?

The last of the sodium smoke cleared, and one of the girls launched herself at Connor, knocking him to the floor. Aneki flicked her whip, slicing through the air barely centimetres above Connor's head, and through the neck of the ghost who was attacking him. It disappeared with a screech, giving him time to scramble to his feet, but when it blinked back into existence, it looked even angrier than before.

JD spun round, slicing with his katana, while Zek got to

work with his scimitar, not moving from his brother. But it was like fighting smoke.

Milly was out of arrows. She pulled out her throwing knives, loading up her fingers as she'd been taught, but what good was any of it? They couldn't keep this up and soon IKIR10 would break through and they would be done for.

Ichi stood before Milly, her hand outstretched. Milly stepped back and back, until she was pressed up against one of the windows. She slashed out with her knife, and the girl blinked into nothing before reappearing even closer. Ichi pinned Milly's wrist to the wall and squeezed so tight that, with a cry of pain, she dropped her last knife. The ice-cold fingers burned her skin.

Blank eyes stared out of the girl's pale face and bored into Milly. Her movements were jerky, almost as if she was fighting against herself. Because she was, Milly realized. Hideyoshi had trapped these girls' souls and was controlling them somehow. But Ichi had broken free of that control before. First, when she'd caused the spotlight to fall, and again when she'd chased Milly down the train – she hadn't been trying to kill her, she'd been trying to get her to listen. And it looked as if she was trying to break free again.

"You have to fight him," Milly shouted. "I know you don't want to do this."

A hand wrapped around Milly's throat, so cold it burned. "*Tasukete.*"

"I'm trying to help you," Milly choked, as the freezing fingers tightened around her throat. She clawed at them, but it was like trying to grab hold of mist. How could something be so strong and so intangible at the same time? Lights started to dance at the edge of her sight: her brain was being deprived of oxygen. Darkness came in pulses, as if someone was turning the switches on and off. With each flash of light, Milly got a frozen glimpse of what was happening. JD slicing. Aneki spinning. Zek ducking.

Slay and IKIR10 were fighting to the death and IKIR10 were winning.

Milly's head pounded, and she knew that she had only seconds before she would black out. She fought to stay awake, to keep thinking. Blue lights sparkled at the corner of her eyes, reminding Milly of something. Something blue and black.

"Tasukete!" Ichi breathed. "Help me."

"Help this!" JD shouted.

From behind Ichi, a blade slashed, the tip passing so close to Milly's face that it nicked the corner of her eyebrow. Ichi vanished and Milly was now face-to-face with JD.

"We have to get out of here!" He grabbed Milly by her injured wrist and pulled her away, just as Ichi reappeared. "Fall back. Everyone fall back."

Connor picked Niv's limp body up and threw him over his shoulder, and ran, while Zek covered his retreat. They made it through the door into the next carriage. JD and Milly followed. Aneki was last through, her chain still whipping. But she needn't have bothered. IKIR10 weren't following. They simply watched them go.

The door closed and a loud clunk sounded as it locked. Milly peered through the window to see nine holograms flicker out of existence.

"No," Milly croaked through her crushed throat. She reached out for the door, hand trying to find the release button.

JD pulled her away. "They're too strong for us."

"I know" – she coughed – "I know how to stop them. It's the—"

Before she could finish, something shook the carriage and they were all thrown to the ground in a large tangled heap.

"What was that?" Zek said, pushing Connor off him.

Milly grabbed hold of the window and pulled herself to standing, then slammed her hand against the door release, ready to throw herself back into the fray. She knew what she had to do to stop IKIR10 and save Tom. They had to destroy Hideyoshi's box and free the souls of the trapped girls.

The door hissed open and Milly went to race forward. An arm wrapped around her waist and pulled her back; JD was dragging her away. Only then did she see that the door no longer led into a train carriage. It opened up on to the train tracks.

The back six coaches of the train had been decoupled, splitting the train in two. Had Milly taken one more step forward, she would have been crushed underneath the wheels.

They were still moving at incredible speed as the momentum of the train kept them going. But without the engine carriage to pull them on, they would slow and stop eventually. Milly watched as the distance between her and the front carriages grew. She tried to pull JD's arms away, but she knew that even if she was brave enough to jump, she'd never make it onto the other carriage now. With every second, the distance grew: two metres, six metres, eight metres…

She heard an ominous clatter and looked down at the tracks ahead. There was a junction point which had shifted, so while the front section had gone straight on, they were now turning to the left.

Milly turned away, burying her head into JD's chest. She couldn't watch as the front of the train sped away into the darkness, taking with it Hideyoshi, Mourdant and any hope she had of ever seeing Tom again.

A new order

With a flicker, all nine of the hologirls were back in the room. Hideyoshi, who had been cradling the black box in his arms, placed it back on his worktable next to Tom's robotic hand and, with dexterous fingers, slid the panels back into place. One by one, the spirit girls blinked out. Ichi was the last to vanish. She stared at Tom, her lips opening a fraction as if she was about to say something. And then she was gone. Back into the box. Back into the darkness.

"Well, now that they're taken care of, we can get back to business." Mourdant turned and grinned at Tom.

Tom roared, writhing against his bindings and trying to get out and help his friends. He couldn't see what had happened on the other side of the door, but he had heard explosions and screaming.

Mourdant completely ignored him and continued as if nothing had happened. "Where was I? Ah yes, offering you the once-in-a-lifetime opportunity to join *Ikiryō*." He pulled a sheet of folded paper out from inside his jacket, and with a flick of his hand, let it unroll. The word *Contract* was written on the top and at the bottom. Tom's full name had already been written on it too.

He twisted in the chair, pulling against the bindings that held him tight. "I'll never join you, ever!"

"Well then, here's my other offer." Mourdant held the contract up by the top corner and threw it over his shoulder. "Have your soul ripped out of your still-breathing body."

Tom went still for a moment.

"Yes, interesting, isn't it? You see, when us demons take possession of a human host, the soul doesn't go anywhere. It quickly withers till there's nothing of it left, and dies. And that's a waste. The Japanese concept for this is *ki* – life force – and they're pretty close to understanding it. The soul, you see, is energy. Pure energy. My research led me to believe that I could put that energy to use. But to do that, I needed to store it. How to do that? I wondered. And then I met Hideyoshi here. This was before I met you boys in Chicago, of course." He patted Tom's head with unnecessary force. "Hideyoshi had found a way to suck the soul out of a body and trap it. A combination of an ancient ritual and modern technology." Mourdant strolled back and forth, hands clasped behind his back, as if he was delivering a talk at a conference rather than explaining how he was killing people. "When I first met him, he'd carried out the procedure on one young girl – a girl he was ridiculously in love with who 'just wanted to be friends'." He made air quotes around the phrase with his gnarled fingers. "Argh, isn't that just the worst? Hideyoshi was there for her, drove her everywhere she wanted, was a shoulder to cry on, but she never wanted more than that. I think you kids call it 'the friend zone'." Again with the air quotes.

"Only losers believe in the friend zone," Tom said.

Mourdant placed a hand over Tom's mouth. "Shush, you're ruining my story. Hideyoshi wanted them to be more than friends. So he came up with a plan. If he couldn't have the girl's heart, he would have her soul. He remembered his old family box and – *tappity tappity* on his computer – turned the words into ones and zeroes. A tweak here and there, and *bam!* Instead of trapping a demon, he was able to trap a human soul."

"It was a success. The girl was left in a coma, of course, but Hideyoshi had what he wanted. He even passed her off as a hologram and showed her off at his university. When I first laid my eyes on it, I knew what I was looking at. Not a hologram at all, but an *Ikiryō* – a lost soul. And if Hideyoshi could do it once, he could do it again, and again, and again. So I brought him under my employ and set him a test. Ten girls. Ten souls."

"What do you want with them?"

"Let me tell you a little story," Mourdant said, spinning a chair around and taking a seat. He placed his feet on the armrest of Tom's chair and leaned back, getting comfortable. "This world, this reality" – he waved his arms around – "it originally belonged to us demons…and then you humans came and spread like bacteria and banished us to the Netherworld. Have you ever been to the Netherworld? Well, it is beyond boring. An eternity of meh. For half a millennia, I've been working to put demons back in their proper place. Ruling over humans. I started small: the black plague. The Spanish Inquisition. Then I got bolder. My most recent plan was to bring across Tezcatlipoca, a demon god, no less, so that he alone could crush all of humanity."

The very mention of Tezcatlipoca sent a shockwave of electric pain through Tom's body.

Mourdant sprang forward in his chair, so his nose was a centimetre away from Tom's face. "You and your little friends put a stop to that one, didn't you? But I am not a demon who will be deterred. I had another plan already under way. A plan to tear a hole in this dimension and bring a whole dark army across from the Netherworld. But to do that, I will need power. Lots of power."

Tom had been using the time while Mourdant was waffling on to try and find a way out. The carriage they were in had two doors and five windows. Kotomi stood in front of the door to the left, but the one to the right was unguarded.

All he had to do was get out of the chair.

"Are you keeping up?" Mourdant tapped Tom on the forehead. "Yes? Good. I need power, energy, and it just so happens that souls are energy. When I saw Hideyoshi and his soul box, it came to me – if I could gather enough souls together and release the force of their energy in one go, pow! It would be like a nuclear soul bomb, blasting a great big hole in the fabric of reality!" He clapped his hands together, looking delighted with himself. "And of course, we couldn't do it in any old place, oh no, it had to be somewhere that the veil between this world and the Netherworld was already thin. So, we're on our way there now. We'll arrive soon, and then the fun and games will really begin!"

"How many souls do you need?" Tom asked, already knowing the answer.

Hideyoshi answered without looking up. "Without the power of the box, we would have needed hundreds, maybe thousands. But the box works like an amplifier, focusing and increasing the energy. I have calculated therefore that only ten souls are required to create the power we need."

"I already have nine, yours will make ten. I did try and ask nicely, but as you refused my offer, we will just have to tear your soul out of you by force. With the girls, I stuck to my usual ways – getting their permission first. Of course, they didn't know what they were giving permission for, but it's not my fault if they didn't read their contracts. But for you, well, you already gave permission to one demon, so we won't need it. And don't worry – once we suck your soul out, we'll find a nice, particularly twisted demon to take over your body. And as for your bandmates – well, they'll be dead in a matter of minutes, when the train they're in crashes over the edge of a cliff."

"You're lying," Tom said, hoping desperately that this was another sick joke by the demon.

"Oh no I'm not," Mourdant said, before mimicking an explosion. "*Boom!* A terrible tragedy, blah blah blah. And Tom Wills, the only survivor, pledges to keep making music in memory of his friends and goes solo under new management. It practically writes itself, doesn't it?"

"You're forgetting Gail," Tom said. "She will find you and stop you!"

"Oh, don't you worry about Ms Storm. I sent some of my very best people to dispose of her. I'm just sorry I couldn't have done it myself – but I have places to be, gateways to the Netherworld to open."

"No!" Tom screamed.

"Oh, yes. Tell me, when will we be arriving at Nara?"

"We're pulling in now," Hideyoshi said.

Mourdant flicked out his arm to check his watch. "Three thirty a.m. and sunrise is at four twenty. Bang on time. This train really is a marvel. Are you finished yet?" He turned to Kotomi.

The demon in the body of Kotomi opened its black eyes and smiled. "Oh, yes. Meet Namahage." She looked up at a black cloud of darkness swirling in the corner of the train. A demon soul, just waiting to take possession of Tom once his soul was gone. No need for permission – he would be an empty vessel.

"Ah, what a wonderful day this is turning out to be! Hideyoshi, when you're done here, bring the box. Come, Kotomi. Leave our demon friend to get acquainted with his new body."

Kotomi opened the door for Mourdant. Where Tom had expected to see a carriage he caught a glimpse of the night sky. Mourdant hadn't been lying. The rest of the train was gone.

Mourdant jumped down from the train. Kotomi went to follow, but paused to blow Tom a kiss. "Have fun."

She slammed the door behind her, leaving Hideyoshi and Tom in the lab.

"It's easier if you don't struggle," Hideyoshi said, adjusting the straps holding Tom. His face twisted into an evil smile. "But it makes no difference to me if you do."

Tom looked at the young man who had once been his friend and knew that one way or another, only one of them was making it off this train alive.

Take off (remix)

"We're going to have to jump," JD said.

They were standing at the front of the train, the wind whipping across their faces. In the distance, they could see signs designating men at work, a bright yellow barrier and flashing amber lights warning people to stay clear, and beyond that, nothing. The train track ahead led to the edge of a cliff and into darkness.

"Where's the bridge?" Zek pushed Milly aside to poke his head out of the doorway. "Who makes a train track going nowhere?"

"It was washed away last week," Aneki said.

"Oh, yeah," Connor said. "I remember DAD flagged it up."

"Now you remember? NOW?" Zek started swearing in Arabic.

Niv, who was sitting up but still drowsy, signed, *What's happening?*

"You don't want to know," Zek said. "You should have stayed unconscious!"

The part of the train they were travelling in wasn't slowing down fast enough. Milly figured it was a matter of minutes before it would go hurtling into the river.

"We're going to have to jump," JD said again, with even more urgency this time.

"But, Tom..."

"We'll go after him. But first, we need to get ourselves off this train," JD said, leaning out of the door and looking ahead. He positioned himself, ready to take the leap off the side.

"Are you crazy?" Zek said, pulling JD back. "We jump off here, we could get sucked under the wheels."

JD stepped away from the edge. "Okay. We go off the back. Go! Now! Go!" He pointed to the back and they all started running, through carriage after carriage, till they arrived at the very last door. Aneki pressed the release button. It didn't open.

"I'm sorry," Kitsune's voice sounded. "I can't let you open the door while we're in transit. There is nothing to see out there. Perhaps I could entertain you with a song instead?"

Kitsune broke out into song, her voice so high-pitched that Milly had to cover her ears.

"Shut up!"

"We're running out of track!" Zek said.

"We're running out of time," Aneki added.

"Get the door open!" JD shouted at Niv.

Niv limped over to the door and ripped a panel off. The wires underneath fizzled with electricity but he ignored it this time, fighting through the pain to keep his fingers moving.

"Come on!" Zek said, the desperation in his voice making it crack.

His twin yanked out a blue wire and plugged it into his computer tablet. He pushed a command and numbers began scrolling across the screen.

"Faster would be better," Aneki said, punching again at the door release.

Connor dug his fingernails into the gap at the edge of the door and began pulling. Aneki helped him but it was no good. Milly grabbed JD's sword off him and jabbed it in the gap, trying to lever it open. The door moved a fraction. She increased the pressure on the sword. With a piercing ring, the blade snapped in two. The door slammed closed again.

Milly looked at the sword grip in her hand and the blunt, broken blade, then looked up at JD.

"My sword," he said, his eyebrows furrowed in a sharp V and his bottom lip bagging.

"I'll get you a new one. If we make it off alive!"

She jammed what was left of the blade in the gap and

tried again. Connor and Aneki both grabbed the hilt and together all three of them pulled.

"Come on!" Zek said, his voice high-pitched.

The door hissed and finally opened. The wind whipped at Milly's face, blowing her hat off, but she didn't have time to worry about her disguise. Connor threw himself out first, hitting the tracks and rolling, over and over, until he came to a stop against a rocky outcrop. Zek wrapped his arm around Niv and the twins went together. Like Connor they hit the ground and rolled.

JD grabbed Milly and leaped, spinning in the air as they flew out of the back of the train so that he landed first. He let out a loud "*Oof*" of pain as they hit the ground. JD had taken most of the impact, and yet it was still enough to slam all the air out of Milly's lungs.

"Are you okay?" she gasped, turning to JD, who still had his hands wrapped around her.

He nodded and she rolled off him. She looked up at the train as it screeched away, heading for the cliff edge. "Aneki!" The girl stood in the doorway, a black silhouette. "Jump! Jump now!"

Milly and all the others were yelling at the girl to jump. She took a step back, and Milly thought she'd lost her nerve, choosing to take her chances on the train rather than risk the leap. The train went over the cliff, carriage after carriage, toppling over the edge. As the final carriage tipped over, its wheels hissing and screeching, a flash of silver cut through the darkness of the train doorway. The train fell away, leaving Aneki hanging by her whip, the tip of which was embedded in a tree that hung close to the track. She swung, suspended above the ground, then dropped gracefully to her feet.

There was a deafening crash and crunch as metal met rocks, and finally a splash as the train was swallowed up by the river below. Milly and the others walked slowly to the edge of the cliff and looked down. The train was a crumpled mess. No one could have survived that fall.

"Bye, Kitsune," Connor said, waving down as what was left of the carriages burst into flames.

"It's a computer-generated fox, Con," Zek said. "It'll be fine. We, however, are up to our necks in goats' droppings."

Niv was sitting on the floor, brushing dust off his face.

"Are you okay?" Milly asked.

Niv gave her two overly enthusiastic thumbs up. *The best.*

Milly helped him to his feet. He seemed okay. No broken bones and he hadn't lost his sense of sarcasm.

JD pulled out his phone. "Damn, no reception. Anyone?"

Each of them in turn dug out their mobile phones and found the same thing. There was no signal.

"Niv?" JD said. "Tell me you have something?"

Niv held up his phone. The screen was cracked and the power off. *Smashed,* he signed, throwing it over his shoulder, over the cliff. *But! My laptop.* He dug around in his rucksack and pulled out his laptop. It was covered in an orange protective case. Milly prayed that it had done its job.

Niv opened it, hit the on button and waited while it picked up signal. *We are...* he signed.

Milly waited, wishing he would hurry up.

...Nowhere.

Zek grabbed the laptop off him. "There's not even a village for miles."

"Where do you think they're taking Tom?" Milly asked.

"To Nara," Aneki said.

"How do you know that?" Milly said.

"I checked the train's destination with Kitsune before we jumped."

"Good thinking. What's in Nara?" JD asked.

"The oldest temple in Japan."

"What do they want there?" Connor said.

Aneki shrugged. "I don't know."

Milly paced back and forth, her hands in her hair. There had to be a way that they could get to Tom. There just had to be. She could hardly think; she could hardly breathe. Every time she blinked, she saw the image of Tom tied to the chair, Mourdant using him like a puppet.

JD and the others were shouting, trying to come up with a plan. But there wasn't one. Tom was gone.

The wind was picking up, buffeting her clothes around

her. It got stronger and stronger and she had to step away from the edge of the cliff for fear it might blow her over. And then she heard a loud *thwup thwup* sound, like something chopping at the air. She looked up to see a black helicopter hovering overhead. The door opened, a rope ladder unrolled all the way to the floor, and someone leaned out.

"Well, come on then," Gail shouted down. "We have a train to catch!"

Hold on

"I wish things could have been different," Hideyoshi said, looking out the window. "But now the train and your friends will be at the bottom of a ravine. Shame. I liked that train."

Tom squeezed his eyes, fighting back the tears. It couldn't be. He couldn't have lost them all. How had he not seen through Hideyoshi? JD always told him he was too trusting. He'd been right, and now Tom had got his friends killed.

Panic clutched at his chest, his breaths came in gulps. *Hold on*, he told himself. *Stay alive. Avenge them.* He closed his eyes and tried to find the stillness that Gail had taught him. He forced himself to imagine water, smooth and calm. But all he saw were dark clouds scudding across a purple sky. He tried the mantra she had taught him, but the words came out twisted – the same words an Aztec priestess had sung on top of a pyramid.

Tom was trying to find peace, but instead, he'd found power. The power of Tezcatlipoca. All this time, ever since the demon god had tried to possess him in Mexico, he'd felt a pulsing echo of its power waiting for him. All he had to do was submit to Tezcatlipoca, and he would be free. He could break out of these feeble bonds, destroy Hideyoshi, kill Mourdant and have his revenge. He would have to sacrifice himself, but it would be worth it.

And yet, Tom knew that if he let Tezcatlipoca overtake him, if he let the demon god cross over, then he'd become Tezcatlipoca's gateway to this world. The only thing holding the god back was Tom's humanity. If he let go of it now, there would be nothing of him left.

There had to be another way to escape. A way where he could keep hold of his soul.

He looked to his left at the robotic hand lying on Hideyoshi's worktable. Had the hand been the real reason he'd not seen the truth about Hideyoshi? Because he was so enraptured with it? From the moment Hideyoshi had switched it on, it had felt like part of him, controlled by nothing but a thought. The interface. Mourdant had taken the hand, but he hadn't removed the interface tucked behind Tom's ear. Tom didn't know what its range was, but maybe there was a chance? The worktable was barely a metre away. And on it, next to the black box, his hand lay, waiting.

Hideyoshi was still staring out of the window. This was his chance.

Tom stared at the hand, so hard he felt his eyes blur, imagining the finger moving, just as he had done when it was attached to him. *Move*, he thought. *Just move.*

Hideyoshi turned around and Tom quickly looked away from the hand. "I suppose we should get this over with," he said as he walked behind Tom and began adjusting the chair. He then placed his black box on the worktable and began clipping wires to the corners.

Tom didn't have long. He took a deep breath and focused on the hand again. The trick, Hideyoshi had said, was not to strain. To just see the hand moving in your mind and it would move. Tom relaxed his mind. The little finger twitched.

Tom fought back a gasp of victory and focused again. The hand moved, the fingers clawing at the metal surface, dragging itself forward, centimetre by excruciating centimetre, closer to the black box.

Hideyoshi, back turned, was typing on a keyboard, getting ready to carry out what he had called the "transferring" process. Lights on the black box pulsed, fading, glowing on and off as if it was breathing in and out. And in the corner of the room, the black shadow of the demon still swirled.

Tom needed more time. He needed to stop Hideyoshi

from completing the process. "Your parents would have been ashamed of you," he said.

Hideyoshi spun around and slapped Tom around the face. "I did this for them!"

Tom gasped with the shock. His cheek stung and he'd bitten his tongue; he could taste the copper tang of blood. But it had been the distraction he needed.

Hideyoshi looked down at his hand, as if it wasn't under his own control, and then looked away, ashamed. "When my parents died, I became obsessed with finding a way to bring their souls back. I'd heard the family stories about the box. How it could summon and trap *oni* spirits. But it was all too mystical. Too random. I needed a process I could trust. And so I began to decode the box." He sighed. "I turned what I realized was a ritual – the position of the symbols as the panels slid, aligning to create what my ancestors called magic – into a program."

Behind the young man, the robotic hand crawled closer and closer to the box. It was barely a fingertip away.

"I failed in retrieving my parents' souls," Hideyoshi continued, "but I realized my box could do something else. It could take the soul out of a living creature. I started small, practising on lab rats, then a fox, until I knew I had it perfected. Then all I needed was a volunteer. I told Kotomi she was helping me with my dissertation. Always so sweet, she was willing to help. I'm not sure she even knew what was happening until it was too late." He laid his hand on the box, and Tom winced, hoping he wouldn't notice that the hand was so close. With gentle pressure, Hideyoshi slid one of the panels forward and with a flash of pale blue light there she was: Ichi – Kotomi's soul.

She stared at Hideyoshi and Tom could have sworn there was rage behind her eyes.

"Always so strong, she has tried to break free a few times. But there is no escape for her as long as the box is safe." He took his hand off the box and turned back to Tom. "And soon, you will join her," he said – just as the robotic hand reached the box and pushed it off the edge of the table. It fell to the floor, landing on the edge of the outstretched panel. There was a sound like the crack of glass, and one of the delicate panels snapped off.

"No!" Hideyoshi cried.

Ichi looked down at the box and then to her hands. She held them up in front of her face, turning them back and forth.

"*Yameru!*" Hideyoshi cried out, backing away. "Stop! Stop!"

But Ichi wasn't listening. Free of his command, she took a step towards Hideyoshi, her slim arms outstretched.

"No," Hideyoshi said, his head shaking furiously. "I didn't mean to. I didn't know what I was doing!"

She took one more step.

"I had to. He made me. Please…" Tears fell down his face, but Ichi clearly felt no pity for Hideyoshi – the man who had torn her soul from her body and trapped it in this box. She grabbed his face in both her hands. Hideyoshi screeched, as if her hands were burning him.

Not burning, Tom realized, they were freezing. Ichi leaned in towards Hideyoshi's face, her head twisting, and placed a kiss on his lips.

Hideyoshi tried to scream but it was muffled by the cold lips over his. Lips that sucked at him. The veins on his face stood out, and blood started to pour from his ears. Tom turned away, unable to watch as Ichi took her revenge.

Finally, the sounds of agony stopped. Tom looked back to see Ichi let go of Hideyoshi. Whatever humanity had been left in the man before was drained out of him now. He looked like an empty shell, while Ichi looked more solid, more real. It was as if she had taken the energy of Hideyoshi's spirit into herself.

She bent down and picked up the black box, a look of pure disgust on her face. This box had been her prison for nearly a year, and now, at last, she was the one in control of it. She twisted it around, trying to slide the panels, but nothing was working.

She then turned to Tom. In a blink, she closed the distance between them and appeared over him. Would she do to him what she'd done to Hideyoshi? Tom had watched

IKIR10 perform, he'd been there while another girl had been auditioned. Had he been complicit in their pain?

Ichi held the box out, and then, to his surprise, she placed it in his lap.

Tom looked down at it. He didn't know how to operate it either. Only Hideyoshi did. But he could try. "Get me out of this chair and I'll help you. I'll help you all."

Ichi tilted her head left then right, looking at Tom. She didn't understand what he was saying.

He nodded at his bindings. "Free," he said. "Set me free."

She reached out and tugged at the leather strap that held him in place. Where her fingers made contact with his skin, the cold burned and he cried out in pain. But soon the strap was loose. He untied the rest himself and jumped out of the chair, holding the box in his left hand. The robotic hand lay on the floor, lifeless once again. He hesitated before putting the box down and picking it up. Hideyoshi had built the hand for him, and Hideyoshi had turned out to be evil. Did that mean that the hand, too, would be evil? He looked down at the young man's body. Tom didn't have time for the morality of it all. He needed his hand back. He slipped it on and sighed as it responded to his slightest thought, fingers stretching and dancing. He held it up to the light and smiled.

Now, the box. He picked it up and turned it over in his hands, trying to work out what to do with it. It was so beautiful, so powerful, that he wasn't sure he could bring himself to destroy it. Then he heard something behind him.

He turned, to see Hideyoshi stand up. Only, it wasn't Hideyoshi any more. Black tendrils disappeared inside the young man's eyes and nose as Namahage, the demon that had been meant for Tom, took over Hideyoshi's body. It quivered and shook, head jerking as it grew and grew, turning slowly red. Hideyoshi's suit ripped at the seams as muscles exploded out of it. Bones cracked as his jaw grew larger, tusk-like teeth jutted out between his lips and two horns burst out of his forehead. Tom could still just about make out Hideyoshi's delicate features beneath the red skin and black eyes.

The *oni* demon took a shuddering step towards Tom. It reached out a clawed hand and, before he could dodge, grasped Tom by the neck and lifted him off the floor. Tom grappled with the iron grip at his throat, trying to pull at the fingers. He couldn't breathe. He couldn't think. Darkness danced at the edge of his vision and was closing in fast.

Let me in, a voice like the sound of cracking bones said in his mind. *Only I have the power to protect you. Only I can save you.*

This was his choice: he could die now, here, his throat crushed by a demon. Or he could become one himself – give up everything he'd fought for, everything he believed in, just so he could survive. But, more than that, he would be worshipped. He would be a god. All he had to do was let the spirit of Tezcatlipoca in.

The *oni* tightened its grip. Tom saw only darkness now.

Let me in.

The instinct was so strong. Tom opened his lips to say the word that he knew would let the demon god break through.

Then something loud slammed on the roof overhead.

A second later, one of the windows smashed, and through it came JD, swinging from a black rope. Another window smashed, and another of the boys landed in the room. One after the other, they came. Slay were here to save him.

The *oni* let Tom go and he collapsed to the floor, gasping for breath. He had so nearly given in. He'd so nearly failed them all. But with the arrival of his friends, hope had rushed into him, driving the darkness out. *Not today, Big-T,* he thought. *Not today.*

He stood up and clenched his fists, ready for the fight. "Okay. Let's do this!"

I'd never leave you

Milly swung through the window, shook the shards of glass off her hair and scanned the room. She could only think of one thing: Tom. Where was Tom? Instead of her friend, all she saw was a huge red-skinned demon with white horns and claws the length of rulers. Its head was bowed, its shoulders braced against the ceiling that was too low to allow it to stand upright. It must have been over three metres tall. The ragged remains of a sleek black suit clung to its huge muscles. She looked back to the demon's face and could make out Hideyoshi's angular features – distorted, stretched and made evil by whatever transformation had overtaken him. The Hideyoshi-demon hardly seemed to notice the band smashing into the room, as all its attention was focused on whatever was in front of it.

There, finally, she saw Tom standing in front of the red demon, his fists raised, the black box by his feet.

Their eyes met across the room. He looked okay: pale, angry, but on his feet, and his eyes shone as clearly as the day she'd first seen him. He smiled. The sickening fear that had gripped her since she'd seen Tom helpless in Mourdant's grasp loosened its hold. Milly felt as though she could breathe again. She wanted to run to him and throw herself into his arms. She'd let so many things stop her before. Now, the only thing stopping her was a giant red demon.

Aneki came tumbling through one of the smashed windows, and as soon as she was up on her feet, she was fighting. She flicked her whip chain, but the demon swiped it out of the way. JD was a moment behind her, charging at it and at the last minute dropping to his knees and sliding between its tree-trunk legs. He slashed out with a knife and there was a spray of black blood, before the demon's right leg buckled. JD flicked back up to his feet and spun around, waiting for the retaliation. But before the demon could respond, the twins had their turn. Moving in perfect harmony, they came at the creature, left and right, their scimitars spinning.

The demon seemed to finally react to what was happening to it. With a howl of pain, it swiped at Niv and Zek, sending them flying. Milly reached over her shoulder and pulled an arrow from her quiver. Gail had given her a new bundle of arrows, but she would have to make every one count.

She nocked the arrow, drew it back and fired, straight

into the demon's chest. It swatted the shaft away as if it was nothing but a mosquito – focusing only on Tom, who was unarmed and helpless. She fired another, which sliced across its cheek, opening up a ragged cut. But still the demon didn't flinch. It took a giant step towards Tom.

Tom crouched down, to protect himself from the blow, Milly assumed. But he quickly stood up again, and now he was holding the box in his hands.

The *oni* paused, as if hesitating. Connor took that moment and threw a grenade at its head. It caught it without looking and threw it out one of the smashed windows. It exploded a moment too late and the bloom of yellow smoke was swept away in the downdraught caused by the helicopter hovering overhead.

Connor tried again, and yet again the demon caught the grenade. This time, it held it in its clawed hand for one, two seconds before throwing it directly at Connor's head. The grenade exploded in front of Connor and the boy threw his hands to his face and fell to his knees, screaming in pain.

The demon turned back to Tom, who was moving the box from hand to hand. The demon's head followed the movement and Milly realized that it wasn't Tom the demon wanted. It was the box.

JD went in for a second attack, slashing open the demon's back with his blade. It merely winced. Aneki lashed out with her whip, wrapping it around the *oni*'s neck. This got its attention. It wrenched the chain away and, with one of its shovel-like hands, picked the worktable up and threw it at JD and Aneki. The table caught them both around the head, knocking them off their feet.

Now there was only Milly and Tom left.

The demon was only one step away from Tom. She had to do something.

"Piggy!" she called out to Tom.

It took him a moment to work out what she meant. But when he did, he smiled again. Just as the *oni* raised a giant fist, Tom pulled his arm back and threw the box. It flew in a perfect arc towards Milly. She dropped the bow and held out her hands. She'd never been good at sports – was always the one to try and hide at the back of the field so the ball never came near her. But this time, the catch mattered more than winning a school game. The box landed in her outstretched arms, its sharp corners digging into her flesh.

The demon roared and started to lumber towards her, its steps shaking the train carriage. Now Milly had the box, it was after her.

She couldn't think. She was frozen, as the red creature charged towards her like a bull. She couldn't let the *oni* get the box, but she had only a second before he would be on her.

There was a flash of light and suddenly Ichi stood in front of Milly, her arms outstretched, facing the *oni*. The demon slammed into the hologirl as if it had hit a wall and was thrown off its feet. She looked more real and was even stronger than before. Ichi was protecting her, giving her the time she needed to destroy the box.

Milly threw it to the floor and pulled out a blade from her belt. She pushed the tip into the crack between two of the panels and prised one out. There was a flash, then there was a second figure standing next to Ichi. The *oni* sat up, shaking his head. Milly forced a third and then a fourth panel to open. *Flash, flash*; two more hologirls. The *oni* clambered to its feet and roared. It charged but IKIR10 attacked in turn, the four souls wrapping themselves around its arms, its legs. The demon roared, struggling against their vice-like grip, still trying to get to the box. Milly worked as fast as she could, and then realized she wasn't alone.

Tom kneeled next to her. He took the box out of her hands and held it in his black, robotic hand.

"Ready?"

She nodded and both he and Milly turned away. There was a creaking, crunching sound. Tom groaned with the strain and then, with a splintering, shattering sound, there was a huge flash of blinding light.

When Milly risked looking back, all nine girls were free. The glowing blue figures reached out and took each other's hands, making a circle around the red demon. One delicate step at a time, they closed the circle. The *oni* spun around and around, trying to find a way out. There was none. The girls leaped and all Milly could see was a glowing ball of light. It got brighter and brighter and then…it was gone.

The demon was gone too. Lying in the middle of the floor was Hideyoshi's human body, a torn suit swamping his frail form. He was dead, his eyes staring, a soft smile on his lips. The fight was over.

Milly looked around as she saw the boys stirring. JD shoved the table off him and Aneki, and they both clambered up. Zek crawled over to where Connor was rocking back and forth, his hands still over his eyes. He gently pulled Connor's hands away from his face.

Connor's skin was pink and raw, his eyes scrunched up, and his face covered in yellow dust. "I can't see. I can't see."

Niv scrambled over and handed Zek a water bottle from his belt. Zek poured it over Connor's face, washing away the sodium. "That's because you have your eyes shut, Con. Come on, open them for me."

Connor opened one eye and then the other. "I never thought I'd be so happy to see your ugly mug!" He hugged Zek, and the two of them stood up.

Milly turned back to Tom. "Are you okay?"

"I'm fine. We're all fine."

She threw her arms around him and hugged him tighter than she'd ever hugged anyone. "I thought I'd lost you."

"I thought I was lost, too," he whispered into her ear. "I'm so sorry. I should have listened to you."

"Hush," she said. She squeezed him even tighter and realized there was something strange about his hug. She let him go and looked down at his arm. The sleek black wrist ended in sizzling wires and shattered plastic. Destroying the box had destroyed his new hand.

"It's okay," he said, reaching up and unclipping it. The remains of the once-sleek black hand fell to the floor.

JD was the second to hug Tom. When he let him go, he punched him in the chest. "Listen to us, next time."

"I know, I'm sorry. I thought I…was better alone."

"Rule one, dude," Zek said.

"Rule one."

Zek gave Tom a slightly gentler hug than the last two he'd had. But before he could pull away, Connor launched himself at them and wrapped them both up in one of his bear hugs. Niv joined in, followed by JD and finally, Milly wriggled her way into the middle of the bundle of boys. Her boys.

When they broke apart, she was glad to see she wasn't the only one wiping tears away from her face.

"Sorry about your hand, man," Connor said, pointing to it on the floor.

Niv picked it up and turned it over, examining it. He signed, banging the top of his left fist with his right.

"He thinks he can repair it," Milly translated.

"Cool!" Connor said. "Can you make it fire darts?"

Only then did Milly remember it wasn't only Slay in the room. She turned to see Aneki holding the crushed box in her hands, kneeling over Hideyoshi's body. Nine souls stood around her, their heads bowed.

Milly stepped closer to Aneki. "I'm sorry."

"Don't be," she said, wiping a tear away. "I said goodbye to my brother long ago."

Milly looked to IKIR10. They flickered on and off, like a broken light.

"Why are they still here?" Tom asked. "They're free."

"Only the five whose bodies are already free of the demons. The other four cannot return until the demons possessing their bodies have been banished. Without the box to sustain them, their souls will grow weaker. They must return to their bodies before dawn or else they will become hungry ghosts, doomed to walk the earth for ever."

"So why are they all here?" Zek said. "If five of them can return to their bodies, what are they waiting for?"

One of the girls spoke in a whisper so faint Milly could hardly hear it. "What did she say?"

"That they won't go until all of them are free," Aneki said.

"So what do we do?" Milly said.

Aneki threw Hideyoshi's shattered box to the floor and pulled her own ivory box out of her bag. The golden patterns glimmered on the cream surface in the low light. Milly saw now how Hideyoshi's was a poor copy of this original box. No technology in the world could match the beauty of its craftsmanship.

"We get the demons the hell out of their bodies."

Before sunset

Tom stepped out of the carriage into the dappled light of the grey predawn light breaking through the trees. They were standing at the entrance to a large park. Trees waved in the light breeze and curious deer peered at them through the slim trunks.

"Ooh, aren't they cute?" Connor said, reaching out to a baby deer. It started and bounded away to its mother.

"In Shinto, deer are seen as messengers from the gods," Aneki said.

"And they're saying 'Get the hell out of here'," Zek said, with a shiver.

Tom felt it too – the sense of unease that permeated the place. His every instinct told him to run, to get as far away from here as possible. But he knew he had a job to do.

A sudden gust of wind tugged at his hair, and the deer scattered, running and leaping for their lives. The helicopter landed and its blades slowed. Gail jumped out of the pilot's seat, carrying a black holdall.

She looked at Tom, then raced over to him, not even bothering to use her cane – which he knew would be causing her pain. She dropped the bag and threw her arms around him, pulling him into a hug. It was over before he even had a chance to return it.

"Never," she said, hitting him, "make me worry like that again."

"I'll try," Tom said sheepishly. "Since when can you fly a helicopter?"

"There are still many things you don't know about me, Tom." Gail reached into her bag and pulled out a crossbow. It was slightly larger than a pistol and had five bright yellow bolts lined up to shoot. "I've rigged it so you can use it one-handed. You reload it with your foot. But basically, you point and shoot."

Tom held it up and took aim. Without meaning to, he twitched the finger of his left hand and an arrow flew dangerously close to Zek's head, thudding into a tree behind him.

"Watch it!" Zek said, running his hand across the side of his head. "Don't mess with the fades."

"And here, you'd better put this on." Gail threw a T-shirt at him. It had *Slay Hard* written on it. Tom slipped out of the shredded remains of his shirt and pulled it on.

"Do you happen to have a spare sword in there?" JD asked.

"What happened to yours?" Gail said.

JD glanced at Milly. "Don't ask."

Gail did have another sword. Not as beautiful as JD's original but it looked just as sharp. "Right then," she said, looking around the park. "Where is Mourdant? I'm going to make him regret the day he was spawned."

"There," Aneki said, pointing up ahead. In the distance – at the end of a winding path marked out by hundreds, if not thousands, of illuminated lanterns – stood a bright-red temple. "Kasuga-taisha."

"He was planning on using the power of the trapped souls to tear a gateway to the Netherworld," Tom said. "But now the souls are free, I don't know what his plan is."

"Mourdant will have backup plans and backup plans," Gail said. "This isn't over yet."

"Then let's go finish it," JD said.

He led the way and, not for the first time, Tom was happy to follow. Physical and mental exhaustion tugged at his every nerve. And yet he had to keep going just a little longer. Milly walked alongside him, looking just as tired as he did, while Aneki and the others walked behind. They all looked broken, but determined. At the back drifted Ichi and the eight other members of IKIR10 – all nine spirits free but not yet safe. They were so faint now, he could hardly see them, like light dappling through the trees. Like him, they only had to hold on for a little longer.

Tom awkwardly placed the crossbow over his shoulder and reached out to take Milly's hand. She interlaced her fingers with his and they held on to each other. As long as she was with him, he could do this.

The path to the temple was lined with small stone carvings which were covered in dark-green moss. The sky overhead had turned pink and orange as dawn crept ever closer, but thanks to the lanterns, the light was as bright as midday.

In front of them, the temple stood waiting. A dark, swirling column was spinning over the roof, like a black tornado sucking light into it and stretching high into the sky.

"He's started," JD said.

Picking up the pace, they raced up the few steps leading to the entrance and stepped inside. Huddled over in the middle of a large courtyard, glowing in the light of the bronze lanterns, was Mourdant. And he'd clearly been busy. He was crouched in the centre of an intricate pattern drawn on the wooden floor in black powder, putting the finishing touches to his design. Tom didn't recognize the symbol and found that he couldn't look directly at it.

Surrounding the square courtyard was a collection of men. Twenty, thirty maybe. Demons, judging by their claws and black eyes. Mourdant must have gathered them all up to act as protection. But they were the least of Slay's worries.

Standing to Mourdant's right was Kotomi. She smiled when she saw Tom and gave him a little wave. To Mourdant's left stood three other girls: the sweet-faced girl he had known as Ishida, and two other girls he didn't recognize, though neither could have been much older than he was. Mourdant had manipulated each of these girls into giving up their soul, by seducing them with promises of money and fame. Each of them stared out at Slay with black eyes. Unlike their muscular counterparts, there was no suppressed rage in these demons, no internal battle taking place. In fact, the demon girls looked bored with everything that was happening, more like they were waiting for a class to start than a ritual to open a doorway to another dimension.

Mourdant stood up and dusted off his hands. He turned slowly, his head rotating first, then his body. "Well, well, what a surprise. Ever so hard to kill, aren't you? Like cockroaches."

"It's over, Mourdant!" Tom said. "The girls are free. You don't have the energy you need to open the gateway." Aneki threw the crumpled remains of Hideyoshi's black box at the ancient demon's feet.

"Sorry about that," JD said. "Oh no, wait – we're not sorry at all."

Mourdant looked down at the box and then back up

at JD. "You kids," he said, shaking his head. "You really are very annoying." He wagged his finger at them, as if they were just a local gang who'd been knocking over his flowerpots.

"Yeah, we make a point of it," Zek said.

"If this was a movie, this is where we'd offer you the chance to come quietly," JD said, readying his sword. "But that's not going to happen."

Mourdant was looking infuriatingly unconcerned. He glanced up at the roof – there was already a cloud of darkness spiralling over his head. Around him, the symbol made from black powder began to undulate, warping and shifting the ground it was drawn on, and making Tom feel queasy. It raised up off the ground, hovering half a metre in the air, spinning, like black snakes swallowing their own heads. Above, the black hole grew wider, and beyond it, Tom saw black hands reaching through the hole, clawing at an invisible membrane that was blocking their way. Demon souls waiting to cross over.

Mourdant reached up, brushing his fingers against one of the black hands. "For centuries I have been waiting for this moment. Soon, my old friends, you shall be returned and together we will crush anyone who stands in our way and the reign of The Mourdant shall last for an eternity! Nothing can stop the return of my dark army!" He threw his head back and laughed.

"About that," JD said. "There is something that can stop you."

"Yeah," Connor said, gesturing at the group with a thumb. "Us."

Mourdant yanked his hand away from the dark cloud and pointed at JD. "You think you can stop my plans. You have no idea."

"You see the box, right?" Zek said, pointing at the lump of black plastic. "That there is your plan all mushed up."

Mourdant smiled in a way that Tom did not like at all. "Kotomi? Don't you have something for me?"

Kotomi stepped forward, and in her hand was a black box, identical in every way to the one Hideyoshi had made.

Mourdant took it from her and tossed it up and down. "I had Hideyoshi make a second box. And now all I need to do is fill it up. Hideyoshi calculated we needed the power of ten souls in order to open the gateway, but I reckon that I could do quite nicely with only..." He turned to them and began counting heads, his lips moving and finger bobbing as he ticked all of them off. JD, Tom, Milly, Niv, Zek, Connor, Gail and Aneki. "Eight." Mourdant smiled. "Get them."

Tom glanced over at Aneki. She had her own box in her bag, ready to pull the remaining four demons out of the girls. However, the demons wouldn't leave the bodies without a fight, so it was up to Tom and the others to weaken them enough so that she could do her work. The challenge, however, was making sure not to kill any of them. Or – maybe even more challenging – not getting killed themselves.

But before they could get to the girls, they had to take out the demon guards in their way. The demons attacked first, all charging at once so that they ended up getting in each other's way. This was only the second time Tom had fought using just his left hand, but he managed to shoot one of them in the neck using the crossbow Gail had given him. Next to him, JD spun his sword, taking out three demons in one smooth motion. Milly fired arrow after arrow – she still wasn't as good a shot as Tom had been, but she managed to dust a few demons that got close. And Aneki was a blur of whipping chain and black silk.

Zek and Niv fought back to back, spiralling around in perfect symmetry without needing to say a single word. It never failed to stun Tom seeing them work together like this, as if the twins could read each other's minds. Gail and Connor were busy throwing grenades.

Tom also caught glimpses of nine pale-blue figures vanishing just as a demon was about to dive and appearing right behind them. The girls of IKIR10 were using the last of their energy to fight.

The circle of demon guards around Mourdant and the demon girls grew smaller and smaller until there were only three burly demons standing between Slay and Mourdant.

"Have some of that!" Connor shouted as Gail threw another grenade into the fray. It landed right in front of the remaining demons, and exploded in a flash of blinding light. By the time the flash had cleared, the last guards were down.

Bodies lay strewn all around the temple, leaking black blood onto the wooden floor. In the middle, Mourdant stood, still muttering, controlling the swirling patterns that surrounded him. But he looked weak, as if the act of keeping the ritual going was draining him. The gateway above his head had grown only slightly larger, and the clawing hands had yet to break through.

Tom raised his crossbow. He'd killed one of Mourdant's bodies before, with an arrow to the eye. He pulled the trigger, firing the last of his bolts. It stopped mid-air, one metre away from Mourdant's head.

Connor shouted and threw himself at the spinning symbol. As soon as he got near it, he was thrown backwards.

"We can't cross it," Gail shouted. "Stay back."

Kotomi and the other girls were also inside the protective circle. She came to the very edge of it and paced back and forth, like a tiger behind bars. She stopped in front of Aneki. "So you're the sister he wouldn't shut up about. I was expecting something" – Kotomi scrunched up her nose, as if smelling something foul – "...more."

Aneki spat something back in Japanese and punched the barrier. She screamed in pain and clutched at her hand.

Tom stepped forward, getting as close to the ritual circle as he could without touching it. The air rippled all around it, creating a shimmering barrier between the ground and the black gateway growing above. But about four metres above the ground, Tom spotted a patch of clear, undisturbed sky. A hole in the barrier! It couldn't be more than half a metre across, maybe even less.

"Um, Connor," he said, pointing up.

"Got ya," Connor said, following Tom's plan. He unclipped a grenade and tossed it lightly in his hand. "It's my last one."

"Make it count," JD chipped in.

Mourdant was on his knees now, his face scrunched up with the strain of keeping the ritual going. The black box lay by his feet, pale blue light pulsing. The four demon girls seemed to realize what was about to happen. They edged away, shouting at Mourdant to do something, but just as Mourdant's barrier was keeping Slay out, so was it keeping them in.

Connor stepped back and pulled back his arm. Slay had often played their own version of basketball, on Agatha, sticking a sucker hoop against one of the windows and throwing anything they could at it. More often than not, the hoop fell off and they resorted to just throwing things at each other. Connor was the best shot. But would he make it this time?

He hefted the grenade once, twice and then threw it in a smooth, high arc. At first Tom thought he'd sent it too high, but as the grenade fell back down, it slipped straight through the gap and landed with a soft thud right next to the black box by Mourdant's feet.

They all waited. The grenade had yet to go off. Mourdant stayed kneeling, looking at the still grenade.

"Connor?" Milly asked.

"Just wait," he said.

"Con, if you forgot to—" Zek was cut off by an explosion that blasted inside the protective dome, and then blew it apart.

The four demon girls screamed, covering their eyes. Mourdant had been knocked unconscious. As soon as he hit the floor, the spinning, swirling symbol disintegrated into a pile of black dust, and the gateway overhead shrank down to nothing, before vanishing with a *pop*. Shards of black plastic were scattered all across the floor: the black box had been blown to pieces.

Kotomi lowered her hands from her eyes. Her perfect make-up was ruined and bloody tears ran from her eyes. She licked at a drop of the red blood. "So, Aneki, what are you going to do now? Kill me?"

Whack! Aneki punched Kotomi so hard it knocked the demon clean off her feet.

"Kill you? No," Aneki said. "Hurt you? Yes."

Kotomi scrambled to her feet, blood pouring from her nose now too. She spat out a single white tooth and smiled again.

"If you want Aneki," Milly said, stepping forward, "you're going to have to go through me." She threw her bow to the floor and held up her fists. At first, Tom thought Milly must have lost her mind, that the frenzy of the fight had overtaken her. But as he saw Aneki slip her hand into her bag, he realized what Milly was doing. She was buying Aneki time to get the box ready.

"It will be my pleasure," Kotomi said, and charged. The two girls fought: punching, dodging and kicking. Milly was weaker, but the training she'd been doing for the last month seemed to have paid off. She blocked a punch from Kotomi and grabbed her arm. Twisting, she wrenched Kotomi's arm around her back and drove the demon to her knees.

Tom wanted to step in and help, but he couldn't risk hurting Kotomi any more than they had to. There was still a chance that the true Kotomi could be returned to her body. Tom could no longer see the souls of the girls, but he felt a cold presence behind him.

There was a scream. Kotomi had spun out of Milly's grip and now had her pinned to the floor. Tom hesitated, uncertain what to do. He raised his crossbow. He had one last bolt. If it meant killing Kotomi to save Milly, he would have to do it.

"Easy," Gail said, resting her hand on his, and lowering his weapon. "She's got this."

Milly wrapped her legs around Kotomi's waist, and, with a shout, she flipped the demon girl over onto her back and started raining blows down on her. Gail was right, Milly did have it. But there were still the other three demon girls to take care of. Tom heard a cracking yell and looked over to see Connor running towards Ishida. She was a tiny thing, but fast and smart. As Connor got close, the demon girl ran up him, grabbed his neck between her legs and flipped him to the floor. Luckily, Gail was ready behind her when she landed. She brought her cane down on Ishida's neck and the demon girl buckled. JD and the twins were busy with the two remaining demons. Between the three of them, they had the girls pinned to the floor.

"Now!" JD shouted.

Aneki pulled the gold and ivory box out of her bag and placed it on the ground. She pushed sections, slid out panels and the box clicked and began to rotate on its own. It shifted from a cube into a series of diamond shapes and opened up like a flower. One part popped out of the top. Aneki slammed her hand down on it.

There was a sound like a screeching, howling wind and out of each of the girls' bodies burst a black, swirling darkness. Tendrils reached out, trying to grip onto the bodies they had occupied, but the sucking force of the box was too strong. One after the other, the demon souls were forced inside the box. When the last black thread of a soul was trapped, Aneki slammed the box again. All of the panels slid back into place and it became a cube once more. She fell back onto her heels, as the box fell still, glinting in the orange light of the rising sun.

Aneki raced over to the body of Kotomi. She kneeled down next to her, with Milly on her other side. A hazy blue light settled over the body and sank into it. For a moment, nothing happened. Had they been too late? Were the girls' souls too weak to rejoin their bodies?

Kotomi stirred. Her eyes blinked open as if she was waking from a deep sleep. They were a soft golden brown. She looked around, confused, not recognizing where she was.

"Aneki?" she said. Her best friend threw her arms around her neck and hugged her, sobbing.

The twins and Milly were helping Ishida and the other two girls up. Like Kotomi, their souls had found their way back into their bodies. The souls of the other four girls were also gone. Tom hoped they'd made it home safely too.

JD was standing over Mourdant. He kicked him in the ribs and rolled him onto his back. "No!"

Tom joined JD. "What's wrong?"

JD pointed down at the body on the floor. The man who had once been Nomura lay still, his now soft brown eyes staring out at them. The demon who had possessed him was gone.

"Mourdant!" JD kicked at a stone lantern, sending it rolling down the steps. "He's escaped."

While they'd been watching the girls, Mourdant must have abandoned his host. He could be anywhere now, looking for a new body to occupy.

Tom shook with anger. Mourdant had tortured him, nearly killed him – he'd wanted to make the demon suffer. A dark rage threatened to overwhelm him, and he pushed it down, gathering himself. "Next time, we'll be ready," he said. "Now we know he can be in any body, we'll know what to look out for."

"Next time," JD said, resting his hand on Tom's shoulder. Then he pulled his friend into a hug.

It was over quickly, but Tom noticed JD brushing aside a tear before he turned away and started instructing Connor and the twins on how they should deal with the demon bodies.

"So," Milly said, coming to stand next to Tom. "What do we do with that?"

She pointed down at Aneki's box. It shimmered gold in the lantern light. It looked so beautiful, so peaceful, it was hard to imagine that there were nine demons trapped inside.

"We can't let this get into the wrong hands," Gail said.

"Aneki, your family have kept the box safe for generations. What do you want to do with it?" Tom said.

"It has controlled the destiny of my family for too long. I say we destroy it."

"Can't we use it to save other people who have been possessed?" Milly said. She was thinking about how, when her mother had been possessed, she'd managed to hold on just long enough to help her daughter defeat the demon priestess.

"This box only traps the souls of demons. I'm sorry, but it can't be used on humans," Aneki said.

"You were right," Milly said to Gail. "There is no way back. I'm sorry, I should have believed you."

"No, I'm sorry. I hoped that I'd been wrong too." Gail wrapped an arm around Milly and kissed the top of her head.

"Won't destroying the box release the demons inside?" Tom asked.

"What are we discussing?" Connor said, as he, JD and the twins rejoined the group.

"What to do with the box," Milly said. "If we destroy it, we risk setting the demons free."

"Nine seriously peeved demons? Could we at least get some rest before having to deal with them?" Zek said.

Niv nodded and signed, curving his right hand into his left palm, as if he were holding something precious, and pulled it towards his body.

"Keep it safe?" Milly said. "But where?"

"I have an idea!" Connor said.

Call me

They were all standing around looking into a dark hole in the ground. Aneki climbed in and placed the ivory box at the bottom. She paused for a moment, saying a silent goodbye, before raising her hands up. Zek and Niv easily lifted her out of the hole and back onto her feet.

They'd returned to the building site in Osaka, the place where they'd fought the schoolgirls when they'd still been possessed by demons.

"And now," Connor said, manoeuvring a bright yellow cement mixer towards the hole, "the finishing touch." He tipped the mixer, and wet concrete slopped into the hole, filling it to the top.

"Seems a shame to destroy something so beautiful," Milly said.

"Beautiful or not, we can't risk those demons getting free," JD said. He was more jumpy than she'd ever seen him, examining the face of every stranger they passed on the way, as if expecting to see Mourdant staring back at him.

"Now we know it can be done," Gail said, "we can work out if there is another way. But for now, this is the safest place for this." She pushed the box under the concrete surface with the tip of her cane. It made one last burbling sound and then the concrete settled flat.

Aneki and Kotomi watched, their arms wrapped around each other. Kotomi, now she wasn't possessed by a demon, had turned out to be a lovely girl. Quick to laugh and to burst into song with her beautiful voice.

"What are you going to do now?" Milly asked them. "Now that you're both free?"

Aneki looked at her best friend. "Actually, Kotomi had an idea."

"Hey, it was *our* idea," Kotomi said, nudging her friend. "So, Aneki showed me the videos of *Ikiryō*. And it got me thinking – no reason why we couldn't do it for real."

"I spoke to Ishida and the other girls, and they're up for it."

"You mean…?" Milly asked.

"Yes – we're going to form our own girl band!" Kotomi placed her hand over her mouth as she laughed with delight.

"And your parents are all right with this?" Gail said.

"Some of them took a bit of persuading," Aneki said.

"Especially the ones who didn't even know that their daughters had auditioned!"

"But when we explained that the girls were the hidden talent behind *Ikiryō's* success, they saw what an amazing opportunity it could be."

"There's a reason Hideyoshi chose them all," Aneki said. "They're all amazingly talented. It's about time they benefited for themselves, rather than having someone else leech off their talent."

"How did you explain why their daughters had been acting so weird lately?" Milly asked.

Kotomi and Aneki looked at each other, and laughed again. "Puberty!" they said as one.

Gail laughed too. "You've already mastered the art of PR spin!"

"Are you going to join them, Aneki?" Milly asked. She could see the girl onstage, using her gymnastic skills to wow the world.

"Oh no, I can't sing," Aneki said. "But *Ikiryō* are going to need a new manager."

"If you need any tips," Gail said, "you know where to find me."

Aneki bowed. "Thank you, Gail-san. That would be amazing."

"And, hey, if you ever want to go on tour again," Connor said, "you can join Slay. Only you can support *us* this time!"

Kotomi laughed, her hair falling in front of her face, and for a moment, with the light of the midday sun shining from behind her, she looked exactly like the photo Aneki had given Milly. Milly pulled the photo out of her pocket and handed it back to the girls. "I won't be needing this."

Aneki took it and then reached into her bag. "And I won't be needing this." She pulled out her whip chain and handed it to Milly.

"What? No, I can't."

"I think you should."

"So do I," Tom said. "You're a terrible shot with the bow."

Milly scowled at Tom, but took the weapon gladly. It felt pleasantly heavy in her hand. She stepped away from the others and gave it a go. The whip chain danced in her hands, like a ribbon. On the first swing anyway. On the second the blade at the end embedded itself in a lump of concrete.

Aneki laughed and came to help Milly set it free. "You'll get the hang of it. Oh, and..." Aneki looked down. "I wanted to say that if you ever wanted a private tour of Japan, well, you have my number."

Milly was about to say how cool that would be, and then the girl planted a quick kiss on her cheek before turning away, shy and blushing. Milly put her hand to her cheek, confused. And then it clicked: Aneki didn't know Milly wasn't Milo. Even as they'd fought side by side, she'd not seen through her disguise and still thought that she was a boy. Milly found herself blushing too. This was one complication of dressing as a boy that she hadn't foreseen. She heard sniggering and saw that Zek was trying to keep a laugh under control. Connor gave her a small thumbs up. Tom was looking at her, an eyebrow raised in mock jealousy. "I…oh, I mean… Sure. I mean, if we're ever in Japan. But I think… Um, don't we have to go?"

"We have to be at the heliport in twenty minutes," Gail said. "We'd better get going."

"Heartbreaker," Zek said, as Milly came to stand with the boys again.

"Shut up," Milly muttered under her breath.

"Are we taking the copter back to Tokyo?" Connor asked.

"Yes, we just have to make a quick stop first," Gail replied.

They said their goodbyes and were about to leave, when Connor had an idea.

"Wait up!" He kneeled down in front of the concrete patch where they'd hidden the demon box and began drawing in the concrete with his finger. When he stood back, wiping his finger on the side of his trousers, Milly could see what he'd written.

Slay woz 'ere.

TRAGIC TRAIN CRASH KILLS
BELOVED TV HOST

National treasure, Nomura, died yesterday in a train crash that also claimed the life of his protégé, Hideyoshi Makoto. Political journalist and lately a popular late-night TV host, Nomura was a household name across Japan. His most recent venture had been as the owner of holographic J-Pop band, IKIR10, who have died along with their inventor. But in an interesting twist, the voices behind the holograms have come forward and created a new girl band called Chikara, which means "power". The girls are currently in the studio, working on their new album.

Tom folded the English language newspaper over and placed it back on the table. It looked like the press had bought the cover-up. Last night, they'd piled both Nomura and Hideyoshi's bodies into the helicopter, flown back to the train crash site and placed the bodies in the wreckage. Then they'd flown back to Tokyo.

It was early morning in the teahouse and the others weren't awake yet. The thrum of the city coming to life outside the walls mixed with the gentle snuffle of Connor's snores. The steam from Tom's green tea drifted with the morning breeze that plucked cherry blossom from the tree above. Tom felt at peace, for the first time since Mexico. He'd tried to deal with everything he was going through alone, too afraid to burden his friends or even admit to himself that he wasn't okay. And not only had he almost got himself killed, he'd also put their lives in danger. From now on, it was rule one all the way. Never go it alone.

"You're up early." It was Gail, dressed in a grey silk kimono and dark glasses.

"Best part of the day, my mum used to say."

"Hmm," she said, taking a seat at the hexagonal table. "She clearly never went to bed at four a.m."

"Or went drinking *sake* till three."

When they'd dragged themselves back to the teahouse in Tokyo, Tom and most of the others had gone straight to bed, exhausted. But Gail had gone out drinking with her Japanese friend Suzume – the owner of the art studio and the reason they'd come to Japan in the first place.

"Hmm," Gail said again, and poured herself a cup of Tom's tea.

"The press bought it," Tom said, showing Gail the newspaper article.

She scanned it without any apparent pleasure, before folding it back up.

"Where do you think he is now?" Tom asked.

"Who?"

"Mourdant."

Gail sipped the tea. "I don't know. I've got every contact I know looking for him. Wherever he is, we won't be so easily tricked next time, now we know what we're looking out for."

"A massive ego inside a small man?" Tom offered.

"I was going to say 'people in positions of power trying to take over the world' – but now that you put it like that, it's pretty much the same thing."

They sat in silence for a while, enjoying the peace. It wasn't to last for long.

"Give it back!" Connor roared.

Zek raced out into the courtyard carrying something. Connor, hot on his heels, was wearing only his boxers. His skin was still a little pink from the sodium grenade and his eyes looked sore. "Give it back!"

Zek leaped over the ornamental pond and came to stand behind Gail, putting her and the table between them.

"What's going on?" Milly stumbled out into the courtyard, rubbing at her eyes. She wore white shorts and one of Tom's old T-shirts and her hair stood up in all directions. He smiled at how cute she was, even without trying. After her came JD and Niv, both also blinking and confused.

"He's got my diary!" Connor said, pointing accusingly at Zek.

"Is that what this is?" Zek said, holding up a black notebook. "I thought it was a toddler's drawing book."

"Argh!" Connor dived across the table, knocking the tea and cups to the floor. Zek was too fast for him. He skipped out of Connor's grasp. But he wasn't too fast for Gail. She stuck her foot out and Zek went toppling over, him flying one way while the diary went the other. Before Zek could grab the book again, Gail stabbed the book on the floor with her cane and pulled it clear of Zek's grasp. She dragged it closer to her, picked it up, and passed it back to Connor. He looked around for somewhere to put it, and then realized he was only wearing his underwear, so made do with tucking it in the waistband of his black boxers.

"I was only having fun," Zek said, getting up and rubbing at his chin, which had connected with the dusty floor.

"You of all people should know better." Gail held Zek by

the chin moving his head side to side to check the injury wasn't too bad. Satisfied he'd live, she pushed him away.

Zek looked properly ashamed of himself. "You're the one who told us to never keep secrets from each other."

"I don't write down my secrets, Zek," Connor said, his red eyes looking even redder.

"What do you write then?"

"I write down my soul."

Zek didn't know what to say to that. None of them did. Connor was like that, constantly surprising them all.

"I'm sorry, Con. I was being a douche." Zek reached his hand out for Connor to shake. Connor grabbed it and yanked Zek into one of his bear hugs. Zek looked a little uncomfortable to be hugging a mostly naked Connor.

Connor finally let him go. "That's okay, but if you try anything like it again, I will break your thumb. Your bass-playing thumb."

Tom straightened up the table and retrieved the broken teacups. Milly came to stand next to him and looked down at the fragments in his hand.

"Have you heard of *kintsugi*?" Milly asked.

"No," Tom said.

"I read about it. It's a Japanese art form of repairing broken pottery with gold." She took one of the broken cups and put it back together. "But it's more than that. It treats the breakage as part of the history of the object, rather than something to be hidden. The idea is that the mended pot is more beautiful for having been broken in the first place."

Tom smiled at her. "I like that idea." He looked down at his stump. He'd not worn a prosthetic since the fight and he was starting to get used to just using his left hand. Maybe that's what he needed to accept: sure, he was broken – but that it didn't matter. "I like not feeling like I have to hide."

"Me too," Milly said, placing the broken cup on the table. "Which is why" – she inhaled deeply – "there's something I want to stop hiding."

Tom's breath caught in his chest. Was she about to tell everyone about them? Not that he was even sure there was a "them" to tell anyone about.

"Gail," Milly said, "what's the best way to make an announcement to the fans?"

And this is me

Milly took a seat on the sofa, with the five boys around her. Gail stood opposite, adjusting the camera stand, ready to livestream.

"Ready?" Gail asked.

"I guess?" Milly said.

"Okay, stream it," JD said.

A moment later, Gail gave them a nod to say they were live.

"Hi," they said in unison, "we're Slay."

"And we promised you an announcement," JD continued.

"Don't worry, the band isn't splitting up," Zek said.

"And Tom isn't going anywhere." Connor threw his arm around his bandmate's neck.

"But there is something we'd like to tell you," Tom said.

They all looked at Milly. She looked down, took off her hat and glasses, then looked back up into the lens. "So, well, my name isn't Milo. It's Milly, and I'm a girl. Surprise!" She waited a while, imagining the fans on the other end of the broadcast, wondering what they would be thinking. Would they be angry? Sad? "I'm sorry that I lied to you."

"That we all lied to you," Tom said, nudging Milly.

"Yeah, we didn't mean to, but…" She'd practised what she was going to say over and over, but now it came to it, she'd lost the words.

"We were trying to protect our friend," JD said.

"We were trying to protect everyone," Tom added.

"But we were wrong. And I hope you can forgive me. I love being a part of Slay. I love these boys as much as I know you all do, and I hope you can accept me as Milly, the way you all accepted Milo."

"So, yeah," Connor said. "Milly's a girl, and so what? She's still awesome and we're still Slay and nothing changes. Thanks for tuning in. See you on the road!"

Connor started waving, then gave Zek next to him a nudge and they all waved at the camera until Gail gave them the thumbs up to say she'd finished filming.

"So, I guess that's it?"

Zek had his phone out. "It's already all over social media."

"What are they saying?" Milly asked.

"Some are freaking out… *How dare a girl be in their band*, blah blah. But most of them seem cool. Ha! A few are saying they knew it all along."

"It will take a few days to blow over," Gail said. "But actually, gender-blurring is pretty hot right now, so…" Her phone started ringing. "That's probably an interview request!"

Milly turned her own phone on and was about to search for her name when she decided better of it. *Never read the comments*, Tom had told her once. *That's where the real demons live.*

She was about to put her phone away when it started ringing. Naledi was video-calling her.

"No. Way!" Naledi shouted, as soon as Milly answered. "This is what you were going to tell me? That you're in a boy band? That doesn't even make sense!" She mimed her head exploding. "I mean…how, what, when? Oh my God, Mills – what are they like? Are they as cute in real life as they look in pictures?"

"I'd say some of us are," Zek said, leaning over Milly's shoulder, so he could be seen in frame. "Hi there." He waved at Naledi.

"Okay, he is seriously cute."

"Thanks, you're pretty cute yourself."

"Zek!" Milly said, pushing him away and moving away from the others. "Nal, I'm so sorry I didn't tell you. It's just all been so wild, and this is only the beginning of it."

"You mean, there's more than you being in the world's biggest boy band?"

"So much more. But I have to tell you in person."

"Are you okay?"

"Yeah, I'm good. Really good. But, Nal, I miss you so much."

"Then get your butt to England so I can hug you."

"I don't know where the tour will bring us next."

"Get packed." Gail had just returned, putting her phone away.

"Hang on a second, Nal," Milly whispered.

Milly lowered the phone, but she could still hear Naledi's voice. "Is that Gail Storm? Can you tell her how much I love her?"

"I put a call out to my contacts all over the world, trying to hunt down Mourdant," Gail said. "And I think we got something."

"Where?"

"London."

Milly picked her phone back up. "Nal, you better get your hugging arms ready, because I am on my way!"

A note from Kim

I have been fascinated by Japan and Japanese pop culture ever since I was a kid and I would stay up way past my bedtime to watch Kaijū movies. They were soon replaced by an obsession with manga and after that came J-Horror. All of those influences have come together in *Slay On Tour*.

I was lucky enough visit Tokyo briefly, but I've yet to explore the rest of the country, so I am eternally grateful to my dear friend Sarah Terkaoui who took me on a tour all over Japan from her living room, right down to describing the smell of the air in Kyoto after the rain. Thanks also to Juno Dawson for creating an awesome J-Pop playlist that I listened to on repeat. And, as ever, endless gratitude to my agent James Wills, the whole phenomenal Usborne team and my amazing readers.

Kim Curran is an author and creative director based in London. She has worked on some of the world's largest brands and charities from EA to UNICEF.

  @kimecurran
@UsborneYA

#SLAY

And find out where Slay's adventures began in...

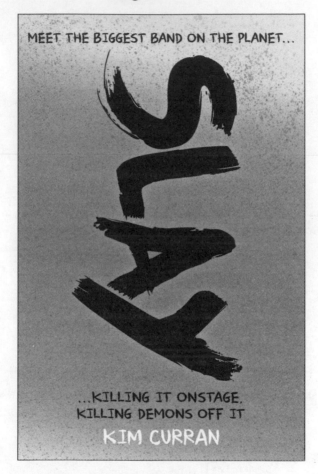

MEET THE BIGGEST BAND ON THE PLANET...

...KILLING IT ONSTAGE.
KILLING DEMONS OFF IT
KIM CURRAN

"Boys as swoon-worthy as One Direction saving the world
from evil? Sign me up!"

Amy Alward, author of THE POTION DIARIES